BOCA
DAZE

STEVEN M. FORMAN

A TOM DOHERTY ASSOCIATES BOOK
NEW YORK

BOCA DAZE

Copyright © 2012 by Steven M. Forman

Edited by James Frenkel

A Forge Book
Published by Tom Doherty Associates, LLC
175 Fifth Avenue
New York, NY 10010

www.tor-forge.com

Forge® is a registered trademark of Tom Doherty Associates, LLC.

ISBN 978-0-7653-2876-2

First Edition: January 2012

Printed in the United States of America

0 9 8 7 6 5 4 3 2 1

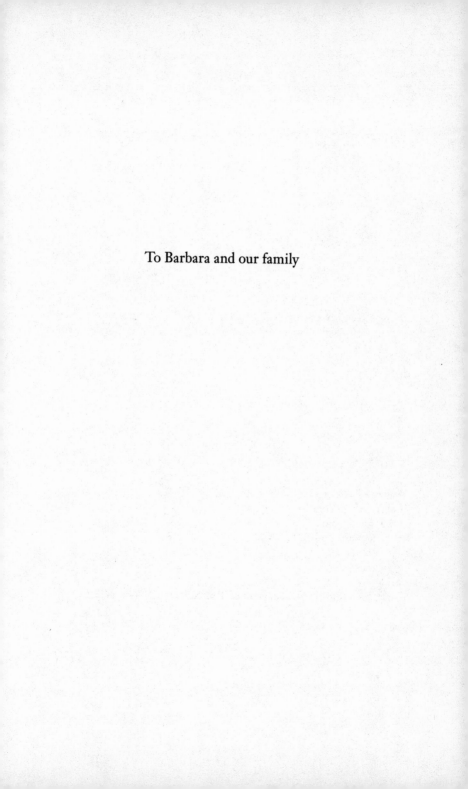

To Barbara and our family

Boca Daze

Acknowledgments

As always, thanks to my agent, Bob Diforio, my editor, Jim Frenkel, and my publisher, Tom Doherty Associates. To my friend Barry Unger for his valuable comments, Steve Brooks and Morris Goldings for legal input, Dr. David Levey for his medical advice, Dr. Glenn Kessler for his psychological perspective, Chief Dan Alexander of the Boca Police Department for his opinions, Police Officers Rosalind Gualtieri and Sandra Boonenberg for helping me better understand Boca Raton's homeless community, and Jeannie Fernsworth for teaching me how to make a Zombie without turning me into one.

Every living thing is born without [a] reason and dies by chance.

—*Jean-Paul Sartre (paraphrased)*

BOCA DAZE

PROLOGUE

The Japanese war flag—sixteen red rays bursting from a rising sun in a field of white—flew over the coral island of Tarawa. At dawn, twelve Allied battleships, sixty-six destroyers, seventeen aircraft carriers, and thirty-five thousand troops launched a withering attack on the tiny atoll. Seventy-six hours later, the Rising Sun went down, Old Glory went up, and thousands of soldiers, from both sides, lay dead. Corporal Herb Brown was not one of them.

Brown, a twenty-one-year-old marine from Providence, Rhode Island, jumped from an amphibious vehicle into knee-deep water off Red Beach One and waded ashore. By the time he reached the beach, eleven of the twenty men from his ATV were dead. Those who survived . . . attacked. A marine running next to Brown stepped on a land mine and disintegrated. Brown saw the dead man's bloody dog tags flutter to the sand and bent to pick them up. A bullet tore through the front of his helmet, knocking it off his head, sending him sprawling on his back. He rolled onto his stomach, facing the ocean. Blood from the gouge on the top of his head trickled into his eyes but he was able to see his helmet a few feet away. A hole was in the front and another in the back. A bullet had passed through his "steel pot," seared his scalp, and missed his brain by a millimeter.

He jammed the M1 helmet on his head and struggled to all fours. Immediately machine gun bullets slammed into his buttocks; two in the left cheek and two in the right. He sprawled facedown into the sand and heard himself scream. A body fell next to him. Brown turned to his right, wiping sand from his eyes and spitting it from his mouth. Private Hugh Stone lay on his back, mouth open, gasping. Stone's insides were outside and he was holding them in his blood-soaked hands. He looked at Brown and winced. They were fellow marines, but not friends. In boot camp Stone, an uneducated kid from West Virginia, referred to Brown as a Yankee Jew boy. Brown, much bigger and stronger than Stone, responded with a one-punch knockout of the smaller man. Their master sergeant enforced a truce, ordering them to "hate each other after the war."

Brown grabbed Stone's shirt collar and began dragging him to the ocean. Brown dug his elbows into the sand and swiveled his hips, painfully squirming toward the shoreline. When he tasted salt on his lips, he knew he was at the water's edge. He felt his fingers being pried from Stone's collar and heard, "This one's alive. This one's dead." He closed his eyes, not knowing who was who.

Herb Brown lived. Hugh Stone died along with fourteen hundred Allied soldiers and nearly five thousand Japanese troops in the three-day battle. When the war ended, marine general Holland Smith was asked if Tarawa had been worth the losses, and he said, "*No.*" When an investigating marine lieutenant asked Brown if he had been shot in the buttocks while retreating, Brown's answer was also "*No,*" but he added a string of curses directed at the officer. His insubordination cost him a medal but he had no regrets.

He returned to civilian life in 1945, married Joan Livingston, a girl he had been dating before the war, and they started a family. He went to work for a clothing distributor in Providence, Rhode Island, and eventually bought the company. Throughout his career he won the respect of the competition, the local unions, and the Providence Mafia. No one ever asked Herb Brown again if he had retreated. Whenever he thought of Tarawa, he wondered why he had lived while so many others had died.

MAY 17, 1980
LIBERTY CITY, MIAMI

Clarence "Big Dog" Walken had just finished unwittingly impregnating his seventeen-year-old girlfriend, Gladys Hightower, when he got a call from Clifford "Free Man" Foster telling him a riot was happening in Liberty City. Big Dog got out of bed, dressed quickly, and hurried to meet Foster without saying goodbye to Gladys.

Free Man and Big Dog ran the nine blocks west to Sixty-second and Seventeenth . . . hoping to do some serious looting. Big Dog needed a TV, Foster wanted a stereo. They wore their black-on-silver Overtown Outlaws jackets.

Look like the goddamn Oakland Raiders.

They found another Overtown Outlaw already at the riot.

"What's happening?"

"People goin' nuts . . . jury found them cops not guilty of killin' Arthur McDuffie."

"McDuffie that motorcycle-ridin' mothuh-fuckah crazy?"

"Yeah, cops stopped him for speedin' then broke his head with nightsticks. Not guilty my black ass."

"Whatchu expect from an all-white jury?"

It ain't fair.

Big Dog shrugged. "Where the TVs at?"

Suddenly the crowd roared. Big Dog saw an old Dodge sedan career into the intersection with a white boy at the wheel, another in the passenger's seat, and a white girl in back. They looked like teenagers. The mob was pelting the car with rocks and bottles. The driver lost control and the Dodge swerved, hit a young black girl standing in the street, and slammed into a lamppost.

Big Dog watched as the three white kids were pulled out of the Dodge and attacked by black rioters. The white boy who had been driving was immediately knocked unconscious by several blows to the head. The crowd left him and turned on the other male passenger, beating him mercilessly. Big Dog saw a middleaged black man wearing a cabby's hat pull the screaming white girl out of harm's way.

Gunshots split the air and the crowd cringed. Big Dog saw the badly beaten white kid who hadn't even been driving stagger backward with blood spurting out of his body. When the barrage of bullets stopped, the boy crumpled to the street like a bloody bag of laundry. Big Dog didn't care. He felt nothing except a sharp pain in his chest. He looked down.

Aw, shit.

The front of his Overtown Outlaws jacket was leaking blood. He'd been hit by a stray bullet.

Now that ain't fair.

Big Dog fell to his knees, crumpled face-first on the pavement, and died. He was twenty years old . . . the same age as the white boy lying dead in the same intersection.

Nine months later Gladys Hightower gave birth to a baby boy she named Clarence, after his father. The Overtown Outlaws took care of mother and child in their own way. They had

Gladys work as a prostitute to feed her baby and her drug habit, and they made Clarence's education a gang responsibility. The streets of Liberty City became his classroom.

When his mother died of a drug overdose in 1991, Clarence could not read or write. But he could disassemble a .38 caliber handgun, clean it, and reassemble it as fast as any other gangbanger. He could cut pure cocaine into rocks of crack and knew a brick weighed a kilo and a kilo weighed 2.2 pounds. He grew up huge and could fight with his fists, feet, teeth, knife, or gun. He was a pure gangbanger; programmed from cradle to crib.

When the Liberty City drug wars erupted in 1998, Clarence was the Outlaws' ultimate weapon. At six foot six, 305 pounds, he was terrifying and fought like a wild animal.

That mothuh-fuckah vicious . . . like a wolf.

When the wars ended, Clarence Walken Jr. was the leader of the pack. He had been born without a father, and some say he had been born without a soul.

He became known as Mad Dog Walken.

CHAPTER 1

BOCA KNIGHTS AND OTHER SUPERHEROES
MID-JANUARY 2006

Some people say I'm a senior-citizen superhero. I'm not. Super-heroes have special powers. I have special needs. Superman has X-ray vision. I'm nearsighted. Batman has a Batmobile. I have a Mini Cooper. Spider-Man spins large webs. I have an enlarged prostate. I was Boston's most decorated and demoted policeman in my prime and the best marksman on the force. Now, I'm just a sixty-one-year-old ex–Boston cop trying to adapt to life's changes. I retired to Boca Raton three years ago, and after solving local crimes and rescuing two damsels in distress, I became a private detective. A young newspaper reporter looking for a story dubbed me the Boca Knight, and the name stuck. I'm a little guy, barely five foot six, 165 pounds. But I'm fearless and that makes me bigger.

I had just sat down at the counter at Kugel's Boca Deli and ordered a cup of coffee when an old man tapped my shoulder and asked if I was the Boca Knight. I nodded. "Eddie Perlmutter," I said, and held out my hand.

"Herb Brown." His hand felt like old iron. "I'm a big fan of yours."

"I'm a big fan of the US Marines," I said, pointing to the SEMPER FI insignia on his cap. "You live in Boca, Herb?"

"I retired here thirteen years ago."

"Enjoying your retirement?"

"Not really," he said. "My wife died five years ago."

"My wife died over twenty years ago."

We retreated to our coffee cups, both of us thinking of lost love.

"When were you in the Marines?" I asked.

"World War Two."

"Did you see action?"

"Yeah, in the Pacific," he said. "Tarawa."

"I never heard of it."

"I wish I hadn't," Brown said.

"Rough?"

"Two thousand Marines killed in three days," he told me.

"How many Japanese?"

"Who cares? I know I didn't kill any. I never got off the beach."

"What happened?"

"I got shot in the ass."

I didn't know what to say . . . but I knew what not to say.

"Aren't you going to ask me if I was retreating?" Brown asked irritably.

"No, but it sounds like someone did . . . and you're still pissed."

"Wouldn't you be?"

"Damn right," I said.

"You would have made a good marine." Herb Brown patted my shoulder.

"I was never in the service."

"You were a street soldier."

"The streets could be a war zone sometimes," I agreed.

"They're worse now with the illegal immigrants."

"I don't talk about religion or politics."

"Me neither," he said. "But I don't like that black senator from Illinois. How would you like having a liberal black man from Kenya as president someday?"

"How do you feel about having a conservative white man from Texas as president today?"

The old soldier smiled. "Good point."

"Hey, Eddie," a familiar voice called. Steve Coleman, a friend from Boston, came up behind me and rubbed my shoulders like a trainer rubs a fighter. "How's my favorite superhero?"

"I'll ask him when I see him," I said. "Say hello to Herb Brown."

They shook hands.

Steve glanced at his watch and ordered a coffee to go.

"What's the hurry?" I asked.

"Investment club meeting in fifteen minutes."

"Has your club ever made money?"

"Never," he admitted. "But that's changing tonight."

"Do you plan to rob a bank?"

Herb chuckled.

"Better," Steve said. "B.I.G. Investments has agreed to take our money."

I stopped in mid sip. "You're making money because someone is taking your money?"

"Not just *someone*. B. I. Grover."

"I never heard of him."

"Everybody's heard of him," Steve insisted.

"I never heard of him either," Herb Brown said.

"He's been making more money than anyone in the investment business for thirty years. He never loses," Steve bragged.

"Everyone loses," Herb Brown said.

Steve smiled indulgently.

"What's his rate of return?" Brown asked.

"Twelve to twenty percent."

"That's unbelievable," Brown replied.

"Yes, it is," Steve agreed.

"Then why do you believe it?" I asked.

Steve patted my shoulder. "Grover is a genius, Eddie. His clients are big-time businessmen, charities, and celebrities. His fund has been closed for years."

"Why is it suddenly open?" I asked.

"It's not sudden. It took us two years to get in. We got lucky."

"Or unlucky," Brown said. "How much did you invest?"

"Twenty guys at two hundred and fifty grand. That's his minimum." Steve glanced at his watch again. "Gotta go, money never sleeps."

Steve was barely out the door when Brown said, "And a fool and his money are soon parted."

"You think he's being foolish?" I asked.

"No one beats the competition all the time. Something isn't kosher."

"A lot of smart investors think he can."

"Who says they're smart?"

"Are you an investor?" I asked Herb.

"Yeah. I've had my money with a rock-solid company named Lehman Brothers for years."

I nodded but the name meant nothing to me.

"Is Steve a good friend of yours?" Herb asked.

"He's my best friend's brother-in-law," I said, referring to Togo Amato from the North End of Boston. Togo had been the best man at my wedding forty years ago and one of my wife's pallbearers twenty years ago. "I'd say we're pretty good friends. Why?"

"You're a licensed private investigator in Florida, right?"

"Over a year," I confirmed.

"Maybe you should do your friend a favor and investigate B. I. Grover."

"Why would I want to do that?"

"If something sounds too good to be true it usually is."

"It's none of my business," I said. "Besides, it's too late."

"It's never too late to help an old friend," my new friend said.

CHAPTER 2

LOOKING A GIFT HORSE IN THE MOUTH

I went home to my live-in girlfriend, the fabulous Claudette Permice. She was a coffee-colored beauty who looked a bit like Halle Berry. She was half-white, half-black, and a little more than half my age. We met two years ago when I was rushed to the Boca Raton Community Hospital with a gunshot wound to my shoulder courtesy of the Russian Mafia. Claudette was my nurse. I wasn't physically attracted to her at first because I had a catheter inserted in my plumbing, but when she unhooked me, I was hooked on her. I loved island girls. Claudette was from Haiti on the island of Hispaniola, and I was already seeing a divorcée from Long Island. The two women were complete opposites. Alicia was like a violin interlude in a symphony, and Claudette was a drum solo in a jazz session. I loved the music I made with both of them, but Alicia wanted to change my tune. That wasn't going to happen at my age.

I told Claudette about Herb Brown.

"He sounds like a nice man," she said, "and probably lonely. Why don't you invite him to dinner one night?"

"Good idea." I got the current Boca phone book from a cabinet. Herb and Joan Brown were listed. She had been gone for five years but he was still holding on to her. I dialed the number and got his answering machine. As soon as I identified myself, Herb picked up.

"I don't answer till I know who's calling," he explained. "Too many solicitors."

I told him why I was calling and he sounded surprised and delighted. We tried several dates and finally picked one a month away.

"Maybe I'll see you at Kugel's in the meantime," Herb said before we disconnected.

Claudette was standing at the kitchen sink when I walked behind her and kissed her cheek.

"Thanks for the idea," I told her. "He was really excited by the invitation."

"I'm not just another pretty face with a gorgeous body." She smiled.

"You're much more than that." I hugged her.

I slept well that night and was at the office early the next morning.

"I want you to do a search on a guy named B. I. Grover," I told Lou Dewey as I walked into his adjoining office. Less than a year ago Lou was a skinny, bucktoothed computer fraud who wore his hair like Elvis and thought like a bank robber. I was arresting him when fate intervened. My heart misfired and raced out of control as it had done many times in my life. Dewey could have run away but he didn't. He stayed by my side and saved my life. In exchange I changed his. We became good friends and business partners after going through major attitude adjustments.

I introduced him to computer wizard Joy Feely, who became the love of his life. We were like a family after that. Joy and Lou moved in together, and Joy moved her computer business into our new office.

"How deep an investigation do you want?" Lou asked.

"Use rubber gloves," I told him.

Lou turned to his keyboard.

Tap, tap, tap . . . Pause . . . Tap, tap, tap . . . Pause. Tap . . . Emphatic tap . . .

" 'Benjamin Israel Grover,' " Lou read aloud.

"Benjamin Israel? You're kidding."

"You like Louie Dewey better?"

"What's in a name anyway?" I asked. "Tell me about Benjamin."

Lou scanned the screen. "Born in the Bronx in 1938. Uneventful childhood, attended Hofstra and graduated with a business degree. No awards. No special recognition. Married his high school sweetheart, Rhonda Tucker, in 1959. Started a small investment firm in 1969 with a borrowed five thousand bucks. The rest is history."

"Sounds perfect."

"Nobody's perfect."

"Keep looking," I said.

I went to my private office, sat at my desk, and pressed the ENTER button on my laptop. Lou had given me the Dell and personally dragged me off the technology bypass onto the information superhighway. A picture of Claudette lit up the screen.

An icon flashed and a voice told me I had mail. I clicked on the voice-mail square.

To: Eddie Perlmutter
From: Jerry Small—South Florida News
Subject: Weary Willie—Call me ASAP.

Jerry was the young newspaper reporter who'd dubbed me the Boca Knight. We had become close during the past two years.

I hit the DELETE button, flicked open my cell phone, read, *You have one message*, pressed the LISTEN button, and heard, "Eddie, it's Jerry. Call me." I clicked to erase the message, thumbed Jerry's speed-dial number, and confirmed the "connecting" signal. I knew how to press buttons, but it was all a mystery to me.

When I grew up, television was beginning, ice delivery was ending, cars had running boards, phone numbers started with a name and a number—Longwood 6, Aspinwal 7, Copley 5—and party lines still existed.

"Eddie, thanks for getting back to me so fast," Jerry answered, using his caller ID to identify me. Jerry was hyper and lived every day as if he were on a deadline. He was only twenty-eight but acted as if he were running out of time. He was too busy and self-centered to be married, and his greatest love was the next story. He would go anywhere and do anything for an exclusive. His bosses loved him because he was always on the job.

"What's up?" I asked.

"You remember Weary Willie, don't you?"

"Sure. You wrote a column about him last year. A homeless nut job who thought he was the sad-faced clown from the Great Depression. Your story got picked up by the Associated Press."

"Willie was found early this morning with the back of his head bashed in," Jerry told me. "He's still breathing but comatose. He could have brain damage."

"I'm sorry to hear it. But why are you telling me?"

"I want you to investigate Willie's attack on behalf of the newspaper. My boss already approved the idea."

"That's police work," I said. "Talk to them."

"I talked to Frank Burke," Jerry said, referring to our mutual friend, the Boca chief of police.

"What did he say?"

"He said his department would conduct a thorough investigation."

"Good, you don't need me."

"Eddie, there are four thousand homeless in Palm Beach County, and attacks happen every day. The police have more urgent things to do."

"Frank will do a good job," I said.

"Of course he will. But Willie's attack will become an ongoing investigation with the police, and with no clues they'll move on. I want you to make it a priority."

"Why?"

"I got to like Willie when I did his interview," Jerry said. "Plus I think we'll sell a lot of papers printing the exclusive story of a Boca Knight investigation."

"So it's business and personal."

"Yeah. Willie was a good guy. I'd like to humanize him and get people to care."

"Where was he found?" I asked, feeling myself getting sucked in.

"Under the boardwalk in Rutherford Park."

"Homeless haven. He was probably attacked by one of his own," I guessed. "Is Willie's condition common knowledge?"

"No, I haven't filed the story yet."

"Can you write an article that says Willie is comatose but stable?"

"Sure. That's basically the truth anyway," Jerry said. "But what's the point?"

"His attackers might get worried. Worried people get careless."

"Is this your way of telling me you'll take the case?"

And that's how I became involved in the case of the Sad-Faced Clown.

CHAPTER 3

THE DOCTOR IS IN

The median age in Boca is much higher than the national average. Violent crime is below the national average. Rape is rare and so is consensual sex.

Boca is benign, but crime is malignant so there was plenty of work for me in the city. I could afford to be selective thanks to my policeman's pension and simple lifestyle. I refused domestic disputes and accepted pro bono work, time permitting. I was already too busy when I chose to be involved with an old nemesis from Boston, Doc Hurwitz.

Doc Hurwitz wasn't a doctor and his real first name was Solomon. Everyone called him Doc because, during the sixties, he specialized in conning Boston doctors. He was much more than a con man, however. In his prime, from 1959 to 1981, he was a bookmaker, horse-race fixer, porno peddler, numbers banker, loan shark, and fraud perpetrator. It was rumored that he killed a couple of people, but that was never confirmed. Doc made money for the Italian Mafia, the Jewish hoods, and the Irish thugs, and his connections made him difficult to convict. I arrested him twice for bookmaking, but both cases were dismissed by two judges who belonged in jail themselves.

Doc was short and slight with a thin, dark mustache and shiny black hair. He was a fast talker, and a sharp dresser . . . described as "slicker than whale shit" by a Gloucester fisherman he conned. Doc looked like a harmless ferret but he was a squirrel with fangs. No one's nuts were safe around him.

Doc was associated with the Cunio twins from East Boston. Rocky "the Repairman" Cunio fixed things . . . such as ball games, fights, and horse races. Rocky's twin, Fabio "the Fireman," was a pyrotechnic artist who set fires for profit. He torched countless delicatessens, Chinese restaurants, and old factories in Boston, and his blazes became known as Cunio Lightning. He was proud to say that no one ever died in one of his fires. In the late seventies Doc and Fabio got involved in a complicated insurance fraud. Doc sold phony life-insurance policies on horses to their owners at Suffolk Downs. Instead of using the premiums to insure the horses, Doc used the money to insure a couple of empty warehouses he owned in Boston. The overinsured buildings were struck by Cunio Lightning one night in 1982, putting Doc in position for a big payday. Unfortunately, the barn area at Suffolk Downs legitimately burned down that same month. Eleven horses perished. The horse owners turned to Doc for their insurance money but the cupboard was bare. Doc and Fabio appeared on the front page of the *Boston Traveler* being led away in handcuffs, charged with arson and fraud. I attended Doc's sentencing, for old times' sake, and watched him receive seven years from an honest judge. He was being led away when he saw me standing by the door. He winked. I smiled.

"See ya, Eddie," he said.

"See ya, Doc," I replied.

I didn't see him for more than twenty years.

"Hello, Eddie," I heard when I answered the phone at my office. "It's Doc Hurwitz. Remember me?"

"You're unforgettable, Doc," I said, surprised. "It's been a long time."

"Over twenty years."

"I wondered what happened to you."

"I served three years for that unfortunate fire misunderstanding in Boston," he explained. "After that I moved to Florida."

"Don't tell me you've been straight all these years?"

"Okay, I won't."

I laughed. "What happened to the Cunio boys?"

"I lost touch with Fabio a long time ago," Doc said. "Rocky died of a massive coronary a few years back watching a Miami jai alai game he'd fixed. He keeled over when his man lost."

"How do you lose a fixed jai alai game?"

"Language barrier between him and his player," Doc told me. "The Repairman was only seventy-three."

"How old are you, Doc?"

"Eighty-one. What about you?"

"Sixty-one," I said.

"Where did the time go, Eddie?"

"With the wind. So what can I do for you, Doc?"

"I want to hire you."

"The last time I looked we were on different sides of the law."

"Look again," he suggested. "This investigation is strictly legitimate."

"I don't believe you . . . but I'm listening."

"Do you know anything about pill mills?"

"No."

"Florida has no state supervision or monitoring system for pain clinics," Doc explained. "Anyone can open a pain-pill clinic anywhere in this state."

"Any doctor you mean?"

"No . . . anyone. You, me, your plumber, anyone."

"Not you. You're a convicted felon," I reminded him.

"It doesn't matter. I can own a pill mill in this state. A chimney sweep can own one. Form a corporation, hire a doctor, and you're in business selling narcotics."

"Sounds dangerous."

"It's deadly and it's big business," he said. "Over a hundred clinics, thousands of users and millions of dollars."

"What's your connection?"

"My twenty-two-year-old granddaughter OD'd on Oxy-Contin a month ago," he said sadly. "She bought the shit from one of these places."

"Doc, I'm really sorry. But what can I do?"

"I want to prove where my granddaughter bought the stuff and who prescribed it. I want to shut them down."

"Why come to me?"

"You were always a crusader, Eddie. If you can close this one operation and put this doctor behind bars, I'll give you a new crusade. I'll help you take down the whole industry."

We set up a meeting for that night. Doc was right. I always was a sucker for a good cause.

Chapter 4

Who Could Ask for Anything More?

I felt rich watching the sun set on Bal Harbour Village. I was sitting on Doc's balcony overlooking the Intracoastal, sipping merlot from a long-stem red wineglass. Doc lived on the top floor of a two-story apartment building with a magnificent view of Bay Harbor Islands, across the Intracoastal. The tropical air was soothing and a breeze swayed the palms.

Who could ask for anything more?

But people do.

"You look good, Eddie," Doc said, sitting on a lounge chair and raising his wineglass. He was also holding slips of paper in his other hand. I didn't ask, figuring he'd get to them.

"You too, Doc." I returned his toast.

"Bullshit," he sighed. "I look old. But I'll bet you could still go a few rounds."

"I retired undefeated. I'd like to keep it that way."

"I was at Boston Arena the night you won the Golden Gloves middleweight championship."

"That was forty-five years ago, Doc."

"I lost a couple of hundred on that fight."

"You bet against me?" I said, laughing.

"That kid Montoya was bigger, older, and more talented than you. But you fought like a maniac and knocked him out. You had a lot of anger."

"It's in my genes. My grandfather once killed a bear."

"You killed your share of animals too," Doc reminded me. "I remember that Chinatown shooting when you got suspended from the force. They shoulda given you a medal for killing that son of a bitch."

He was referring to a night in the seventies when I led a police raid on the Chinatown apartment of Danny Dong, a Boston drug dealer, pimp, and suspected cop killer. I kicked open Dong's front door. By the time I got to his bedroom, he was holding a knife against a teenage prostitute's throat. He threatened to kill her if I didn't back off. I told him, "Take it easy," just before I shot him between the eyes.

"I'd do it again," I said.

"I know."

We sat in silence until I said, "Quite a view," and pointed to the water.

"Tessa used to love it," he said, referring to his late wife.

"How long has she been gone?"

"Two years. And now I've lost my granddaughter."

"I'm sorry, Doc."

"She was my only daughter's only child. Do you remember my daughter, Emily?"

"Not really," I said. "How is she handling this?"

"I have no idea. I haven't seen her in years."

"What happened?"

"Drugs too."

"What about the girl's father?"

"Emily never married Shoshanna's father," Doc told me. "He was a wiseguy from Hartford. He disappeared when the girl was only ten."

"Did you try to find him?"

"I had no idea where to dig," Doc said.

"Sounds like your daughter made bad choices."

"It's my fault. I exposed her to a lot of lowlifes. When you're surrounded by shit, it's hard not to step in it. I tried to save Shoshanna at the end. I put her in rehab down here. She did okay until she found the pill mills. She died from drugs she bought with a bogus prescription at some bullshit clinic."

"What do you want me to do?"

"Follow a paper trail and see where it leads," he said, handing me the papers he was holding.

I shuffled the slips. "These are all blank prescriptions signed by a Dr. V. Patel. Fill in a name and you could use them anywhere."

"Not anywhere," Doc Hurwitz said. "No legitimate pharmacy would fill them. Check out the drugs."

"OxyContin, Percocet, Roxicodone, Vicodin, and Xanax," I read. "Controlled substances."

"They're out of control around here. Shoshanna called me the night she died. She told me she was real sick and asked me to come get her. She gave me the address of a motel in Fort Lauderdale. By the time I got there, she was dead. I found these prescriptions in her pocket."

"Did you go to the police?"

"I don't go to the police. They usually come to me."

"I'm sorry, Doc. It's a sad story. But if you're looking for vigilante revenge . . . I'm not interested."

"Eddie, I told you . . . I want enough proof to close down that clinic and put that phony doctor away for good."

"And you intend to do this legally?"

"You have my word," he said.

In Doc's gangland gibberish, when he gave you his word, there was a fifty-fifty chance he was lying. If he said, "I guarantee it," it meant the game was rigged and he was telling the truth.

"I can't depend on your word," I reminded him.

"Agreed." He laughed. "But if you want to take down the pill mill industry, you'll have to take a chance on me."

I did a risk-reward analysis and decided to take a chance. "Okay, Doc. You got a deal. But I'll be watching you."

"Of course you will."

"Do you know what clinic you're after?" I asked.

He removed a slip of paper from his shirt pocket. He passed it to me. "Patel is listed as the resident doctor at this address, and it's near the motel where Shoshanna died."

"You've already got your man and your place."

"I need ironclad proof," Doc explained. "Patel can claim someone stole his prescription pad, and the clinic can deny they ever sold Shoshanna anything."

I nodded. "Good thinking."

"I think like a criminal."

I glanced at the paper. *No Pain-U-Gain 24 Hour Clinic, 1245 Federal Highway, Ft. Lauderdale, FL. No appointment necessary.*

"What if I can't prove anything?"

"You will," he said confidently. "You're undefeated, remember?"

"When do I get the information on the whole industry?"

"Do I have your word you'll handle my clinic first?"

"I guarantee it," I told him.

"A guarantee is always good from you."

Doc returned with a bottle of wine and a file folder. He

refilled both our glasses, sat down, and shook the folder at me. "This file contains over a hundred dirty clinics. But Shoshanna comes first, right?"

I nodded.

We clinked glasses in a silent toast. Doc knew he could trust me, and I knew I couldn't trust him. Nothing had changed between us. It was just like old times.

CHAPTER 5

GOING THROUGH THE MILL

The next morning I studied Doc's information. The pill mills were loosely defined as "doctors, clinics, or pharmacies providing powerful narcotics inappropriately . . . for nonmedical reasons." Over a hundred unsupervised clinics were in Broward and Palm Beach counties . . . making Florida the top source for opium narcotics nationally. The Hillbilly Mafia transported drugs from Florida to wherever demand exceeded supply . . . such as Appalachia, Kentucky, Tennessee, and Ohio. High-pressure demand combined with low-pressure supervision was a perfect storm for drugs from Florida. Unscrupulous doctors were rarely prosecuted, and the rewards were well worth the fines anyway. OxyContin sold for a dollar a milligram. An eighty-milligram pill cost $80, a small bottle of a hundred pills . . . $8,000. Millions of pills were sold annually in Florida strip malls and office parks by nonmedical corporations.

Overprescribing was good for business. Overdosing only hurt for a little while. Three hundred and fifty pill mill customers died in 2005, but when one kid such as Shoshanna Hurwitz overdosed, another took her place. This particular Shoshanna, however, was the granddaughter of Doc Hurwitz and he could not replace her. All he could do was nail the pill mills that killed her . . . using me as his hammer.

Lou Dewey felt a covert operation was the best way to catch Doc's clinic in the act. By the end of the day he presented me with an electronic listening device called the Intruder.

"With this little beauty," Lou told me, "you can invade people's privacy and ruin their lives from a hundred yards."

Cool.

The device looked like a large handgun with an audio receptor, shaped like a cone, at the end of the barrel. It included a video camera.

"Just aim and shoot," Lou told me.

I can do that.

It was 10:00 p.m., Boca midnight, and the somnolent city was nodding off as I drove the Mini south on Federal Highway toward Fort Lauderdale. Federal is an interminable two-thousand-mile stretch of four-lane, divided highway that connects Fort Kent, Maine, to Key West, Florida. Fortunately I only needed twenty of those miles to reach the No Pain-U-Gain Clinic.

Federal Highway is crisscrossed by countless traffic lights at innumerable intersections and lined with strip malls, strip joints, multiple shopping centers, restaurants, schlocky and fancy office buildings, and Walgreens. I passed through Deerfield Beach and saw a sign pointing west to Wilton Manors. Last year I had a case in that city involving a gay couple kidnapped to Russia, but that's another story.

I saw the No Pain clinic on the east side in a three-unit strip mall. I turned my Mini into a similar mall across the highway where I had a perfect view. No Pain was located between ABC Medical Supplies and Happy Endings Massage . . . both closed for the night. I assembled the Intruder and checked the area. Four empty cars were parked in front, and a bald, stocky man with his left arm in a cast sat on a wooden bench near the door. A long-haired, skinny man with a goatee exited the clinic with a tall, scraggly woman. The couple walked toward a beat-up, old Chevy sedan with a Tennessee license plate.

Hillbillies.

The bald guy got up and limped after them, dragging his right leg.

"Dudes," he called.

"Whatchu want, man?" the long-haired scarecrow answered, opening his car door to get in.

"A little help," the bald guy said, hobbling. "My arm and leg's killing me and my Oxy prescription ran out."

"Don't care," the scraggly woman said, standing on the passenger side. "We got Oxy, eighty milligrams . . . at two hundred a pill."

"Only cost eighty bucks inside," baldy said.

"You ain't inside," the hillbilly said.

"Can you sell me twenty?"

"You got four thousand dollars?"

Baldy nodded.

"Show me the money," the Tennessee trader said.

"Show me the Oxy," the bald guy insisted.

"Man, I got people waitin' in line for this shit back home," the hillbilly said. "You want it or don't you?"

"Can I trust you?"

"Of course not." The seller laughed. "But I can sell you twenty pills for four thousand dollars, trust or no trust."

"The money's in my van," the buyer said, and he limped

toward a rusty panel truck. I noticed he was dragging his left leg
now.

Something wasn't right.

Baldy returned and handed a brown paper bag to the dealer,
who removed the money and counted. When he was satisfied, he
turned to the woman and nodded.

She removed a bag from a leather pouch and tossed it to the
man with the cast. He opened it, took out the contents, smiled,
and gave a thumbs-up. A police cruiser and an unmarked car
screeched into the parking lot. Two uniformed cops hustled out
of the cruiser with drawn guns and ordered the hillbillies to put
up their hands. Two plainclothesmen appeared from the unmarked car. The bald cop had disappeared. "You're under arrest,"
one of the uniformed cops said. "You have a right to remain
silent . . . you have . . ." yada, yada, yada.

"Aw, shit," the hillbilly said.

I tossed the Intruder on the passenger seat, got out of the
Mini, and trotted across Federal Highway. A guy wearing a
sports jacket and tie showed me his badge and said, "Stay back . . .
police business."

"I'm a private investigator," I told him.

"I don't care if you're Dick Tracy. Stay back."

"I'm going to show you my wallet. Stay calm." I removed my
wallet slowly from my back pocket and handed it over carefully.

The police detective read it and smiled. "The Boca Knight.
I heard a lot of good things about you." He handed back the card
and told me his name was Patrick Curley. We shook hands.
"Hey, Antollini," he called over his shoulder. "We got a celebrity
here."

"Who?" the other detective asked.

"The Boca Knight."

"What's he doing here?" Antollini asked, walking over.

"I'm on a case," I explained.

"Luke Antollini," the second cop introduced himself, and took my hand. "What kind of case?"

I gave them a summary minus names.

"Too bad about the girl," Curley said. "Unfortunately she won't be the last."

"Well, at least you got those two pushers off the street," I said, watching the uniformed cops put the dealers in the cruiser.

"They got greedy," Curley explained. "If they drove away without selling, we couldn't touch them."

"What about the clinic?" I asked.

"According to the state of Florida, the clinic did nothing illegal," Curley said as the cruiser screeched out of the lot with the dealers.

"Someone will take their place tomorrow," Antollini told me. "It's a never-ending cycle."

"It has to end," I said.

"Tell the Florida state legislature," Curley said.

"I will," I said, and no one laughed.

Chapter 6

The Sound of Silence

That night Claudette and I were sharing a pizza at Rotelli's on Clint Moore when she asked, "Is something wrong between us, Eddie? We haven't made love in weeks."

"Shhh. The pizza maker doesn't have to know."

"Well, it's true," she whispered. "You're never in the mood anymore. Do you still love me?"

"Yes, I love you," I answered truthfully.

"Then what is it? Talk to me."

I took a deep breath and blew it out slowly. "It's Mr. Johnson," I told her, referring to my talking penis. "We're barely on speaking terms."

Yes, I have a talking penis. All men do. Any guy who says he doesn't is lying. Mr. Johnson started talking to me when I was eleven years old and continued babbling for forty-eight years, nonstop. He became less talkative in the forty-ninth year and was now virtually incommunicado.

"I haven't heard from him in weeks," I confessed.

"Was I with you the last time he showed up?"

"I was by myself."

"You didn't!"

"No," I assured her. "I kept my hands to myself."

"What happened?"

"It was weird."

I told her I was home alone watching an old movie with Ann-Margret when Mr. Johnson popped up.

I love this movie, he said as though everything were normal.

Where've you been? I asked.

Hanging out.

Why haven't I heard from you?

Why didn't you get in touch with me?

I didn't want to bother you.

Same here.

We watched Ann-Margret for a while until Mr. Johnson lost interest and said, *This movie isn't as good as I remember.*

I agree.

I think I'll be going. See ya.

See ya.

When I finished, Claudette took out her cell phone and punched in some keys.

"You're not issuing a press release, are you?" I asked.

"I'm calling your urologist."

"You're overreacting."

"You're underreacting," she said pointedly.

"Dr. Koblentz's office," I heard a voice on her cell phone.

"Hi," Claudette responded. "I'd like to make an appointment for Eddie Perlmutter as soon as possible."

"Don't I have a say in this?" I asked.

"No. Tomorrow morning will be fine."

• • •

Dr. Alan Koblentz and I had become intimate several months ago when he gave me a digital prostate exam and a colonoscopy. Now he was proposing taking our relationship to the next level. He wanted to squeeze Mr. Johnson's head while sticking his finger in my ass.

"Can't we just be friends?" I asked.

"Eddie," Dr. Koblentz said, "a bulbocavernosus reflex test is the quickest, safest way to check your problem."

"Let me see if I have this straight," I said slowly. "You want to squeeze the head of my penis with one hand and stick a finger up my ass with the other."

"That's the basic procedure," he answered casually.

"Will you still respect me in the morning?"

Mr. Johnson seemed indifferent and I started worrying that MJ might actually have "little brain" damage.

According to women, men have two brains: a big one in their head and a little one in their pants. Also, according to women, men don't have enough blood to sustain both brains at the same time. Maybe that was my problem. Maybe I was thinking too much.

"Eddie, you're thinking too much," the doctor said. "This is a very common procedure."

"I know. Some guys swear by it," I said, thinking of my friends in Wilton Manor. "It's just not my thing."

"There are other options but they're more invasive."

"What's more invasive than a finger up my ass and a hand in my crotch?"

"Injections," he told me.

"What and where?"

"Prostaglandin directly into your penis."

"Tell me about the hand-and-finger thing again."

• • •

When Dr. Koblentz finished doing the hand jive in and around my pelvis, I pulled up my pants and asked him to marry me.

"You have ED," he told me, ignoring my proposal.

"An eating disorder?"

"Erectile dysfunction."

"Like Bob Dole?" I asked, referring to the 1996 Republican presidential candidate who lost an election and his erection and got a job as a Viagra spokesman.

"Similar."

"I didn't even run for office," I said. "Is it serious?"

"Nothing we can't treat. Millions of men in this country have ED. In your age range, seventeen percent of the men tested had ED, and by seventy we're talking forty percent."

"There must be a lot of sexually frustrated older women because of ED," I said.

"Not really. A seventy-six-year-old woman threatened to sue me for malpractice unless I stopped prescribing Viagra for her husband."

"She must have been concerned about his health."

"She was concerned about her own health," he explained. "She told me she was a mother of four and a grandmother of twelve and didn't want an eighty-year-old man with a chemically induced hard-on chasing her around her two-bedroom condo."

"Is Viagra that effective?" I asked, embarrassed that I was being outperformed by an eighty-year-old.

"Viagra's just a brand name for sildenafil citrate," the doctor said, going technical on me. "Like Cialis or Levitra. ED is all about blood flow. When a man is sexually aroused, the brain sends an impulse to the arteries in his penis to widen. More blood flows through these expanded arteries and the penis gets hard."

"I remember that."

"If something interferes with that blood flow, it's a problem."

"What interferes with blood flow?" I asked.

"Lots of things. Nerves or blood vessels malfunction, high blood pressure, high cholesterol, heart disease, diabetes, prostate problems, depression, stress, the wrong medicine, or just old age are causes."

"Are you trying to cheer me up?"

"No, I'm trying to get you up." He laughed.

That's not funny.

I went to CVS on Powerline, where a girl who should have been selling me Girl Scout cookies sold me four Viagra pills instead.

"They're for my father," I told her.

I got in the Mini and glanced at my watch. It was nearly seven. Claudette was working late at the Cohen-Goldman clinic, so I decided to take a directionless ride. I drove east on Yamato and randomly selected I-95 South.

CHAPTER 7

ONE OF THOSE DAZE

White lines and exit signs hypnotized me: Glades Road, Palmetto, Hillsboro, SW Tenth Street, and Sample Road flashed by. When I passed Copans Road, I was in a daze, daydreaming of the old days, accompanied by songs on an oldies station. When "Love Potion No. 9" came on, I had to laugh, but then I started personalizing every title: "Ain't That a Shame," "Bye Bye Love," "The Great Pretender" . . .

Did I just see a sign for Martin Luther King Boulevard, five miles?

The disc jockey announced three Rolling Stones songs in a row that were perfect for my condition: "Start Me Up," "You Can't Always Get What You Want," and "I Can't Get No Satisfaction."

The finale featured Jerry Lee Lewis's "Great Balls of Fire" followed by his version of "End of the Road."

I checked my watch. It was a few minutes past eight. I had been driving south for over an hour. It was time to turn around.

I got off I-95 on Seventy-ninth Street and looked for an entrance ramp north. I got lost. Soon I was driving past decrepit buildings and shabby storefronts. I saw the sign LIBERTY CITY AUTO REPAIR and realized I had wandered into one of Miami's most dangerous ghettos. By my third directionless turn I had driven down a dead-end street. My headlights illuminated a group of young, sullen black faces gathered around an old, four-door Buick.

You're not in Boca anymore.

The Buick's headlights went on and I was in the spotlight.

I completed two points of a three-point turn before I was surrounded by nine scowling black men. They wore silver-and-black jackets.

Love them Oakland Raiders, but I gotta go.

I inched forward but one of the Raider fans walked in front of the car and broke the left headlight with a baseball bat.

"Get out of the fuckin'—"

I saw red and I was out of the car before he could finish his sentence. I inherited the red spots from my grandfather, who stabbed a bear to death in the Ukraine the first time he saw red.

"I'm gonna kick your ass," I said to the guy with the bat.

I felt a gun barrel pressed against my left temple.

That changed things.

"One mo' step . . . you a dead," a young voice said.

The gunman couldn't have been more than seventeen. He looked nervous enough to pull the trigger.

Do or die.

I slowly raised my hands in surrender, but when my left hand was nearly to my shoulder, it became a trained weapon. I hit the underside of the kid's gun hand with an upward chop. The gun barrel pointed skyward. In one continuous motion I twisted the gun from his hand and had it pressed against his forehead before anyone reacted.

You see that?

Eight angry black men were now pointing guns at me. I quickly calculated my chances.

I'm gonna die.

I looked at the kid at the end of the gun barrel. He was on the verge of tears. He was just a boy trying to be a man in front of his gang.

No one was moving. I stood like a statue, left arm out straight, pressing the gun between the kid's eyes. Eight guns were pointed at me.

I lose. I'm the best marksman I know, but I figured I could only get off one shot before I was bullet riddled.

You little shit. You should be home with your mother.

I looked at the pistol in my hand. It was an old-time, low-tech Saturday-night special, probably a Ring of Fire MP-25 with six shots. It wasn't much firepower but enough to kill the kid at the end of the barrel. Staring through the gun sight, I was thinking about my funeral when I noticed the safety was on. It was so un-likely I laughed.

"What's so funny?" someone asked.

"The safety is on," I told them, still laughing.

"Ladanlian, you dumb shit," someone shouted at the kid.

"That's how you give it to me, Roach," Ladanlian defended himself to a muscular gang member.

"Here's the safety, kid," I said, taking the gun off his fore-head and flicking the switch to the ON position. "See? Now you're ready to kill someone."

His eyes grew wide.

I tossed him the gun.

He was too dazed to react and the pistol bounced off his chest and clattered on the street.

Roach stepped forward, picked up the junk gun, and waved it at me. "No more fuckin' around."

"I wasn't fuckin' around," I told him.

"Give me your money."

"You want it . . . take it," I challenged him.

He moved closer, aiming the gun at my head. I clenched my fists and thought how sad Claudette was going to be when she learned I was dead.

"*Stop!*" A low voice rumbled.

Everyone froze, including me. A huge black man stepped out of the shadows and brushed the gunman aside. He looked down at me. I looked up at him.

Holy shit!

The man was gigantic; at least seven inches over six feet tall and several lines above three hundred pounds on a scale. He was a block of black granite with arms as thick as banyan boughs. I wasn't afraid of him. I just knew I couldn't beat him.

Then again, my grandfather killed a bear . . .

"Why you give up the gun?" he asked, squinting at me.

"I didn't want to shoot the kid."

"Why?"

"It wouldn't change anything," I explained. "I was a dead man either way. Why take some dumb-ass kid with me?"

He tilted his head trying to get a better look at me. "That dumb-ass kid my nephew."

"Your sister will be very happy," I said.

"She dead. I take care of him."

"You're doing a lousy job."

"Say what?"

"Your nephew was five seconds away from having a hole in his head."

He stared at me curiously. "Where you from?"

"Boca."

"Whatchu doin' here?"

"Wrong turn," I said.

He almost smiled, but didn't. "You a cop?"

"I was . . . a long time ago."

"In Boca?"

"Boston."

He took a step closer and folded his arms across his broad chest.

"You the Boston cop . . . that Boca Knight guy . . . who fucked up them white-power skinheads a while back?"

I nodded.

He looked around the circle.

"That was good," he said, nodding his head.

"Good enough to get me out of here?"

"Maybe," he said, staring at me. "But lemme ax you somethin'. How much money you got on you?"

"About thirty bucks," I guessed.

"You willin' to fight Roach for thirty bucks? He's half your age and twice your size."

"I don't give up anything without a fight," I said. "And I could kick Roach's ass anyway."

"You crazy or something, old man?" Roach asked.

"Crazier than you," I told him.

"You know who we are?" the huge man asked.

"The Oakland Raiders?"

"The Overtown Outlaws," he said. "Everybody knows us."

"I never heard of you."

"We rule Liberty City," he said proudly. "Don't need no Boca."

"Boca doesn't need you either," I told him. "What's Overtown?"

"A symbol."

"What kind of symbol?"

"A symbol of how white people mess with black people," he said.

"I don't understand."

"Check out the history of Overtown," the giant said. "You'll understand."

"You going to let me live so I can check it out?"

"Yeah, you let my nephew live."

"Thanks," I said. "What's your name?"

"Why you care?"

"I make it a practice to know the names of everyone who saves my life."

"I'm Mad Dog Walken."

"What are you mad about?"

"Everything."

CHAPTER 8

OVERTOWN OVER TIME

The following morning I had breakfast with Claudette and told her I had taken a long ride south while she worked late. I didn't mention Liberty City or Mad Dog Walken's last words to me.

"You come here again, I can't guarantee your safety," he had shouted from his Buick after leading me to the I-95 North ramp.

I also didn't tell her the last words I said to Mad Dog: "I come here again, I can't guarantee your safety either."

I heard him laugh as I rode out of sight.

After Claudette finished her light breakfast, I gave her something heavy to digest. I put a Viagra pill on the table. We both stared at the blue diamond.

"Is that what I think it is?"

"If you're thinking it's an erector set . . . you're right," I told her.

"How do you feel?"

"I haven't taken a pill yet."

"No, I mean how do you feel about needing a pill?"

"Great . . . I feel great," I said sarcastically. "I can't wait till I need dentures and a hip replacement."

Claudette rubbed my shoulder affectionately. "Want to try a pill tonight?"

"I guess," I mumbled morosely.

"You don't sound very enthusiastic."

"What if it doesn't work?"

"Mr. Johnson is tired, Eddie. He's not dead."

"We'll see," I mumbled.

I got a stress headache driving to the office. I took two aspirin and asked Lou Dewey to do some research on Overtown.

We met for lunch at my desk, unwrapping tuna sandwiches from Subway.

"Tell me about Overtown," I said.

"It was a first-class black community a long time ago," he said. "Jackie Robinson vacationed there. Ray Charles made his first record there. Now it's a ghost town . . . dead and buried under I-95."

"Overtown was built under a highway?"

"No, a highway was built over Overtown."

"Whose brilliant idea was that?"

"White politicians in the sixties," Lou said.

"Didn't they care about the residents?"

"Actually . . . no. They built highways right through the heart of the place and displaced thousands of people."

"Where did all those people go?"

"Liberty City . . . mostly," Lou said.

I thought about Mad Dog's words about Overtown: *It's a symbol.*

"Why are you interested in that place?" Lou asked.

I told him about my adventure in Liberty City with the Overtown Outlaws.

"You tangled with Mad Dog Walken?" Lou sounded impressed.

"You've heard of him?"

"Only from today's research. He's a drug-dealing gang leader."

"That sounds right."

"A stone-cold killer," Lou added.

"That sounds wrong."

"Why?"

"I'm still alive."

"He didn't kill you because you didn't shoot his nephew and you stood up to those white-power skinheads last year."

"A stone-cold killer wouldn't care about that," I said. "They live to kill. I'm guessing Mad Dog kills to live."

"So do animals."

"He's no animal," I insisted. "Animals don't need reasons. Mad Dog uses reason."

"Are you trying to justify him?"

"He can't be justified any more than the people who built a highway over him."

"You sound like a social worker," Lou said.

"You can't bury a community under steel beams and concrete highways and expect something good to grow there."

"Now you sound like a farmer."

"I can use your opinion as fertilizer," I said.

Lou scowled at my joke. "Let's change the subject. Did you see Jerry Small's article about you and Willie in the paper this morning?"

"No. What did he write?"

"About how South Florida tops the national list for attacks on the homeless—"

"That's old news," I interrupted.

"It was an introduction to the Boca Knight's new crusade on behalf of the homeless."

"With reference to his exclusive rights to my story, no doubt."

"No doubt."

"What did he say about Willie?"

"He said he was in a coma but stable," Lou told me. "What are his chances of waking up, by the way?"

"Not good."

"Why didn't Jerry report that?"

"I asked him not to," I said. "Whoever attacked Willie thought they left a dead man in the sand. Let them worry about Willie waking up. Worry leads to mistakes."

"Sometimes you amaze me, Eddie." Lou sounded sincere.

"Sometimes I amaze myself."

Chapter 9

All the Lonely People

I decided to visit my comatose client at the Boca Hospital. He was on life support in intensive care. I showed the nurse my detective's card.

"I saw your name in the paper," she said, smiling. "He's in room 321."

I opened the door to Willie's room and saw a raggedy old woman in a long black coat leaning over his bed. She was holding what looked like a pencil in one hand and a jar of something in the other. I immediately thought of a needle and a deadly poison.

I hurried across the room and wrested the objects from the startled, frail woman's hands. She had been holding an artist's paintbrush and a small jar of paint.

I glanced at the man in the bed. The back of his head was swathed in a serious white bandage, but a silly red ball was on his nose and his mouth was partially outlined with white paint.

"I'm fixing his makeup," she explained.

"Who are you?" I asked.

"Three Bag Bailey." She pointed to a backpack and two dirty canvas bags on the floor.

"What's in the bags?"

"Everything I need," she told me.

"In just three bags?"

"Don't need much."

Fair enough. "What are you doing here?" I asked. "How did you get in?"

"I snuck in. Been doing it every day since he got here. I found Willie on the Rutherford beach the other night."

"What were you doing at Rutherford in the middle of the night?"

"I live there."

Okay. "What did you do when you found him?"

"I called 211 on my cell phone."

"You have a cell phone?" I asked, recognizing the emergency number for the homeless.

She nodded. "My sister gave it to me."

"You have a sister?"

She nodded. "She lives here in Boca."

"In a house?"

She nodded.

"Why don't you live with her?"

"Don't want to. I'm more at home homeless."

Okay. "Do you know what happened to him?"

"Are you a cop?"

"I'm a private detective working on Willie's case."

"Who hired you?"

"Jerry Small, a local newspaper reporter."

"The guy who wrote nice things about Willie?"

"Yes," I said. "He wants me to find out what happened to him. Can you tell me anything that might help?"

"Are you gonna tell the cops?"

"Maybe."

"Then I ain't talking. I'm afraid of cops."

"Okay," I said, deciding to obstruct justice rather than pass a lead. "I won't tell them."

"Promise?"

"Promise."

"I know Willie wasn't attacked in the park," she said.

"How do you know?"

"He hated the place . . . stopped going there a long time ago."

"You think Willie was attacked elsewhere, then moved to the park?"

She nodded. "Make people think he was mugged in a homeless park by another homeless person."

That's exactly what I thought.

She nodded and turned to the man in the bed. "Can I finish his makeup?"

I handed her the brush and paint.

"When you're done, you want to do lunch?" I asked, thinking I might get more information for my case.

"If you're buying."

Chapter 10

The Early Bird

I drove to the Bagel Barn on Glades Road near the hospital. The little deli was aflutter with a flock of squawking Early Birds. Over a thousand endangered species live in South Florida. The Early Bird is not one of them.

Bailey held her hands to her ears. "It's so noisy."

"Feeding time," I answered, finding two empty seats at the counter. Bailey sat next to me, still holding her hands over her ears.

A fat lady wearing stained, fully stretched stretch pants patted her helmet hair and looked down her nose at my raggedy friend. Bailey wasn't much to look at with her scraggly hair, random teeth, tattered clothes, and wrinkled, rutted skin. I wondered why the fat lady was looking down her nose at someone else's appearance. Did she think she looked better because someone else looked worse?

Out of the corner of my eye I saw Bailey stuff a fistful of artificial-sweetener packets into her pocket. The waitress behind the counter scowled.

"I'll take care of it," I promised.

She nodded. "What'll you have?"

"I don't like tuna fish," Bailey said, squinting at the menu.

"Don't order it," I told her.

"What's an Early-Bird Special?"

"A discounted meal if you eat between certain hours," I explained.

"What if you're not hungry during those hours?"

"Hunger has nothing to do with it," I told her.

"That doesn't make sense."

"Order something," I told her, not wanting to discuss South Florida traditions.

"I'll have a tuna fish sandwich."

What? "You just said you didn't like tuna."

"I did not," Bailey said seriously.

A little mental illness goes a long way.

Bailey ate like a bird; a condor. She hunkered over her plate and didn't surface until the pickles, chips, and tuna were gone.

"The free lunch at Missionary Church is better than this," she decided, stealing regular-sugar packets.

"Don't be ridiculous," I told her.

"Guess what we had for lunch yesterday?"

"Osso buco," I joked smugly.

"Who told you?"

"C'mon, Bailey. Who serves braised veal shanks in a soup kitchen?"

"Boca." She used half the city's name as a full explanation.

I thought her answer had merit. "Where does this fancy food come from?"

"Publix and Whole Foods donate a lot," she said, naming two supermarket chains. "So do other restaurants in the area . . . way better than this."

She pinched her nose for emphasis.

"You ate everything on your plate," I reminded her.

"Beggars can't be choosers."

Good point. "Who cooks at the soup kitchen?"

"Volunteers from Boca."

"I heard the homeless aren't welcome in Boca."

"We're not welcome anywhere," Bailey sighed. "Most people look away from us . . . but some look after us."

"No one looked after Willie the other night," I said, getting up from the counter and paying the bill. "Do you have any idea where Willie might have been attacked before getting dumped at the park?"

"I heard through the grapevine he liked to sleep at the bottom of the stairs behind St. Mary's Church. Maybe he was there."

"What time did you find him in the park?" I asked, walking outside.

"Exactly two thirty in the morning. I saw the time on my cell when I called 211."

"Was he conscious?"

She shook her head.

"How fast did the police get there?"

"Fast."

"Did you talk to them?"

"No, I don't talk to the police, I told you," she said. "I hid in the banyans and watched the hospital ambulance take him away. I waited a few hours, called the hospital, found out he was alone, and headed over."

"How far is the hospital from the park?"

"Rutherford's off A1A north of Mizner."

"That's miles away," I said. "How did you get here?"

"Walked some . . . borrowed a bike."

"You mean you stole a bike."

"I'll return it. I left it behind the hospital in a safe place."

I drove Bailey to the back of the hospital. No bike.

"Some son of a bitch took it," she said, sounding surprised. "Can't trust anyone these days."

"I'll drive you home," I volunteered.

"I'm homeless."

Duh, Eddie. "Where to then?"

"Rutherford Park."

Bailey led me along the elevated boardwalk that cut through the tropical vegetation of the park and ended at a locked gate. Beyond the gate, a flight of stairs led down to the shore of Lake Boca; across the water tall apartment buildings promised excellent views. For the people living low in the weeds of Rutherford Park, I imagined those apartments must have seemed as far away as the twilight moon overhead.

"This is where I found him." Bailey pointed down at the sand about eight feet below us. "Facedown, back of his head busted open . . . barely breathing."

She looked as if she would cry.

Don't cry. I hate when women cry. Why do they do that?

"How do you get under the boardwalk with the gate locked?" I asked.

"I can pick locks. It's a good skill to have if you're homeless."

Bailey shuffled to the gate, removed a small wire from her oversize overcoat, fiddled with the gate lock briefly, and it popped open. We walked down the stairs.

It was dark and damp under the boardwalk.

"You sleep here?" I asked.

She nodded.

"Alone?"

"Who would want to sleep with me?"

I didn't answer.

"I usetabe good-looking," she told me.

Everybody used to be something.

It was growing dark and I heard rustling in the woods around us.

"Are you okay staying here alone?" I asked.

"I'm a survivor."

"I'm sure you are. How long have you been living in the street?"

"Maybe thirty years."

"Where are you from?"

She shrugged, indicating she'd rather not say.

I changed the subject. "If Willie was attacked somewhere else and driven here, that means someone strong had to carry him from a car down this long boardwalk. It was probably two guys."

I looked up at the boardwalk and pictured Willie slung over someone's shoulder, then propped up on the railing and shoved off. He would have flipped over once on the way down and landed face-first in the sand.

"Thank you for all your help, Bailey. How can I get in touch with you?"

"Call me on my cell." She gave me the number.

Wireless in Boca. Cool.

Chapter 11

Pre–Morning Mass

Claudette was working late at the clinic again so the apartment was empty when I arrived home. My Viagra erector set would remain untested for another night. I was relieved and depressed because I was relieved.

I didn't sleep well and at four thirty I drove in predawn darkness to Second Avenue in search of St. Mary's. The Mini didn't have GPS, but when I saw a ten-foot-high cross perched on a peaked roof, silhouetted against a predawn sky, I said, "You have arrived at your destination."

I turned off my headlights and turned into the parking lot. The white church was dark. God was closed. I drove behind the building, shut off the engine, and took my ND Hyperbeam flashlight from my glove compartment. I went to the staircase Bailey had described and descended the twelve concrete steps below ground level to a locked metal door.

Add breaking and entering to obstruction of justice.

I picked the uncomplicated Tylo lock using an equally un-complicated kit I carried in my wallet.

The door opened inward, and I beamed light around a storage room filled with stacked boxes. I tiptoed across the room to a door secured with a standard Schlage lock. It was easy pickings and I entered an adjoining office. My flashlight revealed two antique desks facing each other, cluttered with papers. Computer screens were on each desk, and several filing cabinets were against the walls . . . nothing unusual. Suddenly the beam illuminated the bloodstained, lifeless face of a bearded man. I retreated two startled steps, caught the calves of my legs on a chair behind me, and fell hard on my back. I rolled over professionally and stood up reaching for the Glock nine-millimeter in the back of my waistband. I aimed the gun and the light in the direction of the dead man. He was still there . . . motionless like a statue . . . head slumped on his shoulder.

I've seen this man before.

I illuminated one section at a time until I got the total picture.

"Jesus Christ," I sighed, and that's exactly who it was . . . hanging on the wall.

This is a Catholic church . . . dummy. He belongs here. You don't.

I approached one of the desks and debated picking the lock of the center drawer. Concluding that Willie's head had been shattered and his body moved for a reason, I decided to break and enter again.

"Follow the money," I said to myself, and picked the lock. I found a ledger in the middle drawer, removed it, and flipped through the pages. Columns of numbers, both large and small, filled the ledger. A dollar sign preceding each sum. It represented a lot of money from a poor box, even for Boca.

I glanced at my watch. I had been there long enough. I returned the ledger and locked the drawer. I exited the way I entered, locking each door I had opened. I hobbled up the steps, got in the Mini, and drove off.

It was only 6:00 a.m. when I arrived at the office and found Lou Dewey already at his desk.

"You're in early," I said.

"I never went home," he sighed, looking up from his computer. "I've been here all night researching B. I. Grover."

"And?"

"I have more to verify, but based on what I found so far . . . I believe the man could be running a Ponzi scheme." Lou referred to the old scam where early investors are paid high interest rates from the money of new investors without any actual profits being made. "I came across another name too, Bernard Madoff. I think he may be even bigger than Grover."

"Forget Madoff for now. Focus on Grover. How long before you'll know for sure if he's a bad guy?"

"A few weeks," Lou said. "But, as a former bad guy myself, I can sense these things and I sense a bad result."

"I thought Grover was supposed to be a genius?"

"Maybe he's a genius at fraud."

"Everyone praises him."

"Not everyone," Lou disagreed. "Some people see him as God's T-bill, but some see him as the devil's disciple."

"Why doesn't everyone see the same thing?"

"Greed can be blinding," Lou said.

"What about the thousands of clients he has all over the world."

"If I'm right . . . they're thousands of frauds or fools. Or they're in on the con."

"Steve Coleman just invested and he's no fool. He's a very successful man."

"You can be a successful fool."

"Why hasn't someone blown the whistle on Grover already?" I asked.

"Someone did . . . years ago. A fraud specialist named Harry Chan. He submitted a damning report on Grover to the SEC and they ignored him."

"Why?"

Lou shrugged. "The human condition. Sometimes people look away when something is too horrible to be real or too good to be true."

"I have to tell Steve Coleman about this."

"Wait, I could be wrong. But, honestly, I think it's just a matter of time."

"How much time?"

Lou shrugged. "Not much. Taking money from small groups like Steve's is uncharacteristic, which means he needs cash. That's not a good sign."

I stood up. "I don't care if Steve won't listen to me. I have to tell him."

"Let me finish my research before you say anything to anyone. I don't want to be wrong."

"Okay, I'll wait, but work fast," I said, sitting down again.

"What are you doing here so early?"

I told him about Bailey, my visit to St. Mary's, and the ledgers full of money in the priest's desk. "Something's not kosher at that church," I said. "I think Willie stumbled into a con game and had to be shut up."

"A Catholic priest would never do something like that."

"You're kidding, right?"

"On second thought . . ."

CHAPTER 12

IN MEMORY OF THE SIXTH GRADE

I stood at the bathroom sink staring at the diamond-shaped, electric-blue pill on the counter. I looked in the mirror and saw a short, rugged-looking man in good shape for his age . . . with erectile dysfunction.

"No more carefree erections for you," I said to the mirror. "You're not in the sixth grade anymore."

I still remembered the day Mr. Johnson, my talking penis, made his first public appearance. I was retrieving a pencil I had purposely dropped on the classroom floor so MJ and I could look up the skirt of the girl sitting next to me . . . when the teacher called my name.

Not now, I begged MJ silently as I stood up. Defiantly he stood up with me. Mrs. Thompson, the teacher, did a double take as I approached her at the blackboard, and she took a step back when I reached for the chalk in her hand. A friend of mine in the class whispered, "Boner," and all the other boys laughed.

Some girls covered their eyes . . . some didn't. Mr. Johnson took notes for future reference. I got the math answer wrong but I didn't care. I had a new best friend.

I know a dog is supposed to be man's best friend, but Mr. Johnson became mine. I could have chosen a dog. A dog is loyal. Mr. Johnson was not. A dog can learn tricks. MJ could only sit up and beg. A dog follows his master. I followed my Johnson.

He got me in a lot of trouble but I always forgave him. When we were young, we would lie awake in bed at night and talk for hours about the wondrous things we would do when we grew up . . . and then we did them. We let the good times roll and thought they would never end. But they did. The thrill was gone and Mr. Johnson's one eye was growing dim. I knew I would out-live my best friend unless I did something drastic. I took the pill.

"Did you take the pill?" Claudette asked an hour later when we got into bed.

I nodded.

"And?"

"Nothing."

"Don't we have to be active for it to work?"

"I don't know. This is my first time."

"Mine too," she said.

"Viagra virgins," I joked, but neither of us laughed.

"Why did you choose Viagra?"

"The Cialis ads show a man and a woman in separate bath-tubs on top of a mountain," I said. "We only have one bathtub, and even if we had two, we couldn't have sex after moving them up a mountain."

"Who could have sex in separate bathtubs, anyway?"

"Another good point," I said. "And who wants an erection to last more than four hours?"

She raised her hand to volunteer. We both laughed.

"I draw the line at three hours and forty minutes," I bragged.

"We'll see," she said, reaching for me.

Foreplay became five-play and we were up to eight-play before I became aware that my nose was running. Viagra wasn't giving me an erection. It was giving me nasal congestion.

"I can't breathe," I told her, gasping.

"I'll be right back." She hurried to the bathroom. She returned with a pill and a glass of water.

"I'm not taking another Viagra. I'll have a hard-on and a heart attack at the same time."

"It's Sudafed for your nose."

I took my medicine.

"Now where were we?" she asked, snuggling close to me.

"If I recall correctly, we were nowhere," I said, feeling useless.

"Oh, really? Then what's this?" she asked, squeezing.

"What's what?" I looked under the covers. "Where did he come from? He never said a word."

"This is no time for talking." Claudette pounced.

I wish I had been there.

In the morning I called my urologist. "I had sex with a stranger last night."

"Was it safe sex?" Dr. Koblentz asked.

"It was with Claudette."

"Who was the stranger?"

"Mr. Johnson," I explained.

"Did you take a pill?"

"Yes."

"The feeling of detachment is not unusual with a Viagra pill," Dr. Koblentz said. "You're dealing with a chemical reaction rather than a purely physical one."

"Actually, I took two pills."

"Two Viagra pills?"

"No, one Viagra and one Sudafed. The Viagra pill opened my arteries and blocked my nose. Plus sex ain't what it ustabe."

"Of course not. You're not who you used to be. You've changed."

"I didn't feel any changes," I said, frustrated.

"Did you feel your hair turning gray?"

"My hair is salt-and-pepper," I protested.

"My point is that you don't feel every change you go through. At least now you can have sex."

"Yeah, but it's weird sex, which was always okay with me. But this is different. Before I took the Viagra pill, I felt guilty for cheating Claudette, but when I took the pill, I felt like she was cheating on me with my own penis."

"Do you think she noticed a difference in you?"

"I think so," I said. "I wasn't very lovey-dovey. She likes that. I just didn't feel it. Mostly I was nervous. What am I supposed to do now?"

"Stop putting pressure on yourself. Adapting to changes is never easy. Think of something else."

I thought about when having sex was easy and finding someone to have it with was the hard part.

Chapter 13

Computer Courage
February 2006

After Lou Dewey had investigated B.I.G. for three weeks, he was convinced Grover was a fraud.

"I can't believe he got away with this con for so long," Lou said, tossing a folder on a pile of folders on his desk. "I was good but this guy is great."

"Are you sure you're right?" I asked.

"Positive. Harry Chan, the investigator I told you about, was one hundred percent right. His problem was, he couldn't relate to average people. He didn't know how to simplify his complicated formulas. He confused people and they ignored him."

"That doesn't make sense."

"Sure it does. First of all, the SEC has a conflict of interest," Lou said. "They're employed by the people they're supposed to regulate. They don't want to find anything wrong."

"That's ridiculous."

"It gets worse. The SEC doesn't have one forensic examiner

in the agency capable of understanding Chan. They wouldn't know a complicated scam if it bit them in the ass. So we have to prove Grover's a fraud in terms the average person can understand. Then we have to take that information to the FBI, not the SEC."

"What happened to Chan?"

"He died in an automobile accident," Lou said. "His whole family was with him."

"You think Grover had something to do with the accident?"

"I wouldn't be surprised."

"If they did something to Chan, they can do something to you," I said.

"I can take care of myself."

"No, you can't. Your girlfriend can beat you up."

"No, she can't."

"My girlfriend can," I said.

"What's your point?"

"Danger is not your specialty. That's my job."

"Look, they're not scaring me off," Lou insisted. "I'm going to bring this sociopath down."

"You seem to be taking this personally."

"I am. I was a con man in the old days. But I was never evil. I never set out to destroy people. Grover is evil. He's going to financially ruin anyone who trusts him and not give a shit. I have to stop him."

"I understand," I said. "I hate guys like Grover too. But if he's dangerous, you'll be out of your element. Let me take your proof to the FBI. Grover can't scare me off."

"I'm not afraid. I'm committed."

"You should *be* committed." A thought occurred to me. "Lou, the truth." I looked into his eyes. "Are you trying to prove you're smarter than Grover?"

"Absolutely," he said without blinking.

I phoned Chief Burke the next day to talk about Lou and Grover. He had an agenda of his own when he answered the phone.

"I heard you were at a pill mill raid a few nights ago in Fort Lauderdale," Frank said as a greeting.

"I was on a case," I explained. "The raid was coincidental."

"What kind of case?"

"The uncontrollable distribution of controlled substances." I gave him Hurwitz's details.

He asked if I trusted Doc.

I said I didn't.

"Is this another Boca Knights crusade?"

I said it was and I welcomed him to join.

He said he was too busy. "Haven't you been reading the papers? We have county officials, local lawyers, and corrupt commissioners being led away in cuffs for fixing state bids for roads, bridges, and canals. Corrupt county commissioners are being indicted . . . not to mention sex scandals."

"You can mention them," I said.

"Do you know Dr. Al Minkoff?"

"He's my dentist. Don't tell me he's dirty . . . especially not his hands."

"We arrested him for stealing four hundred thousand dollars from the Florida Medical Association," Frank said. "He used the money on hookers and a girlfriend."

"His hands are probably diseased. Jeez, I know his wife. She's a hygienist in the office."

"His soon-to-be ex-wife. She's suing for divorce."

"I better cancel my cleaning appointment."

"We arrested the headmaster of Addison Academy for forging parents' signatures and attendance records to get millions of dollars in state aid. It's a disgrace."

"Talking about disgraces, Frank. Can you explain how a

fifteen-time convicted rapist was arrested for attempted rape in Delray last week?"

"Ask the judges," Frank told me. "They released him."

"How about Ira Cantor?"

Cantor was a mental case who had been arrested and released 190 times for crimes and misdemeanors throughout Florida.

"He's in jail again." Burke sighed.

"What did he do this time?"

"He threatened to shoot a motorist for not giving him a ride."

"Was Ira armed?"

"Of course not," Frank said. "But this time the victim is pressing charges. This is going to look very bad for the Boca police force. We've arrested that lunatic fifty out of those one hundred and ninety times."

"In all due respect, Frank, that's horrible."

"I agree. But the police aren't the ones turning him loose. It's the system. His arrests are mostly misdemeanors . . . loitering, prowling, intoxication . . . stuff like that. The victims usually don't prosecute because Cantor never really hurts anyone, he's mentally unstable and his mother always offers to pay restitution."

"So, a potentially dangerous, mentally ill person is put back on the streets one hundred and ninety times?"

"It's the law," Frank sighed.

"It's not justice. He should be in an institution being treated for his problem."

"I agree," Frank said. "But the state of Florida rates forty-eighth in the country for mental-health funding. It's a numbers game. Palm Beach County receives less than a thousand a year per patient."

"What's going to happen to Cantor this time?"

"Unless the victim drops the charges, and it doesn't look like he will, Cantor could get thirty years."

"Thirty years after a hundred and eighty-nine second chances?" I asked. "Where's the sense in that?"

"I said it was legally possible. I don't think it will happen, but it could."

"Florida has to work on consistency," I said.

"Every state has inconsistencies. In Alabama, corrupting morals is only a misdemeanor."

"Why would you know a statistic like that?" I asked.

He laughed.

I told him about Lou's B.I.G. investigation and my concern for Lou's safety.

"Lou's probably got a dose of computer courage," Frank said. "Some people feel indestructible behind a keyboard and monitor. There's a sense of power being anonymous. You'll just have to watch out for him."

"I've already got a full schedule."

"I'm sure. How are you doing with the Weary Willie case, by the way?"

"I've got a few leads but nothing solid," I said.

"That's what I figured. I haven't seen anything in the paper."

"How are you guys doing?"

"I can't talk about an active case," Frank said, "but I can tell you it won't stay active for long if something doesn't happen soon."

The world is all about priorities.

Chapter 14

Late February at St. Mary's

Three nights later, I took my second Viagra pill. It was a different experience from the first. My nose got stuffy again, but this time the Mr. Johnson impersonator talked to me.

Do I know you? he asked.

We met once before.

I don't remember. Was I on drugs?

Yes, like you are now.

When we were done, Claudette went to sleep, my new associate went away, and I went into a mild depression. I still hadn't adapted to change and I sensed Claudette was having trouble too.

My cell phone rang an hour later. It was Three Bag Bailey, my newly appointed assistant investigator.

"I'm watching two big guys walking up the stairs behind St. Mary's," she told me.

"What do they look like?" I rolled out of bed, trying not to wake Claudette.

"Like Brooklyn bouncers. Work shirts, jeans, both wearing Yankees baseball caps."

"What are they doing?"

"Leaving, I think."

"I wonder why they're using the back door," I said.

"They seem to be looking for something."

I heard a sharp, scratching sound, like metal on metal.

"Where are you?"

"Hiding behind the Dumpster in the back parking lot."

"Do you hear that scratching sound?"

"Yeah, it's coming from above me," she said. "But I don't see anything. It's too dark."

"What are the two guys doing now?"

"I can't see them either. They moved out of the light."

I heard a hiss, louder than a snake. "Oh, shit," Bailey screamed. "Get away from me." She cried out in pain.

"Bailey, what's happening?" I shouted.

"Oh my God," she screamed. "Stop."

I heard a gruff, male voice call out, "Who's there?"—followed by the sound of running.

"Call my sister," Bailey said breathlessly. "Tell her I'm going to the baker."

I heard the clatter of metal, followed by an inhuman howl.

I didn't bother to call her name again. I knew Bailey was gone and St. Mary's was probably a crime scene. I should have called the police, but I had given Bailey my word not to.

I was at the church in thirty minutes with my homemade forensic kit and my old Glock nine. The parking lot was empty. The Mini's headlights illuminated the Dumpster. I parked behind it and walked to where I guessed Bailey had been hiding.

My flashlight showed fresh blood on the outer wall. I cursed myself for letting her get involved. The grass behind the trash bin was trampled and I saw a scarf on the ground. I picked it up. It was wet with blood.

This is bad. Call the police.

I gave my word I wouldn't.

You gave it to a slightly demented person. She won't remember.

Maybe not, but I will.

I walked across the deserted parking lot to the side stairwell and played the light on the stairs. I saw nothing unusual but I detected the smell of chemicals. I closed my eyes and mouth and inhaled through my nose. It smelled like a swimming pool or a hospital corridor.

Chlorine. Stain remover.

I took a bottle of premixed luminol from my crime kit. Luminol is used to detect bloodstains after a surface has been cleaned. Next I removed the long-exposure Canon Mark II camera I used for night photography. I sprayed the top three stairs with luminol and waited for the chemiluminescence . . . the striking blue glow that appears when the chemical reacts to the iron in hemoglobin.

Nothing!

I sprayed the next three steps and was disappointed *again*.

Why clean up with bleach if you had nothing to hide?

The ninth step lit up like a glow stick. I fumbled for my camera and snapped two long-exposure pictures. I sprayed again, and the last three steps turned bright blue and the adjacent walls glowed. That meant blood splatter. Weary Willie had been here and bled all over the place.

I struggled up the stairs on old, creaky knees and hobbled to my Mini. I was halfway out of the lot when I remembered Bailey's last words.

I remembered the clattering sound I heard after Bailey stopped screaming.

I could call her sister if I had her cell phone.

My tires squealed as I made a U-turn and raced back to the trash bin. I stood on the hood of the Mini and shone my flashlight into the Dumpster. It was empty . . . except for the cell phone on the bottom.

Bailey, you genius.

I pulled into the parking lot of the Embassy Suites on Yamato just west of the I-95 overpass and opened Bailey's phone. Her speed dial contained three sets of initials: BK, BRPD, and MS. Trying to think like Bailey, I figured BK was for the Boca Knight, BRPD signified Boca Raton Police Department, and MS was My Sister.

I pressed the MS button and a woman's voice answered. "Bailey, is everything all right?"

"This isn't Bailey," I said calmly, trying not to alarm her. "It's a friend."

"Are you a homeless person too?"

"No. My name is Eddie Perlmutter."

"I never heard of you. What are you doing with Bailey's phone?"

"It's a long story. Can we meet?"

"No. I don't know you."

"Bailey wants me to give you a message."

"You can give it to me over the phone." Her voice sounded unsteady . . . like Bailey's.

"She's going to the baker. Does that mean anything to you?"

"Oh, God." She hung up.

I redialed. No answer.

For the last time, Eddie, call the cops.

I gave my word.

You're a schmuck.

Yes, but an honorable one.

Chapter 15

How to Make a Zombie

I got off the phone with Bailey's sister and realized I hadn't asked her name or address.

That would never have happened a few years ago. Damn.

I drove home wishing Bailey's phone would ring. I went to bed disappointed.

The next morning Claudette and I had breakfast on the balcony of my San Remo apartment overlooking a narrow, man-made canal and the sixth hole of the neighboring Boca Heights golf course. I brought her up to date with my cases. She asked me concise, intelligent questions about Bailey, her sister, Yankee caps, St. Mary's money, Doc Hurwitz, and Lou's computer courage. I gave her rambling, inconclusive answers and ended with a question of my own.

"Do you think the girl at CVS knows the Viagra's for me?"

"That's what you're thinking about?"

"I can't control every thought," I said, defending myself.

"There's no fool like an old fool," she said with a sigh, and took a sip of coffee.

I gazed across the thin strip of water at the golf course. Two golf carts and four golfers were about forty yards away from my balcony on an elevated tee. Two women were in one cart and two men in the other. The women talked to each other while the men stretched and took smooth, rhythmic practice swings. A tall, slim man dressed in pink teed up a ball. He took two perfect, rhythmic practice swings, assumed a professional hitting stance, and stood motionless just long enough for an evil spirit to inhabit his body. His actual swing was a lightning-fast blur of iron and wood, striking the ball and producing a sound similar to that of a stick hitting a rock.

The ball screeched over his left foot, bounced wildly down the side of the hill, and splashed into the water. Something live and scaly scrambled from the underbrush and slithered into the canal.

"*Shit*," the pink man cursed, then pounded his clubhead into the ground and shouted, "Mulligan," before repeating the entire process. The results were identical.

"I suck," he cursed, and sulked to his cart.

Claudette leaned toward me. "I understand *shit* and *I suck* . . . but what's a *mulligan*?"

"A magic word."

"Like abracadabra?"

"Sort of . . . but it only works on a golf course."

"What does it do?"

"It makes bad shots disappear and gives you a do-over."

"Isn't that cheating?"

"Not in golf," I said. "If the other three players with you agree that your bad shot didn't happen, it didn't happen . . . and you get to do it again."

"What if they don't agree?"

"You have to live with your mistake."

"Like real life," she said.

I nodded.

We watched foursomes come and go and listened to them.

"Elephant's ass," one man shouted after he hit.

"What's an elephant's ass?" Claudette asked.

"It's high and it stinks," I told her.

She put her fingertips to her lips and giggled. "Golfers are so hard on themselves."

"Self-loathing is part of the game. Listen."

The words floated across the canal on a breeze. *Idiot, Imbecile, Stupid, I can't believe it, I always do that, I never do that, I sliced it, I hooked it, I skulled it, I shanked it, I smothered it, I dubbed it, I picked up, I hit down, I hit it thin, I hit it fat, I quit at the bottom, I came over the top, I suck, This game sucks, I hate this game.*

"They sound so unhappy," she said sympathetically. "Why do they play?"

"Some people do self-mutilation . . . some play golf."

My cell phone rang and I said hello to Lou Dewey, who brought me up to date on his B.I.G. research. "I'm almost ready to go public," he said. "I've narrowed down my explanation to a single question."

"Good. Just don't do anything without talking to me first, Lou," I told him.

He didn't make any promises before he disconnected.

I put down the phone. "I'm really concerned that Lou is going to screw this up."

"Do you think he's right that Grover is a fraud?"

"I don't know what to think. How could one man manipulate so many people for so long?"

"In Haiti they use voodoo," she said.

"Pins, dolls, and chicken heads?"

"Mind control," she clarified. "*Bokos* in Haiti can turn normal people into mindless zombies."

"*Bokos?*"

"Witch doctors."

"You think Grover's a witch doctor?"

"If people follow him mindlessly . . . yes," she said emphatically.

"A Wall Street witch doctor," I said, laughing.

"*Bokos* are not funny," she said seriously. "They can destroy a person's mind."

"I'm sorry. But I can't picture Grover dressed as a witch doctor. He wears two-thousand-dollar suits to work every day."

"If he has the power to control people's minds, he is nothing more than a well-dressed *boko*."

"Voodoo doesn't exist on Wall Street," I told her.

"You must be kidding."

"Let me rephrase that. There are no zombies on Wall Street."

"Ed-eee," she whined as if she were talking to a slow learner.

"Okay, maybe Wall Street has black magic and mumbo jumbo," I conceded, "but that doesn't make Grover a *boko*."

"If he makes zombies, he is a *boko*."

"How do you make a zombie, anyway?"

"By paralyzing a victim using poison from a puffer fish," she said cryptically.

"Or in Grover's case . . . shit from a bull," I said, going with the flow.

"Yes." She smiled. "The victim is paralyzed and mesmerized by the venom, but still fully awake. The poison eventually causes neurological damage resulting in the loss of the victim's ability to reason. The *boko* then fills the victim's head with crazy ideas and superstitions. Lastly, the poor soul is buried alive in a shallow grave with just enough air to last one night. The next day, shortly before death, the victim is uncovered. From the grave emerges a sensory-deprived, dehydrated, brain-damaged zombie."

"Conditioned to believe whatever the *boko* says," I completed her sentence.

"Exactly." She patted my knee like a proud teacher. "The *boko* creates zombies and rules them by fear."

"Grover doesn't use fear," I said, pointing out a discrepancy.

"Yes, he does. He uses the fear of being left out of something too good to be true. Everyone has different fears."

Benjamin Israel Grover . . . a *boko* . . . mesmerizing people by burying them under a pile of bullshit and not letting them up for air until they've lost their humanity and sense of reality?

Why not?

Chapter 16

City of Pearls

To find Bailey I had to learn the habits and haunts of Boca's homeless. I knew where Bailey slept but not where she lived. I asked Chief Burke for help. He assigned me to his information officer, Sergeant Iris Adler, for a briefing, and Officer Rosalind Dowd for a tour. I met Sergeant Adler in her office at police headquarters. She was thin and fit and looked young enough to be my daughter.

"What can I tell you, Mr. Perlmutter?" she asked.

"What's the police policy toward the homeless in Boca?"

"We use the *Pottinger* decision of 1988. Are you familiar with that?"

I said I wasn't.

"In 1988 a class-action suit was filed against the City of Miami on behalf of the homeless. A man named Michael Pottinger was one of the plaintiffs. The suit claimed the city routinely harassed

homeless people, destroyed their property, and violated their con-
stitutional rights. After a lengthy trial the homeless won."

"Who said you can't fight city hall?" I quipped. "What was
the judgment?"

"The city was ordered to change police procedures. Con-
tracts were written and thorough record keeping was ordered.
An advisory committee was formed to enforce compliance."

"Was there a monetary award?"

"Six hundred thousand dollars . . . about fifteen hundred per
plaintiff. But the suit was about change, not money."

"Did things change?"

"Absolutely," she said. "The biggest change was police can
no longer arrest the homeless for performing life-sustaining
bodily functions in public."

"Do you have to make a lot of judgment calls?"

"Someone always pushes the envelope. We try to enforce
the law sensibly."

I heard a knock on the open door and turned to see another
policewoman young enough to be my daughter.

"Officer Rosalind Dowd," Adler said, "meet Mr. Eddie Perlmutter."

Dowd's handshake was firm. "The Boca Knight. It's a pleasure. Are you ready for a tour of the back roads of Boca?"

"Ready."

As promised, Officer Dowd drove to areas in Boca seldom
seen. We started in Pearl City, located west of Federal Highway,
near upscale Mizner Park.

"Pearl City is Boca's oldest black community," she said,
pointing at small, faded houses. "It was originally built in 1915
for black laborers working on the construction of the Boca Re-
sort. This part of Pearl City was declared a historical district
just a few years ago."

She stopped by a huge tree with enormous protruding roots.

"This banyan is called the Tree of Knowledge. Generations of people in Pearl City sat in its shade and learned. It was so revered that when Glades Road was widened, they diverted the street around the tree to save it."

She showed me a modest memorial bust of Martin Luther King, isolated and alone at the end of a nondescript street.

We exited the neighborhood and drove north on Dixie, crossing Glades. "Dixie Manor is part of Pearl City too." She pointed at rows of one- and two-level apartment buildings. "Originally it was built as army barracks during World War Two and was acquired by the Housing Authority in 1978. They were rehabbed into Section Eight housing after that along with Lincoln Center, just north of Glades."

She waved to a couple of black kids on bicycles. They waved back.

"How's the relationship between police and residents here?"

"The historical district is peaceful. Generations of black families have been living there for years. Dixie Manor and Lincoln Center are more transient, and drugs are the main problem there."

"Why is it called Pearl City?"

"I think Hawaiian pearl pineapples were farmed years ago."

We made more twists and turns, and Officer Dowd continued pointing out places of interest.

"The Friendship Missionary Baptist Church over there has a soup kitchen run by Boca Helping Hands, a charitable organization. A lot of homeless eat free."

Three Bag Bailey told me.

"Who qualifies for a free meal?" I asked.

"Everyone who wants one. Helping Hands wants to teach poor people to be self-sufficient, but they have to feed them before we can teach them."

I checked my watch. It was nearly 11:00 a.m. "Can we take a look?"

"Sure." She parked near the church.

Several people, black and white . . . poor and homeless . . . were gathered outside the church. Some looked worn and forlorn. Some looked feral. Some smiled at Officer Dowd, some didn't. Everyone looked at me curiously, trying to decide if I was there to help or to eat.

The dining area was a small, rectangular room crammed with packages and people. Paper bags of groceries were lined up like soldiers on two long wooden tables that ran the length of the dining area. Each bag had a name attached.

On the other side of the room were three rows of tables with enough chairs to seat about thirty people. The kitchen area was bustling with enthusiastic helpers who seemed to be delighted to be there.

Officer Dowd introduced me to a bulky, middle-aged woman wearing a stained apron. Her hair was short and frizzy, and I noticed a pencil stuck behind her right ear. She smiled when she heard my name, shook my hand, and patted my back. "Welcome."

"Thank you," I said, looking around. "This is a busy place."

"Last year we served over five thousand meals in this place and delivered over seven thousand more to homes," she told me proudly.

"I'm impressed."

"Thanks," she said enthusiastically, and called out to her fellow workers. "Hey, everyone, we've got a visitor. It's the Boca Knight, Eddie Perlmutter, and he's impressed by what we do."

People stopped working and actually applauded, making me feel guilty for not being as enthusiastic as they were. Greetings were shouted at me from around the room, and I waved self-consciously.

I was introduced to the head chef, who gave me a bear hug. "How you been, Eddie? Long time no see."

He looked familiar but nothing clicked.

"Harold Trager," he said. "Coolidge Corner . . . Brookline. My father, Al, owned a deli there."

"Harold, I thought you looked familiar," I said.

"I should. I used to throw you out of my father's deli all the time."

"You look great, Harold. I didn't recognize you. You're so thin now."

"Are you saying I was fat?" he said, laughing.

"No. You had big bones."

"Elephants have big bones. But thanks anyway."

"It's good to see you," I told him. "By the way, why did you throw me out of your father's deli all the time?"

"You and your Golden Gloves buddies used to hang out at a table and order nothing but cream sodas. We needed the table for real customers. Everyone else in the deli was afraid of you, so my father told me to throw you out."

"You weren't afraid of me?"

"I was scared shit of you, but my father scared me more."

"What's for lunch today, Harold?"

"Osso buco," he said proudly. "It's my specialty."

"So I've been told."

We stayed through lunch but didn't eat. Officer Dowd mingled easily with the people while I kept out of the way and watched. Despite the crowded conditions, there was no pushing or shoving. I noticed a long line of filled paper bags marked "hygiene kits" under the tables. I looked inside a bag and saw toothpaste, soap, shampoo, toilet paper, dental floss, Q-tips, and several miscellaneous personal items. The kits were marked with names, and I watched as each bag was claimed and carried away. When the room was empty, except for the volunteers, I checked my watch. It took about an hour to feed over thirty people and provide home supplies to many more. It reminded me of Thanksgiving: hours of preparation for a meal that ended in minutes.

I saw two unclaimed bags and mentioned it to Officer Dowd. She checked the name and said someone who looked out of place would show up for them. When the room was nearly empty, a neatly dressed, middle-aged man entered and signed for his bags. He was about to pick them up when he recognized me. He looked uncomfortable.

"You're the Boca Knight, aren't you?" he asked, walking toward me.

I nodded and extended my hand. "Eddie Perlmutter," I said with a friendly smile.

"Lincoln Tucker," he said, shaking my hand. "I was at your rally years ago."

"That makes you a Boca Knight too."

"I don't feel like one. I never thought I'd be in this position."

"You don't have to explain yourself to me," I said.

"I can't explain myself to me. I useta own a clothing store . . . Big Man of Boca . . . ever heard of it?"

"I never looked for a big man's shop?" I said, and laughed.

Tucker smiled.

"What happened to your business?"

"A bad economy and a national chain put me out of business," he said. "Now I'm just trying to survive until something else comes along."

"Never give up, Lincoln" was all I could think of to say.

"I tried so hard but here I am. It doesn't seem fair."

"Life isn't fair."

"Any advice?" Lincoln Tucker asked as he picked up his two bags of charity.

"Try again. Never give up."

Officer Dowd and I returned to the car and continued our tour.

"That's the Wayne Barton Center and the Florence Fuller Center across," she said.

I looked out the window. "What's their purpose?"

"Education facilities. They teach the poor how to break the cycle of poverty."

"How about the homeless?"

"They're welcome," she said. "But the homeless usually drop out of society because of trauma or mental illness. Most don't want a way back in. Why are you so interested in our homeless? No one told me."

"I'm investigating an attack on one. And I'm trying to find another one."

"Good luck with that," she said, shaking her head. "Florida is number one in the nation for attacks on the homeless, and nearly half those attacks are done by other homeless people. Can you tell me who you're looking for?"

"No. It's confidential. Sorry."

"I understand. Mind if I ask you another question?"

"Mind if I don't answer?"

"No. It's up to you," she said. "Is it true you were Boston's most decorated policeman?"

"One of them. I was also one of the most demoted. I did a lot of things I'm not proud of."

"I'll bet you did a lot of things you were proud of."

"I always tried to do the right thing," I told her. "Sometimes my methods were questionable."

"Did you ever kill a man?"

"Yes, it's a matter of public record. But no one ever killed me." She laughed.

She pointed at Grace Community Church and told me free clothes were available there.

"Do you think I need them?" I joked.

She laughed again.

"Let me ask you a question," I said, reversing roles. "Where would you look for a hiding homeless person?"

"A bus station. Most homeless are transient. We encourage them to leave town. We feed them, clothe them, and put them on a bus. It's called Greyhound therapy."

"Good thought. Anywhere else?"

"Parks, soup kitchens, hospitals . . . Baker centers—"

"What kind of centers?" I interrupted.

"Baker centers. Medical clinics that evaluate mental health under terms of the Baker Act. They also supply medical assistance like an emergency room."

Tell my sister I'm going to the baker.

"Can anyone go to a Baker center?"

"Yes. Originally people were brought to a Baker clinic involuntarily to determine if they were a potential danger to themselves or others. In 1996 the act was expanded to include people seeking voluntary admission and evaluation."

"Are there Baker centers in Boca?"

"They're in most of the public hospitals," she said.

"Any private facilities?"

"I only know of one," Officer Dowd said, turning into the parking lot at police headquarters. "It's on Boca Rio Road, near the turnpike."

She parked the cruiser and I jumped out, hurrying toward my Mini.

"What's the rush?" she called after me.

I turned around and walked quickly back to her. "I'm sorry," I said, shaking her hand. "But I have to run. Thank you for your help."

"Where are you going?"

"To the Baker."

CHAPTER 17

THE BAKER

The Boca Rehabilitation Clinic on Boca Rio Road was a privately owned facility treating Baker Act patients. No receptionist was at the reception desk when I arrived so I let myself into the in-patient area. I found a room marked BAILEY and entered without knocking.

She was in bed, unconscious, looking as if she had finished second in a two-person knife fight. Her forehead, cheeks, arms, and shoulders were crisscrossed with stitches to close deep gashes. Her eyes were swollen shut and her breathing was labored. At least she was breathing. I remembered a tough Boston cop named McPhee, six foot four, 240, who survived shootings, knifings, riots, and car crashes . . . only to die of a staph infection from a small cut on his foot. Bailey was more than a foot shorter than McPhee and at least 140 pounds lighter, yet she'd survived a date with Mac the Knife. Go figure.

"Who are you?" a frightened woman's voice asked from behind me.

I turned and saw a younger, neater version of Bailey. "I'm
the man who called you on Bailey's phone," I said, and walked
toward her.

She inhaled deeply, clenched her fists, and screamed until
her face turned red and her breath ran out. Without pausing, she
gulped in more air and screamed again. I didn't try to stop her,
figuring whoever came to rescue her could rescue me from her. A
nurse I recognized burst into the room and pointed at the human
alarm system.

"Kayla, stop screaming," she ordered.

Kayla stopped.

"Eddie, what are you doing here?" Nurse Joyce Weinberg
asked. I knew her through my personal nurse, Claudette.

"I'm on a case," I told her.

"Who is this man?" Kayla asked the nurse.

"He's a private detective," Nurse Weinberg vouched for me.

"Why does my sister need a private detective?"

"She doesn't," I said. "She was helping me with a case."

"That's ridiculous. She can't help herself," Kayla said.

"How did you get into this part of the clinic?" Nurse Weinberg asked.

"I let myself in," I said. "No one was at the front desk."

"Oh my God," Kayla said, rushing to Bailey's side. "You have
to increase security."

"Your sister is not in danger here," the nurse assured her.

"This guy just walked into her room," Kayla said adamantly.
"Any madman could walk into this room and attack her again."

"She wasn't attacked by a madman," Nurse Weinberg said.

"Of course she was." Kayla's voice grew louder. "Look at her
injuries. What kind of a wild animal does this to a helpless old
woman?"

"A raccoon," Nurse Weinberg said.

Kayla's jaw dropped and a long pause followed.

"A raccoon?"

"That's what Bailey told us when she came in here covered with blood," Nurse Weinberg said. "We treated her for rabies, distemper, and infection and the drugs worked in no time."

Racoons made sense to me. Florida was loaded with raccoons. The little bandits don't fear humans and they're big fans of garbage. I figured Bailey had been spying on the two fat Yankees fans from behind a Dumpster when the raccoon struck. Bailey and I heard scratching sounds before she was attacked, and they were probably claws on metal. She was on the phone with me at the time and must have thrown her phone into the Dumpster after shouting clues. Next, I figured she stole another bike and pedaled her wounded body several miles to the Baker center.

"Are you sure it was a raccoon?" Kayla asked.

"I'm sure," Nurse Weinberg said. "We did all the blood tests."

"They don't usually attack humans," I said.

"Why a raccoon?" Kayla asked.

"She was near garbage," I answered.

Kayla choked back a sob, sniffled, fussed with her sister's bedding needlessly, then dejectedly walked out the door.

Nice going, schmuck, I said to myself.

"You have a way with words," Joyce said. "A bad way."

"I suppose I could have been more tactful."

I found Kayla sitting on a bench in the corridor. I sat next to her. She looked haggard.

"A raccoon," she said, looking at me helplessly, shaking her head. "My sister was fighting with a raccoon over garbage."

"That's not exactly what I meant. Sorry."

"I'm sorry I blamed you."

"I would have blamed me too, before I blamed a raccoon," I told her.

She held out her hand. "I'm Kayla Carr."

"Eddie Perlmutter. I never knew Bailey's last name."

"Her married name is Sweeney."

"She was married?" I asked, surprised. I never thought of Bailey having a husband.

"It's a long, sad story."

"I'll listen."

Kayla told me a long story with a sad beginning and ending, and the middle part wasn't a lot of fun either.

CHAPTER 18

I HEARD IT THROUGH THE GRAPEVINE

"Joyce Weinberg told me you were a real smooth talker last night," Claudette said at breakfast the next morning.

"Apparently the nurses' grapevine never sleeps."

"What happened?"

I told her about the Pearl City tour and the Boca Rio clinic. She said I was a genius to figure out the Baker clue and I agreed. Then I told her the Carr family saga, starting with the parents.

"What a burdensome gene pool," Claudette said when I finished. "An alcoholic father and a manic-depressive mother . . ."

"And the apples didn't fall far from the crazy tree."

Bailey became an alcoholic at an early age. She was drunk as a teenager, drunk as a young adult, drunk when she became a thirty-five-year-old, first-time bride, drunk the night she got pregnant, and drunk the night she drove her car into a stone wall and ended her pregnancy. When she regained consciousness, she learned her baby had died and her husband had disappeared. She recovered from her injuries and disappeared too.

"How did she get someone to marry her in the first place?" Claudette asked.

"Kayla said it was timing and circumstances."

Bailey got reacquainted with a former high school classmate who became a widower when his young wife died of cancer. He had remained single and lonely for several years until he saw Bailey at a high school reunion. Her exuberance made him feel alive again, and he asked her on a date. Unaware that her party moods were fueled by substance abuse, he made three big mistakes. He fell in love with her, he made her pregnant, and he married her.

"Poor man," Claudette said. "I wonder what happened to him. No one just disappears."

"Jimmy Hoffa did," I said. "Besides, it was about thirty years ago . . . like in the middle seventies. He's probably dead."

"Not necessarily. Bailey's still alive."

"Barely . . . and what's your point?"

"Maybe they could reunite after all these years," Claudette fantasized. "Wouldn't that be romantic?"

"He'd probably strangle her."

"You're no fun," Claudette said with a pout. "Did Kayla ever get married?"

Kayla never married. She suffered from melancholy as a child and was painfully lonely. Her teens were lost to the depression she inherited from her mother, and she battled with suicidal tendencies. In her twenties Kayla had to care for her deteriorating parents while her sister lived a carefree, happy-hour lifestyle. In her early thirties, after both parents had died within six months of each other, Kayla was appointed executor of their small estate and kept what few assets remained. Bailey was drunk at both funerals.

"What a sad story," Claudette said.

"Yeah, culminating in a raccoon attack in a garbage Dumpster."

"You can be a real idiot sometimes."

"I know."

CHAPTER 19

THE HOMELESS AND THE CLUELESS
EARLY MARCH

Dr. Glenn Kessler was my mandatory Boston Police Department psychiatrist when I was a crazy young cop. He retired from the force long before I did and became a bestselling author of self-help golf books. His first book was a bestseller. I consulted with him on occasion about my cases and decided to call him concerning the homeless.

"Eddie, good to hear your voice," he said.

"You never said that before," I reminded him.

"You're a kinder, gentler Eddie Perlmutter now."

"An older, slower Eddie Perlmutter maybe. Is bad golf still happening to good people?"

"Thank God bad golf never ends," he said cheerfully. "We're in our second printing."

"Congratulations. Do you think you can still analyze non-golfing psychos?"

"I think so. Try me."

"I have a case involving a homeless man and woman. I'd like to understand them better."

"Did you know there are homeless golfers? It's in my book. They're players without a home course."

"That must be terrible for them," I said. "But the homeless I'm talking about are more traditional. They don't have homes."

"How unusual."

I told him about Weary Willie and Three Bag Bailey.

"They're both classic cases," he said. "She doesn't feel worthy of a relationship or a home. She probably can't forgive herself for something terrible she did in the past."

"That's her. What can I do to help her?"

"You have to encourage her to forgive herself. And that won't be easy."

"Okay," I said. "And what about the clown impersonating Weary Willie?"

"He's not impersonating anyone. He's living someone else's life so he doesn't have to live his own. He probably suffered an emotional trauma at some point and ran away to start over. It's called a dissociative fugue."

"That sounds about right too. He can't be helped though. He's in a coma."

"Comatose people just don't listen," Kessler joked. "The thing is, Eddie, you have to deal with each homeless case individually. They've suffered a personal trauma that put them on the streets. There are no set answers or magical solutions. Sorry. Got anything else?"

"I have a case concerning pill mills in Florida. Ever hear of them?"

"Sure. Terrible business. Some doctors don't care how they make money, and the state of Florida gives them a license to steal. That's a legal matter for the state of Florida to resolve, not me."

"We're investigating a Catholic church—"

"Altar boys again," Kessler moaned.

"Not that I know of. I don't know what kind of case it is yet. Forget it."

"Anything else?"

"Our biggest investigation is financial fraud," I said. "But that's not your field."

"I'm an investor. What company are you investigating?"

"I'd rather not say. Our investigation isn't conclusive yet."

"I understand," he said. "I feel very fortunate to have done so well using the same investment company for years."

"Who do you use?"

"B.I.G. Investments," he said proudly.

Oh, shit. What am I supposed to do? Should I tell him or not? I felt I had to tell him. "That's the company I'm investigating."

"What for, making his clients too much money?" Kessler laughed.

I didn't laugh with him. "No, for fraud."

A prolonged silence followed. "You're kidding, of course?"

"I'm serious," I said.

"Were you hired to investigate him?"

"No. We're freelancing."

"Is this another one of your Boca Knights crusades?"

"I suppose it is."

"You're wasting your time," Dr. Kessler said. "B.I.G. has been investigated by the best of them and no one found anything wrong."

"If you're referring to the Securities and Exchange Commission as the best of them, I disagree."

"They're good enough for me," Kessler said, sounding unhappy with me. "I've been with Grover for over ten years and made a small fortune. People have built hospital wings and donated millions of dollars to charities with the money they've made from this man."

"What if they're false profits? What if he's a fraud?"

"Be very careful with that word, Eddie. If you start an unsubstantiated rumor, you could ruin a lot of innocent people, including me. But you must be wrong. I've withdrawn substantial profits."

"If he's a fraud, you may have to return the money. But I haven't accused anyone of anything yet."

"No, but you're making me nervous," Kessler said. "I'm going to call the guy who put me into this fund and hear what he has to say."

"He's going to tell you everything is fine."

"I'll call you back."

An hour later, Kessler called me back. "My man says everything's fine and he wants to talk to you."

"You told him about me?" I asked, surprised.

"Yes, and I gave him your office number. I thought you'd like to hear his side of the story."

I didn't bother to tell him that the last guy who investigated Grover died a violent death.

"Who's your adviser?" I asked.

"Jimmy Hunter. You'll like him."

"I don't think so. So you're leaving your money with Grover?"

"Actually, I invested more," my highly educated psychiatrist said.

Now I believed in *bokos*.

Chapter 20

Big Game Hunting

Jimmy Hunter called fifteen minutes later.

"What took so long?" I asked.

He chuckled. "I try to address all allegations immediately."

"We haven't alleged anything."

"And I want to keep it that way. I suggest we meet as soon as possible."

"Why are you concerned about a small-time detective agency like ours?"

"You're being modest, Mr. Perlmutter. You're well known in South Florida, and we have many high-net-worth clients there. Mr. Grover has a winter home in Palm Beach with family and friends in the area. We'd like to avoid needless negative publicity . . . especially in his backyard."

Sounds reasonable. "I have to talk to my partner."

"That would be Mr. Dewey?"

"Yes, it's his investigation. Give me your private number. I'll call you back."

I entered the adjoining office without knocking. My mistake. Lou and Joy were locked in an embrace . . . kissing passionately.

"Can't you do that at home?" I asked.

"We did," Lou said, breaking away.

Joy looked like Lou with big boobs. They were made for each other.

I told Lou about the Kessler and Jimmy Hunter phone calls. "So much for a sneak attack," I said.

"That's okay," Lou said. "I got Grover anyway and I know about Big Game Hunter. He runs a feeder fund and he's a scumbag."

"What's a feeder fund?"

"He raises money for master funds that do the actual investing," Lou explained. "Feeders are supposed to research masters and spread their clients' money among the best of them to reduce risk. They're also expected to closely monitor the accounts."

"It sounds legit," I said.

"In theory. In practice, it can be a license to steal." Lou grabbed a stack of files on his desk, shuffled them, found the one he wanted, and handed it to me. "Research on Big Game Investments."

I hefted the thick folder. "How about a summary?"

"Hunter invests one hundred percent of his clients' money in B.I.G.," Lou said. "He's selling access to Grover, who pays him huge commissions for the referrals."

"Why does Grover pay huge commissions if he's in such demand?"

"Investors don't know. They think they're getting into an exclusive club, but Grover needs new investors desperately. A

Ponzi scheme doesn't make real profits so it needs new cash constantly. A good feeder can raise billions, and Grover needs those billions to survive. If new money stops flowing, the Ponzi pyramid collapses. Considering the magnitude of Grover's fund, it would be a financial apocalypse."

"You're exaggerating?"

"Maybe a little," Lou said. "But it will be the end of the road for a lot of people. Thousands of trust funds, charities, institutions, and individuals will be destroyed. Here, look at this list of investors just from Palm Beach County."

Lou handed me a thick folder and I didn't bother to ask where he got it. I sifted through the pages, seeing a few names I recognized. "He has a lot of money from Jewish organizations and pension funds."

"Keep going," Lou said. "There's plenty of individuals there too. Maybe you'll see some names you'll recognize. He's going to destroy them all."

I continued reading, stunned by the number of individuals who had put their faith in B. I. Grover. I began focusing on Boca, looking for familiar names. "I do know some of these people," I said to Lou sadly. I shifted my attention to Delray Beach and came across a name that stopped me. Delray Vista Investment Club 550, LLC.

"Damn," I said.

"What's wrong?"

"Remember the case we had in Delray with a condo association?"

"The haunted-elevator case?"

I nodded.

"How could I forget?" Lou asked. "I was with you most of the time on that one."

"Their investment club is on this list."

"Oh, jeez. Do they list the names of the individuals?"

"There's twelve units listed here," I said. "That's all of them. Can we do something?"

"Nothing. I'd go to jail just for hacking the list. We have to keep our mouths shut."

"Remember the Paretsky kid?"

"Sure, Noah," Lou said, "the kid who helped put a man on the moon but couldn't control a two-story elevator."

"He meant well though."

"All those people meant well."

"I hope you're wrong about Grover," I said.

"I'm not." Lou took the folder away from me. "Don't torture yourself. It's better you don't know."

"Grover's a piece of shit. I'll tell Hunter you don't want a meeting."

"Of course I want a meeting," Lou said, raising his voice. "Give me his phone number."

What?

I handed him the number. He punched the buttons and put on his speakerphone. I got a bottle of water from the refrigerator and sat in front of his desk.

"Jimmy Hunter," Big Game answered his private line.

"This is Lou Dewey," Lou said gruffly. "I understand you want to meet."

"Yes, I do, Mr. Dewey," Hunter said politely. "May I call you Lou?"

"No."

"All right," Hunter said. "When can we meet?"

"Whenever Mr. Grover is available."

I was in mid-sip and spewed water on the Big Game folder.

Hunter took a moment to reply. "I think we have a misunderstanding. I'm asking for this meeting, not Mr. Grover."

"I understand perfectly," Lou said. "You want to meet and bullshit me about your split-strike strategy and Grover's uncanny genius in timing trades. You want to deny any dishonest front-running and show me the same flow charts and forecasts that baffled the SEC years ago. Forget it. I'm not interested."

Hunter sounded shaky when he asked, "What are you interested in, Mr. Dewey?"

"The answer to one question."

"What's the question?"

"That's between Mr. Grover and me," Lou said. "But you can tell him I'll stop my investigation if I receive an acceptable answer to that question."

"I'll have to call you back," Hunter said, and hung up.

"What question?" I asked Lou.

"I want to save it as a surprise. You'll love it. Trust me."

"I'd trust you with my life. But I don't trust your judgment worth a damn sometimes. Why do we want a meeting with Grover?"

"I want the satisfaction of looking him in the eyes when I nail him," Lou said.

"Let me remind you this is business, not personal."

"It's personal to me."

"You're never supposed to tell your enemy what you're planning."

"Duly noted," Lou said, blowing me off.

Within a half hour Hunter called back. "Mr. Grover agrees to a five-minute, one-question meeting," Hunter said over the speaker. "You're invited for cocktails at his Palm Beach home the day after tomorrow at seven fifteen. I'll be there too."

"Why would you fly all the way from New York to attend a meeting that might only last five minutes?" Lou asked.

"It's a good excuse to visit with Mr. Grover and spend some time in Palm Beach," Hunter said. "I already reserved the penthouse suite at the Breakers facing the ocean. There are worse ways to spend my time."

"Suit yourself," Lou said, and disconnected.

Lou stood up when the call ended and slapped his desk with the palm of his hand. "We got him!" he exclaimed.

I had an uncomfortable feeling Grover had us.

Herb Brown came to dinner that night and brought Claudette a box of chocolate. She liked him immediately. We made small talk until the subject became his deceased wife.

"She was the other half of me," he said. "I haven't felt whole since she died."

"How long were you two married?" Claudette asked.

"Fifty-six years."

"That qualifies you as an expert," Claudette said.

"There are no marriage experts," he said. "We all make mistakes."

"What did you do wrong?"

"I overprotected her. I never talked about the war or the battles I fought in business. She never knew that the Providence Mafia came closer to killing me than the Japs. I shut her off from things she should have known. It wasn't fair. If I could do it again, I'd tell her everything."

"You could learn a lot from this man," Claudette said to me.

We talked about his two sons. One was a confirmed bachelor and a professor of economics at Washington University in St. Louis. The other had been married three times and was currently single. Herb had no grandchildren.

"Do you have a close relationship with your sons?" I asked.

He smiled. "Let me put it this way: I saw a movie years ago where an actor, trying to explain his relationship with his sons, said, 'One I put through college, and one I put through a wall.' I think that sums up my relationship with my sons. Children aren't easy."

"So we've heard," I said, which led us to a conversation of

the advantages and disadvantages of having children. We didn't arrive at a conclusion.

Claudette sent Herb and me to the balcony, where we drank coffee and talked about anything that came to mind. He told me about his war injury and I declined his joking offer to show it to me. I told him I had followed his advice and was investigating Grover, and he seemed confident I would find something.

The conversation turned to sports and I learned that Herb had boxed successfully in the Marines. "I knocked out a lot of guys," he said. "I still like to watch the fights on television."

I told him about PAL and he seemed mildly interested. "I'd like to attend a show."

"Would you like to help coach?" I asked.

"I'm too old."

"No you're not. You're in great shape."

"I guess I must be," he said. "I've outlived all my friends. The last friend I had here was a Tom Coates from Chicago. He owned a bar called Boca Magic. He was a marathon runner."

"Sounds like an interesting guy."

"He was. Unfortunately he dropped dead jogging in Sugar Sand Park."

"That's sad," I said.

"That's life. After the war I always wondered why I had lived when so many around me died. After I married Joan and had children, I told myself I was saved for them. Now she's gone, the boys are on their own, my best friend died, and I'm still here wondering why. What's my purpose now?"

"We'll just have to wait and see."

Chapter 21

We're Off to See the *Boko*

Lou spent the next two days reviewing his B.I.G. files while I worked on my other cases, which seemed to be going in circles. The DNA samples I took from the back stairs of St. Mary's Church proved to be tainted by bleach and were useless. The two large Yankees fans Bailey had seen at the church did not reappear when I staked out the place. My surveillance at No Pain-U-Gain yielded nothing new, but Lou hacked into government files and found Dr. Venu Patel through his Social Security number. Lou got a complete history on Dr. Patel along with his picture and Fort Lauderdale address. Patel was a seventy-two-year-old widower who lived in a small, old house on A1A across the street from the beach. It didn't look like much but, based on location, had to be worth a fortune. Lou's computer search revealed that Patel had purchased the property at a reasonable price over twenty years ago when his wife was still alive and paid off the mortgage five years ago.

I chose a Monday morning to stake out Patel's house, figuring that weekend parties would make a big dent in his customers' inventory and business would be good. I brought a beach chair and watched the house from the vantage point of a tourist. I was there for three hours and saw several men enter and leave, each carrying a briefcase.

At noon Patel appeared in the doorway and I folded my beach chair and leaned it against the beach wall. I followed him at a professional distance while he walked two blocks south and one block west to the Roxie Diner. He sat at a table outside the restaurant; it looked as if it had been reserved for him. I went into the diner and sat at the counter where I could see him. Within an hour, six men separately, each carrying a briefcase, had approached him. Patel greeted each man with indifference, and he barely looked at the documents they presented. He scribbled on small notepads they handed him and slid them back across the table when he was done. He was handing out prescription slips like chewing gum. I was reminded of the slips that killed Shoshanna Hurwitz.

I estimated he signed at least fifty slips in an hour, casually dispensing death but not breaking Florida law. This had to stop, but it would have to wait until we had had our meeting with Benjamin Grover.

Lou and I drove to Palm Beach on I-95 North for our scheduled evening appointment with B. I. Grover. The last time I had driven on the interstate I went south to Liberty City and met Mad Dog Walken.

Talk about different worlds.

Lou suggested we take my Mini. "Let them underestimate us," he said.

We got off on Southern Boulevard so we could get a glimpse of Mar-a-Lago, the mansion built in 1927 for cereal heiress Marjorie Merriweather Post. Lou and I had never been on Palm Beach Island before, and we gawked like tourists.

"There it is," he shouted, pointing to the Mar-a-Lago tower as we crossed the Intracoastal bridge. We could see the rear of the mansion from the elevated waterway. Lou opened a travel book and read to me: " 'Mar-a-Lago, built in 1927, one hundred ten thousand square feet, fifty-eight bedrooms, thirty-three bathrooms, twelve fireplaces, and three bomb shelters.' That's a lot of Cheerios."

"Grape-Nuts," I corrected him.

"Right . . . but why three bomb shelters?"

"Some people hate Grape-Nuts," I guessed.

We turned north on South Ocean Boulevard in front of the pre–Post Toasties castle. To our right was the Atlantic Ocean.

"Amazing," Lou commented. "Look at those giant hedges."

"Yeah, they hide the houses."

"And the people," he said, pointing at an American flag flapping high above the hedges. "I read that Trump wants to replace that pole with one thirty-eight feet taller."

"How high is that one?"

"Forty-two feet, the zoning limit," Lou said. "Palm Beach is threatening an all-out war against Trump."

"That would explain the three bomb shelters."

We passed a sign for Worth Avenue, the exclusive retail area of Palm Beach.

"Wanna go shopping?" Lou asked.

"I can't afford to feed the parking meters on Worth Ave."

We glanced at Royal Palm Way, which was lined with regal royal palms.

"Awesome," Lou said, and I couldn't disagree.

The road jogged west on Barton Avenue and became South County Road. We saw the spectacular façade of the Breakers Hotel to the east at the end of a long private driveway.

"Let's take a look," I said, turning the Mini onto the impressive approach.

"I bet they've never seen a car like this here before."

"Let them eat their hearts out," I said, looking at the imposing, twin-peaked hotel. I parked at the valet stand under a portico. I got out of the car and tossed my keys to an appalled valet.

"Be careful," I told him. "It's a collector's item."

"Yeah, a garbage collector," Lou said, and laughed.

As the valet lowered himself into the Mini, I told him we would only be a few minutes.

"The manager will be pleased to know that," he said.

Cute.

Lou and I walked the red carpet into the hotel. He opened his tourist book again and read, " 'Built by Henry Flagler in 1896.' "

"That was the year my grandfather left the Ukraine," I said.

Lou flipped papers with his thumb. "It doesn't mention him in the book. . . . 'Originally built as an adjunct to the larger Royal Poinciana Hotel, the Palm Beach Inn was renamed The Breakers in 1901 because of its closer proximity to the ocean.' " His voice trailed off as he read to himself, moving his lips. " 'Burned down in 1903,' " he resumed reading aloud, " 'rebuilt and reopened a year later, burned down again in 1925, rebuilt and reopened in a year again. However, this time they used concrete instead of wood.' "

"A stroke of genius," I said. "Now, let's do this tour fast before they throw us out."

"I've never been thrown out of a finer place."

We scurried through the lobby, hurried past the Tapestry Bar and raced through the Circle restaurant. We walked carefully by the pool, sidestepping several drunks at happy hour, and caught a glimpse of the Atlantic.

Where are the breakers?

We were moving briskly through the lobby when I noticed that we didn't look out of place after we got out of the Mini. I was neatly dressed in khaki Dockers and a white, fake Polo shirt. Lou wore his best 1950s black Elvis ensemble. Our clothes were outdated but not outclassed. The people in the lobby were dressed as if they woke up in the morning and asked themselves . . .

How can I look my worst today?
Let's see.
I have a fat ass. I think I'll wear stretch pants.
I have a scrawny ass, perfect for baggy jeans.
I have a grubby beard. I won't shave.
I have a great beer belly to hang over a pair of skimpy shorts.
I like sandals with black socks.

Elegantly attired Vanderbilts, Rockefellers, and Morgans were gone forever, and the only Astors at the Breakers now were disasters. In olden days, the hotel guests dressed like kings and queens. Now they resembled court jesters. If Henry Flagler were alive, he'd drop dead.

We blended in at the valet stand until my Mini arrived alongside a $430,000 Maybach.

"How do you like the way she handles?" I asked the same snotty valet as before as I handed him a dollar.

He looked at the wrinkled bill. "A whole buck, wow," he said disdainfully.

"You're right," I said. "That tip is inappropriate." I took back the dollar. "I should give you what you're worth."

I got in the Mini . . . gave the kid the finger . . . and drove away.

The entrance to Via Sonrisa was about two miles from the Breakers. Grover's mansion was the last one on the right, sharing the same beachfront with the Breakers. I gave my name to an intercom box mounted on a pillar and watched the wrought-iron gate swing open majestically. A white coquina driveway meandered through beautiful flower gardens and trimmed tropical foliage. Uniformed gardeners were everywhere, clipping, snipping, planting, removing, improving, and scurrying. Some were riding lawn mowers more stylish than my Mini.

"Business must be good," I said to Lou, who frowned.

"A widow from Scarsdale paid for that front gate," he said cynically. "And a retired CEO from Detroit is paying for the gardeners. They just don't know it yet."

I parked my ride in the circular driveway and was immediately overwhelmed by the abundance of everything: flowers, mosaics, marble, miles of mulch, scurrying domestics, stately columns, and royal palms. A silver Rolls-Royce was being waxed by a muscular young man sporting a B.I.G. logo on his green pullover golf shirt.

Money, money, money.

The main house was one level, over five hundred feet long. Twin two-story buildings stood at either end of the sprawling ranch. The front door looked like a thousand pounds of glass, wrought iron, and rich wood, but it was opened effortlessly by a thin man in a black tuxedo.

"Mr. Perlmutter, Mr. Dewey," he said with a smile. "Mr. Grover is waiting for you by the pool. My name is Roscoe. Follow me, please."

We followed Roscoe through gleaming tiled corridors past lusciously carpeted rooms, fabulous works of art, elegant furniture, amazing chandeliers, and impressive statues. With each display of wealth Lou got angrier.

"This bastard is living like a king with stolen money," he whispered in my ear. "And so are a lot of other people who got into this scam when the pyramid first started. The original frauds got money out when they could. Now it's a different story."

"He's innocent until proven guilty."

"He's guilty," Lou muttered.

"Prove it," I whispered.

We exited the rear of the house onto the elegant tiled deck of an Olympic-size swimming pool surrounded by an acre of lush grass all overlooking the Atlantic Ocean. The sun was low in the sky, the setting was postcard pretty. Three well-dressed men in sport coats were standing by the pool. I recognized Grover from pictures I had seen. Next to him was a tall, dark, handsome, younger man. I guessed he was Jimmy "Big Game" Hunter. I didn't recognize the third man, but he looked a lot like Grover. Behind them on a landing pad was a Robinson R22 Beta 2, two-seat helicopter.

It's a rich man's world.

Grover wore expensive clothes well, but he was small and soft looking. His expressionless eyes looked through stylish tinted glasses perched on a large nose that hooked over a forced smile. His swept-back, silvery mane made him look like the king of the jungle.

The three men waited for us to come to them. We met poolside. Grover smiled. He had capped teeth. He held out a freshly manicured hand. We shook hands. His handshake was decent but his smile was phony.

"Mr. Perlmutter, Mr. Dewey, it's nice to meet you," Grover lied. "This is my associate Jim Hunter, and my neighbor Bernard Madoff." We shook hands. Lou looked as if he were touching slime.

"I have to be going," Madoff said. "Benjamin, we'll talk later." He nodded to everyone and departed. The four of us looked at each other like wary prizefighters.

Roscoe reappeared and asked about drinks. Grover ordered a gin martini, Hunter asked for vodka on the rocks, and I asked for a Diet Coke. Lou asked for nothing.

"I understand you want to ask me one question, and if my

one-word answer is satisfactory . . . you will stop investigating my company," Grover summarized.

"That's right," Lou confirmed.

"I can't imagine any one question . . . or one-word answer . . . that could fully explain my business," Grover said, all the while smiling condescendingly.

"I don't need a full explanation," Lou told him. "I already know how your business works."

"Are you a finance man, Mr. Dewey?" Grover asked.

"No, I'm a con man, Mr. Grover."

Grover raised his eyebrows and Hunter cleared his throat nervously.

"A former con man, actually," I interjected.

"Do you plan to make this an unpleasant meeting, Mr. Dewey?" Grover asked.

"Unpleasant for who?"

Roscoe arrived with the drinks, making an answer unnecessary.

Grover removed a long-stemmed glass from Roscoe's tray and took a sip, closed his eyes, and savored the buzz.

Hunter gulped his vodka and looked uncomfortable. I took the Coke but didn't drink. Lou crossed his arms in front of his chest and stared at Grover.

"All right, Mr. Dewey," Grover said confidently, "what's your question?" He raised his martini glass to his lips again.

"Would you be willing to produce trading slips to me that coincide with the trades you claimed for fiscal 2005?"

"What?" Grover said with alarm, and choked on his martini.

"That's not the one-word answer I had in mind," Lou said.

"I . . . I . . . have thousands of trading tickets," Grover stammered, clearing his throat of a shot of gin, a touch of vermouth, and a jigger of bile. His color had faded from pink to ashen.

"That's not a one-word answer either," Lou said.

"Your question is unreasonable," Grover stammered again. "It's not even a question. It's a request that requires exhaustive work for my firm."

"They should all be on file, cross-referenced," Lou said. "It shouldn't be difficult at all."

"You don't understand the complex nature of what we do at B.I.G.," Grover said.

"Is that a yes or no?"

"It's a *no*. I simply can't expose private files like that. You don't understand."

"I understand perfectly. Thanks for the meeting." Lou turned and began walking toward the ocean. When he realized he was headed in the wrong direction, he changed course abruptly. "How do I get out of here?"

"Can't we talk this over?" Big Game Hunter requested.

"There's nothing more to talk about," Lou said.

"I don't understand," Hunter said.

I didn't have a clue either.

"Ask Mr. Grover," Lou said.

I looked at Grover. His eyes were glassy and frozen in a thousand-mile stare.

"Benjamin . . . ," Hunter said, "can't you just—"

"Shut up, Jimmy," Grover snapped.

As we departed, I watched Grover remove a cell phone from his jacket pocket, punch in one number, wait a few seconds, then start talking. He noticed me watching and quickly turned away. I glanced at my watch and saw it was only seven thirty. Our entire meeting had taken less than a half hour.

We exited the "King Kong" front door and I noticed the Mini looked different. It was clean. The Mini was never clean. A rubber hose lay on the ground nearby. The weight lifter in the green shirt smiled and waved. I waved back but I wasn't happy. I don't like anyone messing with my Mini and I like it dirty.

"Let's get out of here," Lou said, and I could tell he was disgusted.

"What just happened?" I asked as I drove away.

"I just finished the career of Benjamin Grover."

Chapter 22

APOCALYPSE SOON

Driving west on Okeechobee, I told Lou I had no idea what he was talking about.

"Did you see Grover's reaction when I asked him to show me trading slips?"

"Yes. He blew gin through his nose."

"After *that*."

"He said it was too much trouble to gather all that material," I said.

"The trouble is, the slips don't exist."

"That's ridiculous. His trades must have been verified."

"Eddie, listen to me carefully because this is going to be hard for an honest man like you to believe. For the past forty years Grover has been paying greedy people massive sums of money *not* to verify his claims. Feeder-fund managers were paid millions to raise billions and not ask questions. Grover convinced people to believe the unbelievable by either paying them royally or numbing them with bullshit."

Like a boko *with puffer-fish poison.*

I pulled into a large parking lot and turned off the engine. "I want to give you my undivided attention."

Lou continued, "Grover used social contacts, personal connections, greed, and hocus-pocus to create the largest Ponzi scheme in history."

"Can you prove it?"

"Yes, I can," Lou said confidently. "And I'm going to the FBI tomorrow to present the evidence. I have documents that prove Grover claimed B.I.G. made more trades in 2005 than the entire exchange made that year."

"How did you figure that out?"

"I didn't figure out anything," Lou said. "Harry Chan did. His equations proved that for Grover to pay the twelve percent he claimed, trading blue chips, he had to take more positions than actually existed in the entire market that year. All I had to do was explain Chan's complicated formulas in a short, easy-to-understand format. I narrowed it down to the one question I asked Grover. The FBI can ask him the same question and back it up with a search warrant. Brilliant, huh?"

"What wasn't so brilliant was tipping your hand to someone who might be capable of murder."

"You worry too much," Lou said. "This will be over first thing tomorrow morning."

"What if Grover tries to stop you tonight?"

"He won't. For all he knows, I already put out the story."

"For all he knows . . . you didn't."

"I'm not worried," Lou said.

I am.

I asked more questions and he answered them all overconfidently, which worried me even more. After nearly an hour of interrogating and cautioning him I resumed the drive to Boca.

I saw a "Boca—Next 5 Exits" sign and took Yamato west to Military south to Spanish River east. Joy's house was a couple of minutes from the intersection and fifteen minutes, with traffic, to the ocean.

I made a U-turn and stopped in front of their slab ranch. Joy's Cube (the ugliest car I have ever seen) and Lou's banged-up Cadillac were in the driveway. Their garage was filled with old computers, computer parts, heaps of household refuse, Joy's enormous stuffed-animal collection, and things they could not live without but could not say why.

"Are you *ever* going to clean out that garage?"

"No," Lou answered honestly. "As a matter of fact I just put an old mattress in there."

"Why?"

"We wore out the old one," he said with a wink. He got out of the car. "Get some rest. Tomorrow we're going to change the world."

I'm worried about tonight.

I watched him enter the house before I drove away. When I reached the intersection of Spanish River and Military, I got a gut feeling I shouldn't leave. I U-turned again, parked a short distance from the house, and turned off my headlights. I decided to spend the night.

I glanced at my watch. It was only a few minutes past nine. The neighborhood was still awake and well lit. I decided to go to Kugel's for a cup of coffee before my all-night vigil. I called Claudette and told her I was on a stakeout. She accepted my explanation the way an obstetrician's wife accepts her husband's leaving the house in the middle of the night because another woman called saying she needs him. It's part of the job.

Chapter 23

Life's a Dash

I saw Herb Brown sitting at the counter at Kugel's, talking to an athletically built, coffee-colored kid in his late teens. I walked behind them and patted Herb on the shoulder.

"Hey, marine," I said.

Herb turned and smiled. "Hey, Eddie, I was just telling my new friend Teofilo about your boxing career."

"All lies," I joked.

The handsome young man stood and shook my hand. He towered over me.

"Teofilo Fernandez," he introduced himself. "Mr. Brown told me you were an undefeated champion."

"Why were you talking about a broken-down old fighter like me?"

"I told Mr. Brown I was named after a great Cuban boxer," he said proudly.

"Teofilo Stevenson?"

"You know Stevenson?"

"I know *of* him," I said, sitting on a counter stool and ordering a cup of coffee from Dave, the owner. Teofilo sat between Herb and me.

"Stevenson was the Olympic heavyweight champion in '72, '76, and 1980," I continued. "I remember he refused five million dollars to fight Muhammad Ali, saying being loved by eight million Cubans was more important to him than millions of dollars."

"He was an inspiration to many Cubans," Teofilo said. "My father was a boxer too and he idolized Stevenson."

"What was your father's name?" I asked.

"Felix Fernandez," the boy said proudly.

"I don't remember him. Was he in the Cuban national program?"

"Yes, and he won many bouts. He was invited to try out for the 1984 Olympic team."

"Cuba boycotted those games," I said.

"Yes, for political reasons. My father was only twenty at the time and was going to try for the World Games and 1988 Olympics. But during training he started losing endurance and power. By 1986 he could no longer compete. In 1988, the year I was born, he was diagnosed with leukemia."

"What a shame," I said. "He might have been a champion."

The boy nodded. "He had a remission for several years and became a coach for the National Athletic Federation. When I was six, he began teaching me, but he got sick again and died when I was eleven. My mother decided to leave Cuba a year later to join relatives in Miami."

"How did you get to America?" I asked.

"We escaped on a boat. Do you remember Elián Gonzáles?"

"Sure," Herb said. "He was the Cuban kid who survived a boat wreck in the Florida Straits. Two US fishermen found him floating on a rubber tube and brought him to Miami."

"He became a big political issue," I remembered. "He's back in Cuba now."

"My mother and I were supposed to be on Elián's boat the night it left Cárdenas six years ago," the boy said. "The boat was scheduled to depart at four in the morning. We were delayed by bad weather and flooded roads. We arrived just as the aluminum boat was leaving. Two other passengers had already taken our place."

"They left you there?" Herb asked.

"They had to," Teofilo said. "Their homemade boat was flimsy, had a feeble engine, and was already overloaded with twelve people. A big storm was passing through and the water was choppy. They told us another boat was leaving the next morning. We waited in hiding and were able to buy our way onto a much sturdier vessel the next night. After we landed safely in Miami, we learned that Elián's boat had capsized and nine out of the twelve people drowned. That same storm that took their lives saved ours. We felt very lucky . . . but guilty too."

"I understand the feeling," Herb said. "You ask yourself why you lived when others died."

The boy nodded.

"Tell him about Tarawa, Herb," I said . . . and he did.

"That's incredible," Teofilo said at the end of Herb's war story. "Seven thousand people died and you survived."

"That's life." Herb took off his Marines cap, leaned forward, and pointed to the long, thin scar that ran the length of his bald head. "A millimeter here, or in your case, a day there, and we wouldn't be sitting here having this conversation."

"Do you think we were spared for a reason?" Teofilo asked.

"No. I believe everything happens by chance. If I didn't bend down to pick up those dog tags on Tarawa, I would have been dead and buried for sixty-two years already. My gravestone

would have read, 'Corporal Herb Brown, 1922 dash 1943.'" He
used his index finger to make the dash on the invisible monu-
ment.

Herb's dash reminded me of a poem I'd heard years ago during a eulogy at a friend's funeral. I shared my thoughts with them.
"I can't remember all the words, but I remember the meaning.
The dash on a headstone is the most important thing because it
represents a lifetime. We all have a birth date and we all die one
day, but our dash makes us unique."

"Some dashes are better than others," Herb said with a smile.

"Very true. What about yours, Herb?" I asked, returning his
smile.

"My dash became a marathon," he joked, and we laughed.

"Seriously," I prompted him.

"I think I did the best I could with the dash I had."

"What was the best single thing you did," I asked.

"I ducked. It made everything else possible."

"I dodged a few bullets to get here myself," I said.

"I dodged a boat wreck," Teofilo added with a smile.

"Interesting how life works," Herb said. "When I was on
Tarawa, you two weren't even a thought. And here we are at the
same time in the same place."

"Mr. Brown, I think you were saved so you could meet Mr.
Perlmutter one night and me tonight."

"It's a nice thought," Herb said. "But do you really believe
everyone in this coffee shop is here for a reason?"

"I don't know," the young man said. "I only feel that way
about us."

We looked around at the eight other people in the shop. An
elderly man and woman at a table near the front door were not
talking or looking at each other. They sat glumly staring into
space.

"They look unhappy," Teofilo observed.

"Maybe they're disappointed how their lives turned out," I speculated.

"Maybe one of them is sick," Teofilo guessed. "Maybe they're both sick."

"Maybe they're just pissed off being old," Herb said. "I know I am. Most old people are."

"I'm not," I said.

"You're not old enough yet," Herb said.

"Okay, Moses," I said. "How do you explain the four people across the room having a good time? They're in your age category."

Two men, who were old enough to have fought in World War II with Herb, sat with two women who might have been their war brides. They were animated and laughing, using four forks to share one piece of cake.

"There are exceptions to every rule," Herb said.

"Maybe they refused to get old," Teofilo theorized.

"You can't do that," Herb said. "I tried."

"You have to adapt to every stage of your life," I said. "That's what my doctor told me about aging."

I noticed an African-American college kid wearing a Lynn University T-shirt and a New York Yankees cap. He was sitting alone at a table, reading a book. He looked to be about the same age as Teofilo, but I felt sure they were from different worlds. Yet here they were together for one night.

I turned to Teofilo. "What brings you to this place tonight?"

"My mother and I moved to Boca last week after six years in Miami. She was able to get a job as a nurse's aide at Seaside Hospice on Hillsboro. I am picking her up after her work. I took a drive to learn my way around and saw this place."

"Totally random," Herb said. "Couldn't your mother find a job in Miami?"

"She had a job. She wanted to leave Miami for personal reasons."

"Was she a nurse's aide in Miami too?" I asked.

"Yes. In Cuba she was a registered nurse, but not here. In America, Cuban registered nurses become nurse's aides, and Cuban doctors become nurses. It's sad."

"What will you do in Boca?" Herb asked.

"I'll get a job."

"What about school?" Herb asked.

"We lived with an uncle in Miami so I could afford to go to high school there. But now we are on our own and I need to make money."

"Do you have any friends in this area?" I asked.

He shook his head no.

"Do you still like to box?" I asked, thinking of the Boca Police Athletic League program.

"I haven't done it in years." He smiled. "But I loved it."

"I'm involved with a boxing program in Boca," I said. "I could help you get started there and meet some kids your age."

"That's a great idea," Herb said.

The kid's eyes lit up and he smiled just as the front door crashed open.

Chapter 24

Walking on Broken Glass

The threat of mortal danger can paralyze people . . . or energize adrenaline junkies like me to come alive at death's door. And death was at the door of Kugel's: four apparitions, each wearing a black ski mask and brandishing an AA-12 shotgun. They wore short-sleeve shirts showing tattooed arms. They were hiding their faces but not their skin color, letting everyone know that black men were holding the guns.

"Oh my God," one of the women at the table of four said. "It's a robbery."

No, it's not! I thought. *Drum-fed, automatic, AA-12 fire-breathing dragons take lives, not money.*

Move, Eddie!

I rolled off the stool and simultaneously reached behind my back for the Glock nine-millimeter in my waistband.

Boom! A shotgun erupted before I hit the floor. Someone

screamed. Three more explosions, in deliberate succession, rocked the room . . . three more screams.

Why single shots? An AA-12 can discharge five twelve-gauge shells per second.

I heard the sound of gooey splatter hitting walls.

I knocked over a table and dove behind it with my Glock in hand. One gunman saw me.

Boom!

A window shattered above my head. I peeked around the corner of the table, saw the shooter's thigh, and put a hole in it.

He screamed, blood spurting through his pants as he went down, shouting, "Someone's got a gun."

The remaining shooters went ballistic, lighting up the restaurant with an awesome display of firepower. I scrambled along the floor like a combat soldier and took cover behind the front counter. I saw Dave, the owner, lying there, dead. He had nearly been decapitated by a blast to the throat. He was a nice guy trying to make a living. Now he was dead.

When the bombardment stopped, I heard footsteps approaching.

"Where you at?" a shooter growled.

He thinks I'm on the floor hiding . . . or dead. He'll be looking down.

I stood up, fired three shots into his ski mask, dropped to the floor again, and rolled toward the kitchen. The two remaining shooters filled the air with shotgun shells and flying glass, but I was already behind a baking oven.

When the shooting stopped, one of the rattled gunmen said, "I think we got him."

"Why don't you check it out, man," another said.

"Why don't you?"

"Get me outa here," the man with the hole in his thigh wailed. "I'm bleedin' like a pig."

"Yeah, let's go before the cops come," one shooter warned the others.

I heard grunting, groaning, and the cracking of glass underfoot. I crawled to the front counter and looked over the top. I saw the limp body of one shooter, his ski mask drenched in blood, being lifted and draped over the shoulder of another shooter, who then stumbled toward the door. A third assassin limped in that direction . . . clutching his thigh. The fourth killer was covering their retreat, waving his AA-12 wildly. He saw me peeking over the counter and fired automatic bursts in my general direction. I ducked under the counter again. Shattered stainless steel and wood flew over me. Suddenly my forehead was on fire and I toppled onto my back.

Don't pass out or you're a dead man.

I struggled to my knees, held the Glock over the counter, kept my head down, and fired in the direction of the front door.

"Son of a bitch," the shooter shouted, and blew more of the counter to pieces.

The sound of a siren pierced the air.

"C'mon, man," one of them called from outside the store.

I heard the sound of running . . . and finally the screeching of tires.

I stood up, staggered to the door, and saw a car speeding away. I aimed my gun and pulled the trigger. I hit a random car in the lot.

I collapsed in front of the store, losing my grip on reality without losing consciousness. I saw blue pant legs.

"This guy took a bunch of shotgun pellets in his forehead," a voice said.

"Hey, that's Eddie Perlmutter," I heard another voice.

Do I know you?

"Body parts all over this goddamn place," someone shouted from inside the store.

"Don't disturb the crime scene," another cop called out. "Just look for survivors."

"I've got a live one under a dead one over here," someone shouted.

Who?

I felt myself being lifted and shifted onto a stretcher. A tube was in my arm and someone was wiping my forehead with something that stung like hell. I squirmed.

"Relax, Eddie," a soothing voice said. "Everything will be fine."

No, it won't.

"You're okay."

No, I'm not.

Chapter 25

Stay with Me

I was whisked from the ambulance and wheeled into the hospital.

"Stay with me, buddy," an anxious male nurse urged.

Where would I be going?

A frazzled doctor shone a light in my eyes, pressed his fingers to my neck, and listened to my heart through a stethoscope. He instructed someone to give me a shot of something and told them I was well enough to be left alone while they checked other victims. His confidence in my survival made me feel better. The painkiller made me feel nothing. I took a nap.

I woke up vaguely aware of a bright light overhead and someone poking at my forehead.

Feels like an operating room.

"He's got splinters near his eyebrows," I heard.

"He's lucky he didn't lose his eyes."

"He's lucky to be alive."

Why don't I feel lucky?

"More pellets on top of his head."

"What a mess."

The next thing I knew I was being wheeled again and my forehead was throbbing.

"Give him another shot and leave him there," someone directed. "We've got incoming."

I saw a stretcher whisk by . . . a bloody face . . . burned skin . . .

Lou?

Another stretcher with more blood.

"Her leg looks bad."

Joy?

"What happened?"

"Home gas explosion."

"Get them both up to surgery."

I passed out.

I woke up in a hospital bed. The clock on the wall read four o'clock. It was still dark outside. I had only slept a few hours.

My forehead burned, my body ached, and red bubbles were popping in front of my eyes like bloody balloons. I was having an *intermittent-explosive-disorder* episode without an intermission. The red remained and my memory was clear. Prior to pieces of the countertop nearly blowing my head off, my IED had been a lightning bolt, a violent explosion that did its damage and was gone. The current feeling was more like a forest fire that spread, intensified, and smoldered but never truly went out. I had never learned to control my old craziness, and now I had a new one to deal with.

An intravenous needle in my left arm was attached to a tube, attached to a plastic bag hanging from a portable stand next to my bed. An identification tag on the stand told me I was in the intensive care unit. I suddenly had a flashback of bloody bodies on stretchers. Were Joy and Lou in the hospital or had I been hallucinating? Had I heard something about Joy's leg and Lou's burns? Did I really hear something about a gas explosion or had I been imagining things? I had to know.

I pulled the needle from my arm and swung my legs over the side. I sat on the edge of the bed and waited for the room to stop spinning. It didn't. I stood up but had to sit down again. I waited a minute, stood again, and took a few tentative steps. Eventually I made it to the door and into the corridor. An identification sign with my name was on the wall next to my room. There would be signs for Dewey and Feely if they were really there. I sidestepped along the tile floor with my back and the palms of my hands pressed against the wall jailbreak style. The corridor was long, and every room had a name tag on the wall next to each door.

I heard voices and stepped into a darkened room with the name TATUM on the door. Two nurses passed, talking about the Florida state legislature being in session for sixty days and doing nothing. They didn't notice me. Mrs. Tatum coughed, called out an unidentifiable name, and was silent again. I shuffled out of her room.

Good night, Mrs. Tatum. I hope you find whoever you're looking for.

I edged around a corner and saw the name DEWEY on the wall. Across the hall was FEELY. I hadn't imagined things. The blood and gore had been real.

I shuffled into Lou's room and stood by the bed. He was propped on his right side, and I could see he was burned on the back of his head to the base of his spine. There had been a gas explosion. I swallowed what would have been a sob . . . if I cried.

"I'm here, Lou," I whispered, and touched his shoulder lightly. I moved silently from his room and across the hall to Joy.

The outline of the sheet covering her body clearly showed

that Joy's right leg was gone below the knee. I swallowed hard again. She was on her back and did not appear to have suffered significant injuries to her face. I noticed her right hand and arm were heavily bandaged, but her left hand and arm were not. I tried piecing the puzzle together.

The explosion must have originated in the garage from the gas water heater. The master bedroom was at the other end of the house. The junk probably saved their lives. The blast started on the left side of the house meaning the explosion would have traveled from left to right, reaching the master bedroom last.

I closed my eyes and saw the scene through the red spots and tried to picture the incident.

Explosion! Flare! Fire! Flames! Joy and Lou are blown out of bed. He is injured on the back of his body and the left side. Her right leg was demolished and her right hand and arm were badly burned. What did these strange injuries tell me? After a minute they told me everything.

I'll be damned. I can't believe it.

The overhead lights came on and startled me.

"What are you doing?" a gruff voice demanded. A tall, bearded orderly was approaching me from the doorway. "You're not allowed in here."

"She's my friend," I explained.

He grabbed my right wrist and looked at my hospital identification bracelet. "And you're my patient, Mr. Perlmutter. You have to go back to your room."

"Let go of me," I said, twisting my wrist free with expert ease and surprising him. I was vaguely aware of more red dots.

"Let's go," the orderly said, annoyed. He put a firm hand on my shoulder and attempted to guide me away from Joy.

I raised my right arm quickly, striking the underside of his left arm and forcing his hand off my shoulder. I didn't want to fight. I just wanted to stay with my friend.

"Son of a bitch," the big man snarled, and reached for me again.
Reflexively I pushed the heel of my hand into his chest. He
stumbled backward, tripped over his own feet, and fell.

"Sorry," I said, dizzy from the exertion.

"Help in room 754," the orderly shouted twice as he struggled
to his feet. He came toward me again. "Calm down, Mr. Perlmutter." He extended his hands toward me. Two more orderlies appeared at the door and rushed me. I collapsed in their arms.

"Give him a sedative," one of them said.

Not another one!

It went black again.

I opened my eyes and saw the hands of the clock pointing
straight up at twelve. Sunlight filtered through the narrow opening of the vertical window blinds. It was noon. I had been sleeping for hours. A burly male nurse sat in a chair next to my bed. I
rubbed my eyes. An ocean of red spots was still there, and anger
lurked just below the surface like a shark.

"Welcome back," the big nurse said, and stood up.

"Are you guarding me?" I asked with a hoarse voice.

"I prefer to think I'm protecting you from yourself," he said,
walking to the door. "Perlmutter's awake," he announced to whoever was outside my room.

Police Chief Frank Burke was the first through the door,
followed by a young officer I didn't know.

"You look like shit," Frank said, dismissing the male nurse
with a polite hand gesture.

"I was shot in the head with an AA-12 last night."

"Fortunately it was loaded with bird shot. If it was lead buckshot, I'd be at your graveside instead of your bedside."

"Does Claudette know about this?"

"Everybody knows," Frank told me. "The gas explosion at
Joy's house and the shooting at Kugel's have been all over the news
this morning. I called Claudette."

"How did she take it?"

"Bad. I also had to tell her about Lou's and Joy's condition. She wanted to come right over, but I told her to wait until I met with you and the other survivor, Teofilo Fernandez. I already got his statement."

Teofilo. "How is he?"

"Hardly a scratch thanks to an old man named Herb Brown," Frank said. "According to Fernandez, Brown stepped between him and the barrel of an AA-12 and lunged for the gunman. He took a direct blast to the face and was knocked backward into the kid. When they fell, Brown's body covered Fernandez's and the kid got lost in the shuffle. Herb Brown's head was blown to bits."

"No," I shouted, unable to see through a wave of red that engulfed me. "You said it was bird shot."

"Not all of it apparently. The shooters probably got screwed by their ammo supplier and got a mix-and-match shipment."

"Goddamnit," I screamed, and put my hands over my eyes. I wanted to disappear.

"Did you know Brown?"

"He was a friend."

"What can you tell me about him?" the chief asked.

"He was a war hero," I said in a shaky voice.

"I'm not surprised. He died like a hero. He saved that boy's life."

I removed my hands from my eyes and looked at Frank. "Herb questioned why he had lived so long when so many around him had died," I said. "He wondered if his life had a purpose. Last night he found out."

I looked away from Burke and took several deep breaths to regain my composure. I don't cry, but if I did, I would have, right then and there.

"Have you heard anything about Joy and Lou?" I asked.

"I looked in on them today. Their injuries are not nearly as extensive as they could have been."

I told him about the insulation between the garage and their bedroom.

"They're very lucky to be alive and so are you," Burke said.

"I don't feel very lucky right now."

"Do you feel well enough to give Officer Vladimir here your statement about last night?"

"How about tomorrow?" I asked. "I need some time to think."

"Sure, and while you're thinking, think about this. What are the odds of two business partners being involved in two random acts of violence against them on the same night in two separate locations?"

"That's a good question and you're a good cop," I said.

"Got a good answer?"

"Not yet. But I will."

Chapter 26

What's on Your Mind?

The chief and his assistant started for the door as a man dressed in white entered.

"Mr. Perlmutter, I'm Dr. Levey," the young man said.

"Are you the doctor who covered my forehead with Ben-Gay?"

"No, I wasn't on duty last night."

"We were just leaving," Frank said to the doctor.

"Chief, before you go," I said, "would you authorize a couple of cops to guard Joy's and Lou's rooms for the next few days? I'll pay the overtime."

"Does this have something to do with the question I just asked you?"

"Yes, it does."

"I'll take care of it," Burke said, then departed with Vladimir.

When we were alone, Dr. Levey shone a bright flashlight in my eyes.

"So how am I?"

"You've had a concussion. I'm ordering some tests. How are you feeling?"

"I'm seeing red. Do you know anything about intermittent explosive disorder?"

"A little but I'm not a neurologist or psychiatrist."

"Can I ask you a theoretical question anyway?"

"Sure, and I'll give you a theoretical answer."

I told him about the changes in my IED and the constant red spots I was seeing and asked if he could explain it.

"There's a condition called explosive personality disorder," he said. "It's a chronic version of IED."

"In English please."

"*Chronic* refers to a persistent condition. Unlike IED, which comes in spurts, EPD is always with you and doesn't require a major event to set you off. It's like you're perpetually on the edge but don't go over. Does that make any sense to you?"

"Basically, I got hit in the head and things changed."

"Something like that. But you really need to consult a specialist."

After he was gone, I looked around. I was in a single room. It had a television set mounted high on the wall with a remote-control device on a tray next to the bed. My disheveled, blood-stained clothes were on a nightstand in a plastic bag. I reached for the bag and inspected the contents. The police should have taken everything, but with bodies being rushed in and out, I was lost in the shuffle. In one pocket of my pants I was surprised to find my car keys and wallet. In the other pocket I found Big Game Hunter's business card and my cell phone. My Glock wasn't there, but I had another gun at home for emergency shootings.

I felt dizzy and put my head back on the pillow. My mind

was racing and red spots were popping in my head like corn ker-
nels in a microwave. I closed my eyes and watched the fireworks.
The spots began clinging to one another, expanding into one
oozing, red blob . . . seeping into the corners of my mind, until I
was looking at the world through a bloodred veil.

Chapter 27

Unleash the Kraken

In ancient mythology the gods would unleash a Norse monster called the kraken on their enemies. The beast had enormous tentacles that could reach anywhere and crush anything. Grover, the Jewish God of Fraud, apparently had a kraken too and unleashed it on Lou and me. Now it was our turn.

I am going to kick your kraken's ass, Benjamin.

I got out of bed and put on my bloodstained clothes, looking like a train-wreck survivor. I wanted to leave the hospital, but I couldn't call Claudette. She would never allow me to check myself out. Besides, I didn't want her involved with my new red curtain of rage and psychopaths with AA-12 shotguns. Whom could I call who was crazy enough to get involved with me right now?

Think.

Jerry Small, my newspaper friend, would risk anything for a good story . . . and I could trust him. I called him.

"Eddie, how are you?" he asked with concern.

"I need you to pick me up at the hospital."

"Have you been discharged already?"

"I'm discharging myself."

"You can't do that."

"I'm doing it."

"What if I don't want to aid and abet an idiot?"

"What if I told you there was an exclusive story in it for you?"

"I'll be there in a half hour."

I exited intensive care through a rear staircase, walked down a flight, and took the elevator the rest of the way to the lobby. Jerry Small was waiting for me outside in his SUV. Jerry was a twenty-eight-year-old star reporter for the *South Florida News*. When I broke the Russian Mafia's counterfeit and drug ring a couple of years ago and everyone wanted my story, I impulsively gave Jerry an exclusive. I thought he was a nice kid suffering in a dead-end job for a dying local paper, so I plucked him out of obscurity and made him a hero. We'd been friends ever since.

"Hey, Eddie," he greeted me when I got into his SUV. "You look terrible. You have holes in your head."

"You're very observant. Now drive before they realize I'm gone."

When we were on a main road, he asked, "So what's the story you have for me?"

"It has to be off the record."

"That's not a story," he protested. "That's a secret. I'm a reporter. I expose secrets."

"I need you to keep this confidential until I straighten a few things out or you don't get the story."

"This sucks."

"Do I have your word?"

"You know you do."

"The shooting at Kugel's and the explosion at Joy's house were related incidents."

"Holy shit," he said. "Someone was trying to kill you both?"

I nodded.

"Who?"

"I can't tell you that either."

"You're killing me," Small moaned.

"Sorry. But it will be worth the wait. Trust me."

"I trust you. But what can you tell me on the record? Can we at least talk about the shoot-out? What happened?"

"You know what happened. It's been in all the papers."

"Very funny," he said sarcastically. "I like to uncover news stories . . . not read them in a competitor's newspaper."

"It wasn't as if I could have tipped you off. It was a sneak attack."

"You can make it up to me with an exclusive interview about the shoot-out." He pulled into a parking lot and shut off the motor. He took out a pen and pad of paper. "Go ahead . . . in your own words."

Why not? "I was sitting at the counter at Kugel's last night a little after nine when four guys wearing black ski masks, carrying AA-12 shotguns, marched in and started shooting."

"No warning?"

I shook my head.

"How did you have time to get your gun out and return fire?"

"I was looking in the direction of the front door when they came in," I said.

"But the counter stools face the other way," he pointed out professionally.

"The seats swivel. I was looking at the other patrons in the store with my friend Herb Brown and a kid we just met named Teofilo."

"Teofilo Fernandez is the kid who survived," Jerry said. "Brown is the ex-marine who got shot in the face, right?"

I grimaced and nodded.

"Did you see it happen?"

"No, I was a little busy at the time. Fernandez told the chief that Brown stepped in front of him and took the bullet."

"He saved Fernandez's life," Jerry said with enthusiasm as he scribbled in his notebook. "Do you know anything about him?"

"Yes, and I want you to write about him. He was a US marine in World War Two. He survived the invasion of Tarawa, in the Pacific. He won a Purple Heart and lived another sixty years to become a husband and father. Last night he died a hero saving a young man's life."

"Can I quote you?"

"Yeah, you can quote me."

"So let's go back to the shooting," Jerry said professionally. "The four guys came in blasting. Were you able to get a look at them?"

"They were black—"

"You said they were wearing masks," Jerry said skeptically.

"Yeah, and short-sleeved shirts."

"You are so cool," he said, scribbling. "What happened next?"

"Their AA-12s alerted me right away that they were there to shoot. I dove off the stool the instant I saw them and rolled for cover before they fired their first shot. I stayed covered through most of the attack."

I told Jerry about the gunman I shot in the thigh and the one who took three in the ski mask. I explained how steel bird shot saved my life. "Be sure to write about the bird shot," I said. "I want the gunmen to get pissed off at their ammo supplier and fight with them."

Jerry nodded. "What else?"

"That's all for now," I said, rubbing my eyes. "I'm tired."

"What about Joy and Lou?"

"Later."

He started the car again. "I'll take you home so you can get some rest."

"No . . . take me to Kugel's. The Mini doesn't stand out. Maybe the police didn't see it."

"You intend to drive in your condition?"

"I'm in better condition than most drivers in Boca."

The Mini was in the Kugel's lot fifty yards from the entrance. The right-front headlight was blown out, and two side windows were shattered. I probably did some of the damage myself when I fired at the departing shooters. "Son of a bitch," I said, getting out of the car.

"You and your car need repairs," Jerry said.

"You're right. I have no headlights or windows. I'll take the Mini to the dealer in Fort Lauderdale and get a loaner. I have too much to do to be without a car."

"What about Claudette's car? Does she even know you checked yourself out of the hospital?"

"No. She would have had me strapped to my bed. I'm too dangerous to be around anyway."

I told him about IED and EPD, the strange red veil and people trying to kill me.

"I can't believe you have brain damage and you're in mortal danger and you call me?" Jerry said, shaking his head.

"It's a great story."

"In that case, call me anytime," he said, and drove away.

I was about to start the car when a thought occurred to me. How did Grover's shooters know where to find me? I would have noticed being followed. I got out of the Mini, knelt, and looked under the car.

Damn!

The guy in the green shirt had washed bugs off my windshield and put one under the car.

I detached the transmitter and stood up. It was a ProTrak GPS. I disconnected the wires and put the device in my back pocket.

I'm doing the tracking from now on.

I drove to the Lauderdale Mini dealer. They gave me a loaner in blue.

"You want tinted windows when I replace them?" Tony, in the repair shop, asked. "You're a detective, you should have privacy."

"Tint the windows."

"We'll make the car look like new."

"Can you make me look like new?"

"Too late for that."

CHAPTER 28

LIFE ON MARS

I was relieved Claudette's car wasn't in the lot when I got home. I needed to be alone.

As I got out of the car, it occurred to me that Grover might try a second attack. He couldn't get to Lou, and he didn't know where I was now that the tracker was disconnected. The odds were I was safe for now, but I couldn't help being a little paranoid.

I checked the lock on my apartment door and was satisfied no one had tampered with it. I entered the apartment and went directly to a closet in the second bedroom. I slid two shoe boxes out from under two larger boxes on the closet shelf and carried them to the kitchen. I put the boxes on the table, flipped the lid off one, and removed a handsome handgun made of high-grade carbon steel with a brightly polished blue finish. The Colt King Cobra was a gun for all reasons. It could fire .38 caliber bullets with decent stopping power or discharge high-powered .357

Magnum rounds . . . capable of "blowing your head clean off" according to Dirty Harry, a movie cop. I'd purchased the Colt on a whim in 1982 and hadn't used it much over the years. But I kept it well oiled and ready to use. I figured the police were holding my Glock and the bad guys were holding AA-12 cannons. Now was as good a time as any to give the old Cobra a shot.

In the second shoe box were dozens of rounds of each caliber. I chose Mr. Magnum's deadliest version and slipped one into each of the six chambers of the Colt. I gave the loaded cylinder a spin for good luck.

I stepped onto my balcony overlooking the golf course and thought of the red planet Mars. The Boca Heights fairways were green, but they looked vermilion to me, and the four golfers approaching the tee were all dressed in red, in my eyes. I wondered if I would spend the rest of my life seeing the world through rose-colored glasses.

I used my cell to call Claudette and hoped she wouldn't answer. I got her voice mail and talked at the beep.

"Hi, Claudette," I began, clearing my throat. "I don't know any easy way to say this so here goes. I checked myself out of the hospital. Last night's shooting and explosion weren't accidents. Grover sent assassins to kill us, and Joy was collateral damage. I don't want that to happen to you. It's not safe around me right now. I took a risk and went to the apartment, but I don't want you to go there. Don't visit Lou and Joy at the hospital until I think it's safe. Stay with your grandmother. I'll let you know when this is over."

I disconnected without telling her I loved her. My mind just wasn't working that way. I was focused on survival, justice, and revenge. As I turned to reenter the apartment, I heard a loud, angry scream . . .

"Muthah fuckah!"

The hanging clay pot above my head exploded and pieces flew into my living room. I hit the deck. I hadn't heard a gunshot, but it had to have come from the golf course. I figured it was one of the three surviving shooters from Kugel's.

Rifle, silencer, I thought.

I reached for the Cobra in my waistband, got up, and fired a warning shot in the air to let the bastards know I was armed. There was no return fire. I fanned my gun in all directions. I looked down on the tee and saw four golfers lying facedown, motionless.

Not again. Enough people had already died because of me.

One of the golfers shouted, "Don't shoot, okay?" and stood up slowly, his hands above his head.

What's going on?

"My name's Al Shapiro," the golfer called to me. "I'm a member here. It was an accident. Honest."

The other three got up slowly, holding their hands in the air.

"It was the damnedest thing I ever saw." Shapiro pointed. "Unger over there hit his drive into that rock over there, and the ball ricocheted onto your balcony and broke the pot."

I lowered the gun and the four of them put their hands down.

"Nothing personal, man," Unger shouted. "But you should try an anger-management class."

I shook my head and was walking back into my living room when Unger called to me.

"Hey, man, I think my ball went in your living room. Could you throw it back?"

I turned and took aim. "Forget it," Unger said, and ran to his cart. I watched them drive away.

Pottery shards littered the living-room rug. I picked up a golf ball on the coffee table. It was a TiTech, forty-five-cent ball with the name BARRY UNGER stamped on it.

"Damn golfers," I muttered, and tossed the ball in the trash.

I cleaned up, changed clothes, grabbed a box of ammunition, put my Cobra back in my pants, and drove to my office.

I went to Lou's room, retrieved the Big Game Investments folder, and took it to my office. I sat behind my desk, leaned back, and opened the Hunter file. An eight-by-ten, computer-generated photo of Hunter was on top. He was leaning against a classic '56 Corvette convertible, arms folded in front of him, legs crossed casually at the ankles. He was wearing tan pants and a royal-blue golf shirt. A sweater was draped casually over the back of his shoulders, long sleeves tied stylishly across his chest. His wavy, black hair was slick like a matador's. He looked confident and relaxed, not at all like the rattled, despondent person I had seen at Grover's estate. I set the picture aside and read.

James Jeffrey Hunter, born in New York City in 1950, went to Erasmus High School in Brooklyn, where he was voted Most Handsome his senior year. It was his only honor. I checked the computer using one of Lou's custom-made programs. Hunter was a below-average student with below-average ambition, content to get by on his good looks and easygoing manner. Despite his showing no academic aptitude, Jim's father, a city ward politician, was able to get his son admitted to CCNY and avoid the Vietnam War. The crowning moment of Hunter's college career was appearing as an extra in the movie *Love Story* during a Harvard graduation scene filmed, for some reason, on the CCNY campus. After graduating at the bottom of his class from the Harvard of 135th Street, Hunter got a series of inconsequential jobs. His employment usually lasted as long as it took his employers to learn he was not nearly as good as he looked. It was the same with impressionable women. They tended to love him at first sight but leave him after a second look. Some women didn't see through him soon enough, and he got three rich ones to marry him. Each marriage ended with a disillusioned wife willing to pay Hunter to leave. During the death throes of his third marriage, he met Benjamin Grover at a cocktail party. Grover was introduced to Hunter as the shrewdest investment man on Wall Street, and thus began a relationship that lasted longer than any of Jimmy's marriages.

I dropped the folder on the desk. Grover and Hunter were meant for each other. One was fascinatingly enigmatic. The other was superficially charismatic. One lied. The other sold those lies to people who should have known better. Euphoric investors told friends about Grover's unbelievable returns, and those friends told their friends. Soon everyone believed the unbelievable and wanted to be admitted into B.I.G. land. Perhaps the most unbelievable thing of all was that Big Game Hunter was accepted as a gatekeeper to Grover's Magic Kingdom. Hunter, who had never made a decent living in his life, was growing rich taking other people's money and giving it to a fraud.

My overall impression was that Hunter wasn't evil. I didn't think he fully understood the consequences of his actions. He was a remora . . . riding on the back of a whale . . . going places he could never have gone on his own. Hunter became rich and respected in his world, but I knew he was the most vulnerable target for a counterattack on Grover's evil empire.

It was late afternoon when I called Hunter's cell phone.

"Jim Hunter," he answered.

"Eddie Perlmutter."

Hunter cleared his throat. "I'm a little surprised to hear from you."

"Why's that?"

"We had a rather unpleasant meeting as I'm sure you'll agree. Then this morning on the news I heard you had been involved in a horrible shooting and were in intensive care."

"Don't believe everything you hear on the news. I'm fine."

"I'm glad to hear that," he said, sounding sincere. "But why are you calling me?"

"You're close to Grover," I said, flattering him.

"I understand. What can I do for you?"

"I want you to tell Grover that I got his message last night. Tell him I understood it completely."

"What message?"

"He'll know, ask him," I said evasively. "Tell him there's no need for a follow-up message. We have no further interest in pursuing the investigation."

Is lying to a liar really lying?

"I don't know what you're talking about, but I'm glad you reached an understanding," Hunter said.

"There's more," I said, starting to believe that Hunter was clueless about the attacks. "Be sure to let him know that if he decides to send further messages, I'll answer him in person. If I'm unable to do that for any reason, tell him I'll respond through the mail with all the information I have."

"Will he understand you?"

"You better hope he does, Jim. It's very important to both of you."

"That sounds ominous. What does this have to do with me?"

"Ask Grover when you give him the message," I said, and disconnected.

I hoped I had lied well enough to make Grover think twice about a second attack. I needed time.

CHAPTER 29

BAILEY BAILED

I phoned the Baker center and asked the male receptionist about Bailey.

"Bailey has left the building," he said glibly.

"You're kidding. When?"

"She bailed out sometime after the nine o'clock bed check last night."

I was in a gunfight at the time. "Do you know where she went?"

"The homeless don't usually leave forwarding addresses."

"You're annoying," I said, and disconnected.

Okay, where was Bailey?

I guessed she'd hitched a ride, borrowed a bike, or walked to Rutherford Park last night and slept under the boardwalk. In the late morning she probably went to the Baptist church in Pearl City for Harold Trager's osso buco. After lunch she would have visited Weary Willie in the Boca Hospital for the afternoon, scrounged for dinner, and returned to Rutherford after dark. I would look for her there. Until then I had to plan my next move, and I did a quick review of my cases.

The pill mills case still needed more research before I could take action. The Grover case was on hold pending Lou's recovery. I was in no shape to go after the shooters or bombers, and that case would have to wait while I healed.

The only thing I felt capable of doing was going to St. Mary's Church and hunting for clues. I decided to go in disguise in the event anyone was there who could identify the Boca Knight. I put on a Red Sox cap and pulled it low to cover the puncture wounds in my forehead. I wore a light Windbreaker to conceal my Colt King Cobra tucked inside my waistband against my spine and headed for my Mini loaner. I felt light-headed behind the wheel but Boca has a lot of light-headed drivers.

St. Mary's spire looked beautiful in the twilight, silhouetted against a clear winter sky. I drove past the church and saw a worn-out pickup truck and a late-model Ford sedan parked in front. I parked in the street and took a pair of black-rimmed, tinted eyeglasses from my detective kit and put them on. I was always surprised how much these simple, black-rimmed glasses altered my appearance. I turned my jacket collar up, tugged my cap lower, and walked to the church. The front door was locked. I jiggled the handle several times, then knocked. No one answered. I walked to the side of the building opposite the fateful staircase. That door was locked too. I knocked again. No answer. The back of the building had a few windows high on the outside wall, but no door. I turned the corner and stared at the staircase of doom. I descended slowly and tried the door at the bottom. As expected, it was locked. I knocked loudly but no one answered. I began trudging up the stairs, head down and knees aching.

"What do you want?" a deep voice boomed from above. I knew from the Brooklyn accent it wasn't God. I looked up at a

big man in work clothes wearing a Yankees cap. I started climb-
ing again. As I got closer, I saw GINO embroidered on his shirt.

Behind me the door banged open. I turned and saw another
"Brooklyn-bouncer type" standing below me dressed in the
same uniform as Gino, except he had TONY embroidered above
his pocket. They looked like brothers.

Tony followed me as I climbed. With only one stair remaining, I had to stop because big Gino was standing on it. I looked
up at him and nearly lost my balance. I grabbed the handrail to
steady myself.

"I almost fell," I said to him. "This staircase is dangerous."

"Most people don't use these stairs," Gino said defensively.
"They're no problem. Now what are you doing here?"

"This is a Catholic church, isn't it?"

"Yeah, so?" Gino said.

"So I'm a Catholic," I lied. "I'm new in town and I'm looking to join a Catholic church. I saw the cars parked out front so
I figured someone was here. I tried every door."

That got him thinking and I used the opportunity to push
past him to level ground. I still had to look up at him. When his
brother joined us, I was looking up at twin towers.

"I was hoping to meet the priest and talk to him about what
the church has to offer," I continued lying, enjoying myself. "Who
are you guys?"

"We're the priest's cousins," Tony told me. "We help out
around here. Who are you?"

"Eddie Monroe from South Boston," I lied again. It was easy.
"Is the priest in?"

"He ain't here," Gino lied right back at me.

"Are you a Red Sox fan?" Tony asked, pointing at my hat.

"No. I hate the Sox. I'm a Yankees fan like you guys. I won
the hat on a bet."

"Good man," Gino said, and they both lightened up.

"Where you from?" I asked.

"Bay Ridge," Tony said. "Right near the Verrazano Bridge. Ever heard of it?"

"Sure, great town," I said, never having heard of the place. "When will the priest be in? I need to make a confession."

"You been doin' a lot of sinnin'?" Gino asked.

"I can't seem to stop. How about you?"

"I never confess to nothin'," Tony said.

"Look man, we're busy," Gino said. "Why don't you come to Sunday mass and meet the priest then."

"That's a good idea. I love a good Sunday mass. See you there."

Chapter 30

Under the Boardwalk, Part 1

I drove from St. Mary's to Kugel's. The scene of the crime was sealed off with yellow DO NOT CROSS tape and lit with portable, police-issue FoxFire spotlights. The bloodstains, broken glass, and splintered wood were still there.

When I approached the tape barricade, a patrolman I knew ordered me to stop: "Off-limits. Crime scene."

I removed my Red Sox cap and tinted glasses. "It's me, Sarge. Eddie Perlmutter."

"Eddie," Sergeant Tom Dowd said, surprised. "I didn't recognize you. I thought you were in the hospital?"

"I was, but I'm fine. Anything I can do to help around here?"

"I can't let you in. The crime scene is still secured."

"Okay, I'll just look around?"

I stood outside the lines watching the police take pictures, bag evidence, and search for clues. The place looked like the

Alamo, filled with bullet holes and bloodstains. It was a miracle I had survived. I thought of Herb Brown. It was a miracle he survived Tarawa, lived sixty more years, and died saving a life in a Boca deli.

Go figure.

After a quick surveillance I drove to Rutherford Park to look for Bailey. A full moon was the only light on the boardwalk, so I played the beam of my flashlight on the uneven floorboards. As I neared the locked gate, I heard rustling in the bushes. I wasn't worried. Whatever was in the underbrush had more to fear than I did.

I picked the gate lock and descended the steps to the sandy beach. I shone my light under the boardwalk and saw a shadowy figure lying there.

"Stop, I have a gun," Bailey said in a shaky voice.

"No, you don't."

"Eddie?"

"It's me, don't shoot."

She scrambled into the light and smiled into the beam. The stitches on her face had not been removed and she had a Bride of Frankenstein look. She was surrounded by cats of various sizes, shapes, and colors. I estimated ten of them.

"I thought you were in the hospital," she said, crawling closer.

"I thought *you* were in the hospital."

"I started feeling better so I took off."

"Me too," I said. "Are these your cats?"

"They're no one's cats. They just sleep here."

"How do you feed them?"

"They feed themselves," she said. "Fish wash up onshore, plenty of mice and birds live here. I feel bad when they kill birds, but at least it's natural."

"Did you sleep here last night?"

She nodded.

"I went to the soup kitchen for lunch, then went to the hospital and sat with Willie the rest of the afternoon."

"What do you do there all day?"

"I talk to him," she said. "I tell him stories."

"He can't hear you, Bailey."

"We don't know that for sure."

"Any change in his condition?"

"No. He just lays there."

"Did you have something to eat tonight?"

"I ate some leftover food from the trays in the hospital corridor. Then it took me almost two hours to get back here. I couldn't find a bike anywhere."

"You have to have your stitches out," I said, pointing at her scars.

"Next time I visit Willie, I will. But never mind me. I heard you were shot. How are you?"

"I may have a little brain damage, but no big deal."

"That's good," she said, already on to her next thought. "As soon as I feel stronger, I'm going back to St. Mary's and learn more about those big fat Yankee fans."

"I already did. Their names are Gino and Tony. They're Father Vincent's cousins and they take care of the church."

"Like janitors?" she asked, sounding disappointed. "I was hoping they had something to do with what happened to Willie."

"I think they do."

I told her how Tony and Gino had sandwiched me on the staircase. "I almost fell backward myself. If I had fallen, I would have landed on my head when I hit the stairs. That's what I think happened to Willie."

"Do you think they pushed him?"

"Maybe."

"If they pushed him it's murder," she said. "If he fell, it's an accident."

"Either way, I want to know why they moved him. Why didn't they just call the police and report an accident. They must be hiding something."

"What could a Catholic church be hiding?" she asked.

"You must be kidding me."

Chapter 31

Under the Boardwalk, Part 2

"I'm uncomfortable," I told Bailey.

"Lie down." She patted the space beside her, shooing away a few cats.

"I am a little tired." I yawned.

She gave me one of her three bags as a pillow, and I stretched out next to her. I folded my hands on my chest and breathed deeply. I listened to the bugs and a cat purring in my ear.

"Can you explain this?" I asked. "I have a nice two-bedroom apartment and a beautiful girlfriend across town, and I'm lying under a damp boardwalk in a park for the homeless. Why's that?"

"Circumstances."

"How's your sister?"

"She's in a shell hiding from the truth," Bailey said.

"We all do that."

"Not me. I face the truth every morning."

"You face reality but not the truth," I disagreed. "To face the truth you need to include the past and the future."

"I wasted my past and I don't have a future."

"I think everyone has a future. We just can't predict it."

She moved closer to me and put her head on my chest. I sensed she just wanted to be close to someone.

"I can hear your heartbeat," she said.

Her hair smelled clean; the rest of her smelled like unwashed laundry.

She was snoring before I fell asleep.

Loud noises woke me. Bailey's head was still on my chest.

"Shhh," she warned.

The cats were alert but silent.

I listened to scuffling on the boards above my head, then a thud. I heard a man groan, followed by laughter that sounded like human donkeys braying.

"Get up, you old bum," a loud male voice ordered.

"What's going on?" I whispered.

"Homeless bashers," Bailey said. "They come looking for bums to beat up."

"Sounds like they found one."

"Probably found him outside the park and hauled him in."

I hate bullies. I've hated bullies all my life. I moved Bailey's head off my chest and sat up.

"Don't go up there," she said.

"I have to."

I remained under the boardwalk and scrambled about twenty yards away from Bailey's nest. I rolled onto the beach near the steps and looked up. I could see four silhouettes holding flashlights, kicking at an inert body on the boardwalk.

"Get off our streets, you scum," one of them shouted, and

kicked hard. I heard a weak groan from the man being beaten. He was still alive but they were doing their best to kick the life out of him.

I hurried up the stairs quietly, picked the lock, and walked onto the boardwalk. They still hadn't seen me, but they heard my footsteps. Four flashlight beams lit me up. I must have looked like hell with all those holes in my head.

"Hey, look, we got another one," a voice announced, and they laughed, sounding like hyenas this time. I didn't respond or stop walking. When I got closer, I did a policeman's survey. A squat, fat kid was closest to me. He wore baggy jeans low on his hips. He would be slow and clumsy. No problem. A kid with a baseball hat on backward was next. He wore shorts, a baggy sweatshirt, and combat boots. He was holding a metal pipe in his hand and I figured I had to disarm him fast. The third was a baby-faced girl who looked excited to be with the boys but scared to be with me. She didn't worry me.

"Welcome to the party," the fourth one said. He was the biggest and wore a bandanna on his head.

"I don't suppose you guys would just leave if I asked you real nice," I said, seeing red but thinking clearly.

They laughed in unison and annoyed the hell out of me.

Baggy Pants swung a roundhouse right at me.

He was slower than I anticipated. I sidestepped the punch easily, using his momentum to shove him forward against the wooden railing. Before he could turn around, I pulled his baggy pants down to his ankles and pushed him sideways. He stumbled over his jeans and fell on his back. I heard the air rush out of his mouth.

The kid with the baseball cap and metal pipe came at me, poised to strike. I stepped toward him, grabbed his raised wrist, twisted it into an unnatural position, and took the short pipe from his hand. I rapped him on top of the head just hard enough to make him howl and drop to his knees holding his head with both hands.

"Jesus Christ," the girl with the baby face cried, and ran off into the darkness.

"I'm gonna cut you up," the bandanna boy snarled, and I saw he was holding a knife.

"Never tell the enemy what you plan to do," I said.

"Is that so?" He lunged forward, slashing at my stomach with a sweeping motion. I was too fast for him. I stepped back and the knife passed in front of my abdomen from right to left. He was about to swing it left to right in a backhand motion when I whacked him with the pipe across the forehead. Blood spurted and he collapsed next to his friends. I picked up the knife he had dropped and threw it into the trees.

"And now for the best surprise of all," I said, pulling the Cobra out of my back waistband and aiming it at them.

"Holy shit," the chubby kid said. "Don't shoot."

"Why not?"

"Because we'll never come back here again," the kid with the baseball cap said.

"Yeah, that's right, man," the chubby kid said, still trying to untangle his pants.

"Shut up," the kid with the bloody bandanna said. "That's a fake gun."

I pulled the trigger and blew apart the wooden railing above their heads.

Oh my God.

Holy shit.

"Satisfied?" I asked.

Three heads nodded.

"Good. Now I have a decision to make. I can shoot you, turn you in to the cops, or let you go."

"Let us go, man," the chubby one said.

"We promise we'll never come back here," the one with the baseball hat said.

"What about you, tough guy?" I asked Bandanna Man.

He nodded.

"Okay. I'm going to let you go. But it's not because I believe you won't come back, and I sure as hell don't feel sorry for you. I'm letting you go because I want you to tell your friends what happened here tonight. Tell them about this .357 Magnum, and let them know there's plenty more guys like me sick of guys like you ganging up on the homeless. They've been beaten enough already. Understand?"

Three nervous nods followed.

"Now get your dumb asses out of here while you still can."

They scrambled to their feet and ran off into the darkness.

"You think they'll be back?" Bailey asked, standing behind me.

"I don't know. How long have you been there?"

"Since you blew the railing down. Why didn't you just show them the gun in the first place. You could have frightened them off without a fight."

"I didn't want to frighten them off. I wanted to send a message. Hey, what happened to the guy they were beating?"

"He's crawled away," she said. "I think you scared him off too."

"But he was badly hurt."

"He's used to being kicked when he's down."

"Maybe. Maybe not," I said.

"By the way, your forehead is bleeding."

I touched my palm to my head and felt the sticky ooze of blood. "No big deal," I told her, but my knees buckled and I grabbed the wooden railing. "I guess I am a little out of shape."

"You better rest," she said, taking my arm.

She walked me down the stairs and under the boardwalk. "Get some sleep," she said as she covered me with the one blanket she had and slid under it next to me. A cat licked my wounds while several others snuggled next to me.

"They like you," Bailey said, watching her feral pets pet me.

"I don't like them. I'm a dog man. Are you cold?"

"I've been colder." She put her head on my chest again.

"Is my heart still beating?" I joked.

"Loud and clear," she said in a sleepy voice.

"That's good to know." I closed my eyes.

CHAPTER 32

RED ALERT

When I opened my eyes in the morning and Bailey was gone, I felt like a one-night stand. I sat up and checked my watch. It was six thirty, the sunlight was weak, and a ten-foot alligator, with his mouth wide open, was thirty yards away from me at the water's edge.

"Holy shit," I said, brushing a cat off my chest and scrambling out from under the boardwalk. I pulled my Colt and aimed it at the gator. If he made a move for me, I'd shoot first and turn him into a pair of shoes later. I noticed two cats walking on the gator's back and felt less threatened.

"Eddie, don't shoot," Bailey said, appearing out of nowhere. "Allie is old and harmless."

"His mouth is open like he wants to eat me whole."

"That's how he suns himself. He's not interested in you. The lake is stocked with fish and he eats all day."

"What about the cats on his back?" I asked. "Are they safe?"

"They're too fast for him and they know it. Put the gun away."

"Where were you just now?" I asked, sticking the Cobra back in my pants.

"In the ladies' room washing up. You want a toothbrush? I have an extra."

I was brushing my teeth in the public men's room when my cell phone rang. It was Chief Burke.

"It's about time you answered," he started the conversation. "I called you a bunch of times last night."

"I turned off my phone."

"Why?"

"I spent the night at the home of a homeless woman and didn't want to be disturbed."

"Your head injury is worse than I thought," Frank said.

"What's up?"

"Your friends Lou and Joy are up."

"How are they?"

"Physically they'll survive. They've got second-degree burns, concussions, and it appears that Lou lost some hearing in his left ear. You know about Joy's leg."

"Did anyone tell Lou about Joy?"

"That's when the screaming started," Frank said.

"I'll get there as fast as I can."

I offered to take Bailey to the hospital, but she asked to be dropped off near Pearl City. "I'll scrounge for some breakfast at McDonald's," she said. "Then I'll walk to Friendship Baptist for lunch. Chef Trager is making knishes today. You want me to bring you one?"

I passed.

When I got off the elevator at intensive care, I saw Chief Burke. "How is he?" I asked.

"They put both of them to sleep with medication a few

minutes ago. They couldn't control them any other way. They could be out for a while. I'm sorry I had you rush over."

"That's okay. I should have been here for them last night."

"You should have been here for yourself last night," Frank said. "You're not in such great shape either."

"I have things I gotta do, Frank. I have no time to rest right now."

"You ready to tell what's going on?"

"Not yet."

"Well, I've got something to tell you," Frank said. "We found things at Joy's house that indicate the explosion was no accident."

"What did you find?"

"Fragments of a Teflon-coated wrench were embedded in the fibers of a mattress that was leaning against the garage wall. A Teflon-coated tool leaves no evidence of tampering . . . no scratches or scrapes on a gas pipe. Whoever did the tampering knew enough to use the right tool but didn't clean up before the blowup. Very unprofessional."

It was a last-minute job.

"A small piece of electrical wire was found connected to a lightning-arrestor wire. An expert would have used combustible sodium wire that disintegrates at two hundred degrees . . . leaving no evidence. These guys missed that too. We're looking for more."

"Nice work."

He nodded. "You weren't really with a homeless woman last night, were you?"

"Not in the biblical sense. I went looking for a client who lives in Rutherford Park."

"So you're the guy." Frank pointed at me. "I should have known. A patrolman picked up some stoned punks this morning on Federal babbling about being attacked by a crazy man at Rutherford Park."

"It's a dangerous place. I hear kids go there to beat up the homeless."

"They said this guy was about ten feet tall," Frank said with a smile.

"That leaves me out."

"How's your head?"

"I'm having hot flashes and seeing red all the time. My behavior is unpredictable. Outside of that I'm fine. How's Joy?"

"Stable but she refuses to see anyone."

"Even Lou?"

"Especially Lou."

"That's bad. What does her doctor say?"

"You can ask him," Frank told me. "He's in with her now and should be out soon."

A few minutes later a tall, dark, middle-aged doctor in a white coat exited Joy's room. "Chief Burke," he said, holding out his hand, "you're still here."

"She's a good friend," Frank said. "Eddie Perlmutter, meet Dr. Barry Unger, Joy's surgeon."

"I know Dr. Unger."

"Have we met?" the doctor asked.

"You hit a golf ball through my window. It had your name on it."

"Oh, yes." He looked at me. "I remember. Are you armed?"

"Always, but I'm taking an anger-management class. I'm much better."

We laughed and shook hands. "How's Joy?" I asked.

"She'll survive her injuries, but I'm very concerned about her. She's an emotional wreck. She won't allow us to examine her and she refuses to move. Normally we have an amputee in a wheelchair within two days, but she won't budge. We can't begin her rehabilitation without her cooperation."

"Will she get better with time?" I asked.

"I'm concerned she could get worse. She seems to have lost her will to live. She's said several times she wishes she was dead."

"What's her physical condition?"

"Surprisingly promising," Dr. Unger said. "We amputated below the knee, which means she has a functioning knee joint. With a properly designed prosthesis and a lot of hard work, she could walk again, maybe even run."

"Have you told her?"

"Of course. But she's not listening. She just stares off into space. We can't help her unless she helps us." The doctor looked at his watch. "I have to go. I'll be back later."

"Is there anything we can do?"

"Try to get her to work with us or she's going to wither away," he said, and moved on.

"Lou's the only one who can get through to her," I said to the chief.

"But she won't talk to him," he said.

"I'll figure out something."

After Frank went back to work, I went to Lou's room, sat down on a comfortable chair beside his bed, and watched him sleep. When I woke up two hours later, he was watching me.

"Hey, Lou," I said in a groggy voice, and sat up straight from my slouch.

"Where were you?" he asked, sounding like a little boy who was lost and found. Tears were in his eyes.

"I got here as soon as I could, Lou."

"Joy lost her leg," he told me, choking on the words and covering his eyes with his arm.

"I know." I bit my lower lip. It's a good thing I don't cry.

"Can you believe it . . . *a gas explosion*?" he said incredulously. "What are the odds of that?"

He had no idea the explosion was manmade. No one except

Frank Burke and I suspected anything. Jerry Small had a hint . . . but Lou didn't have a clue.

Should I tell him?

Would he want me to tell him?

Would I want him to tell me?

Yes!

"Lou, I have to tell you something that's going to upset you. Do you want to hear it now . . . or wait until you're feeling better?"

He removed his arm from his eyes. "Tell me now. I can't feel any worse."

That's what you think.

I started with the end of our meeting with Grover and told him everything. He didn't interrupt once, though his facial expressions told me what he was feeling. When I reached the part about the shoot-out at Kugel's, he looked at my injured forehead. "I didn't even notice," he said sadly. "I'm sorry."

"It's okay. You've got a lot on your mind."

"Are you seeing red now?"

"All the time. I hardly notice it anymore."

"Jesus, Eddie, look what I did," he said, his voice cracking and his hands trembling. "Nine dead, you're hurt, Joy—"

I interrupted him, "We did it together. I should have stopped you."

"No, it was my fault," he insisted. "You warned me a meeting with Grover was dangerous, but I didn't listen. I wanted the satisfaction of looking the son of a bitch in the eye when I told him. It was stupid."

Yes, it was.

"We were both stupid," I said. "I let you do it. We underestimated Grover."

"I overestimated myself."

"Whatever," I said dismissively. "What do you want to do now?"

"Nothing," he said, turning away from me. "I can't take a chance with Joy's life again."

I told him about the police guards I hired and my stall call to Jim Hunter. "I don't know if Grover called the dogs off or not," I said. "But after you release the story, Grover has no reason to come after you. The damage will be done."

"I'm not doing anything until I talk to Joy. And she won't talk to me. I'll have to give her more time."

"According to her doctor, the last thing she needs is time to lay in bed feeling sorry for herself." I told him what the doctor said.

"She said she wanted to die?" he asked, horrified at the thought. I nodded.

"I have to talk to her," he said. "Why won't she see me?"

"You want my opinion? I don't think she wants you to see her. You're her whole world and she doesn't think you'll want her with one leg. She'd rather die."

"That's ridiculous. I love her more than anything in the world."

"You have to tell her, not me, Lou."

"How can I tell her anything if she won't talk to me?"

"She doesn't have to talk to you. You have to talk to her."

"You're right, let's go," he said, throwing off his covers, swinging his legs off the bed, and falling on the floor, screaming. He had pulled the intravenous needles out of his arms and torn the urine catheter from his bladder and urethra.

Holy shit, Mr. Johnson said, sympathetically. I hadn't heard from him since the last Viagra pill.

Two nurses ran into the room and saw Lou on the floor holding his groin and moaning. "Jesus, God," one of the RNs said. "He broke the balloon off his Foley catheter. I've never seen that before."

They started lifting Lou and he started screaming. I left the room and waited in the corridor while he was reconnected, soothed, and drugged.

"What the hell happened?" one of the nurses said as she waved me back into his room.

"He got upset. He tried to get out of bed."

"Well, he can't. He's attached to a bunch of stuff. If we want to move him, we have to take all his attachments with him. No more excitement, understand? We just gave him some pain pills."

I nodded.

When I reentered Lou looked at me sheepishly. "I guess I'm not cut out to be a hero."

"After what you just survived, you're my hero."

"What do we do now?" Lou asked, his eyes growing glassy from painkillers.

"First we figure out how to move you without giving you a sex change."

"I'd appreciate that." His eyes began to close. The drugs were doing their job.

"Then we'll worry about step two, getting you in to see Joy. We'll do it."

He smiled and fell asleep.

Chapter 33

Nurse Eddie

While Lou slept, I wandered the floors and corridors of the hospital formulating a strategy. I borrowed a male nurse's green, baggy uniform from an open linen closet and put it on in an empty men's room stall. The round surgical linen cap covered the red spots on my forehead, and the surgical mask covered most everything else. Incognito, I wandered into the maternity ward and froze when someone grabbed my arm.

"Hey, Doc," a beaming, red-faced young man said to me. "Would you mind taking a picture of me and my new son?"

"Not at all," I said, relieved.

A black female nurse, inside the nursery, held up a screaming Caucasian baby boy who could have been anyone's except hers or that of an old Chinese woman standing next to me. I was handed a camera, snapped a picture of the beaming father and screaming son, declined an IT's A BOY cigar, congratulated everyone, and hustled away. I passed a woman in a wheelchair and got an idea. Her wheelchair had a portable IV pole attached that carried three intravenous bags.

Perfect.

I saw a similar wheelchair against the wall, without a lady in it, and borrowed it just before I got on the elevator. No one gave me a second look on the ride up to intensive care, and I confidently pulled my face mask down for the duration of the ride. I got off the elevator wheeling the chair in front of me.

Head down, mask up.

I walked to Lou's room. He was still sleeping. I was sweating like a pig. I took off the uniform and hid it in the closet. I sat in the chair next to the bed and took deep breaths. A real male nurse entered the room, nudged Lou awake, and took his vital signs. He seemed satisfied and nodded to me as Lou closed his eyes again.

"A friend?" the nurse asked.

"My best friend," I confirmed. "I've got another friend on the floor named Joy Feely. How's she doing?"

"Not so good. She lost a leg, you know."

I nodded.

"She won't talk, eat, nothing." He sighed. "She won't even let me take her vital signs. She hides under her blanket. They're going to have to do something about her before she makes matters worse."

"Can I visit her?"

"We're not allowed to let anyone in to see her. Those are her orders, not the doctor's."

"What if you don't see me entering the room?" I said with a wink.

"I can't stop someone I don't see," he said understandingly. "But all visitors have to check in at the reception desk to get in the ward."

"I'm already in the ward."

"Indeed you are," he said, giving me a thumbs-up and departing.

I was leaving Lou's room when two cops arrived. I recognized them from police headquarters and they knew me.

"Hi, guys. Are you here to guard Feely and Dewey?" I asked.

They nodded and one of them said, "Chief Burke said we're working for you."

"Come back in an hour," I said. "I may have different instructions for you."

"We'll go to the cafeteria and hang out," the other cop said, and handed me a card with his cell phone number. "Call if you need us."

I located Joy's room, four doors away. The door was closed. I returned to Lou's room and nudged his shoulder. His eyes opened slowly. "What?"

"I'm busting you out of here."

"Where we going?" he said, still groggy from the drugs.

"Joy's room."

"Okay," he said, placing his hands over his crotch. "Just be careful."

I moved his intravenous bag and catheter tube to the wheelchair holder. Lou edged himself off the bed into the chair. Miraculously the transfer went without a hitch. He watched and smiled as I put on my Nurse Eddie disguise. "The things we do for love," I said, pulling up my face mask. "Do you have any idea what you're going to say to her?"

"I'm going to ask her one question," Lou told me, still sounding mildly under the influence.

"The last time you did that we almost got killed."

"I'll do better this time."

I wheeled him to Joy's room. Her door was closed. I knocked.

"Leave me alone," we heard a weak voice say.

I opened the door and pushed Lou into the room.

She was lying in bed, looking out the window, away from us. "I told you to leave me alone," she said, and turned.

"Hi, Joy," Lou said, and waved timidly.

"Go away," she said, starting to cry. "I don't want to see you." She pulled the covers over her face like a frightened child. "I don't want to see anyone."

Lou motioned for me to push him closer to her bed and I did. I could see where her leg was missing under the covers. I don't cry but I almost did.

She sensed that we had moved closer. "Go away. Please. I don't want you here," she pleaded.

"I understand, Joy," Lou said calmly.

"No, you don't," she said, her head still covered. "Go away."

"Okay, I'll go away if you answer one question for me."

"No questions," she said, her voice muffled by the blanket. "Get out."

"You only have to give a one-word answer. And I'll leave."

Oh, boy, this sounds familiar.

"My one-word answer is *no*."

"I haven't asked the question."

"I don't care, go away," she insisted.

"Not until you answer my question."

"Just one word and you'll leave?"

"One word," he confirmed.

"You promise."

"I promise."

"Okay," she agreed, still hiding under the blanket. "Ask your stupid question."

"Will you marry me?"

Wow! That's some question.

Dead silence. Her eyes peeked above the covers. "W-what?"

"That's not an answer," Lou said.

"You don't want to marry me," she said, stunned. "I'm a cripple."

"You lost part of your right leg. You're not a cripple. You'll walk again and I'll walk with you."

"But I'm a one-legged freak now." She wept.

"Are you kidding me? You could win the One-Legged Miss America contest, you're so beautiful."

Don't push it, Lou.

Joy lowered the blanket below her chin. Tears were streaming down her cheeks. "Don't make fun of me, Lou," she said, sniffling.

"I'm not making fun of you. I'm proposing to you."

"You don't mean it."

"Yes, I do. And what happened to the one-word answer I wanted?"

"Why would you want to marry me? I'm a mess."

You're making progress, Louie.

"Because I love you and you love me," he said. "We can take care of each other. It will be great."

"My stump is repulsive."

"Your stump is incredibly sexy," he said with a sly smile. "It's kinda kinky."

"You're an idiot," she scolded him, and almost smiled. "It's ugly."

"Nothing about you is ugly," he insisted. "I think you're the most beautiful woman in the world. Will you marry me, Joy Feely?"

She reached for him with both arms. She was crying. "Yes, I'll marry you, Lou Dewey."

Chapter 34

The Panhandle

I called Claudette from outside the hospital.

She answered the phone without saying hello. "If you're not calling to say you miss me and want me by your side, I'm going to be very upset."

"I miss you. But it's too dangerous to be by my side right now."

"Are you forgetting I cut a man's head off with a machete before I left Haiti?"

"You have my permission to cut off Benjamin Grover's head."

"I'm serious," she said. "I want to help you."

"And I want to protect you."

"I can take care of myself," she insisted.

"That's what Lou Dewey said just before his ass caught on fire."

"No one's going to set my ass on fire except you."

"My point exactly," I told her. "And the safest place for your ass right now is at your grandmother Queen's house. No one's going to infiltrate Osceola Park."

"You're right about that. Queen has mobilized the entire neighborhood," Claudette said. Queen was Claudette's maternal grandmother from the black side of the family. She was ninety-something years old and she loved me.

"Good. So Queen agrees with me."

"She always agrees with you," Claudette said.

"Did she tell you to listen to your cute little white boy?"

"You know she did."

"Take her advice," I said.

"But I want to help you."

"You are helping by letting me do what I do best without having to worry about you."

"You're just saying that."

I could visualize her pouting. "I'm saying that because I love you."

I heard her sniffle. "I love you too. If you die out there, I'll kill you."

"I'll try to stay alive."

"You better. How are you feeling?"

"I'm a little tired and my behavior is totally erratic," I said. "Yesterday I fired my Colt in the direction of the golf course. Fortunately I didn't hit anything, but I scared the shit out of four golfers."

"Did they give you a mulligan?"

I laughed.

"What about the red spots?"

"It's a red veil and it's always there," I said. "But it's not like IED. I don't explode and forget what I did afterward. I'm on edge all the time, constantly on alert. I just don't know what the hell I'm going to do next."

"You need a doctor."

"When this is over, I'll see one," I promised.

"How are Lou and Joy?"

"They came off the critical list today."

"Why didn't you tell me right away?" she said, raising her voice.

"You didn't give me a chance."

"Can I visit them?"

"Not yet. I have two guards posted outside their rooms. I'm not satisfied the danger is over."

"How's Joy handling things?"

"She's very happy," I said.

"How can she be happy? She lost a leg."

"Lou asked her to marry him. He said prostheses turn him on."

Claudette was silent for a moment, then said, "I love that man."

"He's special. Even though he almost got us killed."

"He got carried away," she said, defending him.

"We all got carried away."

"What are you going to do next?"

"I haven't figured that out yet," I admitted.

"You better call me and let me know or I'll come looking for you."

"I promise," I said to my lover and best friend.

I went back to the intensive care ward and arranged for Lou to be moved into the same room with Joy with the consent of their doctor. I put both cops outside their door. "Be careful," I told them. "Either nothing is going to happen or all hell is going to break loose."

When I was ready to leave, Lou and Joy were in adjacent beds, holding hands.

I kissed Joy good-bye and told Lou he was too ugly to kiss.

"Lou and I want you to be our best man at our wedding," Joy said.

"Since there's no one more qualified . . . I accept."

"We're going to ask Claudette to be the matron of honor," Joy said. "But don't tell her. I want to ask her myself."

"I know she'll be an honored matron," I said.

What now? I asked myself, sitting in the rental car, outside the hospital. The fight at Rutherford had proven I wasn't in fighting condition and should lie low for a couple of weeks. All my cases were stable. Weary Willie wasn't going anywhere, Bailey was self-sufficient, Gino, Tony, and Father Vincent could wait, Doc was being patient, and Lou and Joy were protected. I was the most vulnerable, so the best move for me was to get out of town and rest. But where should I go? I couldn't just sit around doing nothing for two weeks. I went for a drive to think things over. Within minutes I had a plan. I went to the body shop and picked up the Mini, which wasn't cosmetically ready but was safe to drive again. I was advised not to take it, but I explained I was going on a trip and felt most comfortable in my own car.

I got on Florida's Turnpike north to Orlando for two hundred and thirty miles and merged onto I-75 North for another one hundred and seven miles. A hundred miles more and I saw signs for Tallahassee. According to the nurses at Boca Hospital, the state legislature in Tallahassee was in session for six weeks. The police I met during the raid on the No Pain-U-Gain Clinic told me the state legislature could change laws governing pill mills. I went to Tallahassee for RR&R . . . Rest, Relaxation, and Research.

It was early evening when I checked into the Studio Deluxe Motel a few miles from downtown Tallahassee. The room was neat and clean, with a mini-kitchen. I flopped on the bed and put my hands behind my head and considered my situation.

I knew no one in Tallahassee. I didn't know what Florida district I lived in or the name of my state senator or representative. I didn't have a change of clothes, a toothbrush, or a razor. I was hungry. I had a Visa and a MasterCard. No problem.

Chapter 35

Mad Mick Murphy, Part 1

The man at the reception desk gave me directions to the nearest Wal-Mart. I bought shirts, pants, and underwear for the next two weeks. I asked a Wal-Mart associate if there was a restaurant or bar where the legislators hung out after a daily session.

"That would be the State House Steak House, not far from here," the octogenarian said, and he gave me directions.

I found the restaurant easily. It was the kind of establishment I avoided in Boca—dimly lit, rich, dark paneling, and big-time prices. The elegant dining room was empty. The manager told me they served food in the Legislature Lounge and pointed the way. The high-top tables and low-slung booths were unoccupied, and only one person sat at the far end of the bar. I took a stool at the opposite end and nodded to the solitary bartender, whose name was William according to his name tag. I ordered a burger and a Coke and looked around. Pictures of Florida State athletic teams were on the walls, and one large, signed photo of an older man in a maroon baseball cap.

"Who's that?" I pointed.

"Bobby Bowden," William said, punching my order into the computerized cash register. "Head coach of the Seminoles for thirty years."

"Best damn coach in the history of college football," the other patron in the bar said.

"Right you are, Mick," William responded, putting my Coke in front of me.

"Why is it so quiet here?" I asked. "Isn't the legislature in session?"

"Yeah, we're normally very busy at this hour," William said. "Tonight the crowd of legislators got here early and left early. Don't know why."

"I can tell you," the only other person at the bar said. "The legislature began a discussion at the end of the day on breast-feeding in public and decided to sleep on it."

William and I laughed.

"Mick's a journalist from Key West," William told me. "He knows everything about Florida politics. He returns here on the first Tuesday following the first Monday of every March when the legislature convenes. He's like a migrating duck."

"Quack," Mick said.

"Another Jameson's?" William asked.

"Of course," Mick said. "My glass is half empty."

"It's half full," I said, working my way into the conversation.

"Spoken like a man who gets free Coke refills." Mick smiled good-naturedly. "I have to pay for each Jameson's . . . except when William feels charitable."

"I'll buy you a Jameson's if you tell me what a Jameson's is," I offered.

Mick beamed. He stood and approached me, glass in hand. "You don't have to buy me a drink," he said with a smile. "I just like to joke with William."

Mick was a good-looking man, ruddy faced, slightly taller than average with an athletic build. He had a full red beard and long red hair that looked like it were cut by a friend at a barber school. His clothes indicated that he'd rather be sailing.

"Jameson's is a good, affordable Irish whiskey," he told me, never losing his smile. "John Jameson started producing his whiskey in 1780 at the Bow Street Brewery in Dublin. Now it's made in Cork. The recipe calls for two kinds of barley, one malted . . . one not. The brew is cooked in a 'pure pot' still, which gives it a smooth, sweet taste."

"You've sold me," I said. "Make that two Jameson's, William."

"I don't want to corrupt your morals," Mick said.

"I was drinking whiskey before you were born. I just never made it a habit."

"No one's perfect," Mick said.

We clinked our glasses and took a sip.

Not bad.

"Liam Michael Murphy," he introduced himself, and held out his hand. "My friends call me Mick. Those who know me best call me Mad Mick."

"Eddie Perlmutter," I said as we shook hands.

His eyes grew wide. "Were you a cop in Boston?"

I nodded.

"I'll be damned. I wrote about you a hundred years ago. I'm from Boston originally . . . Southie." Mick referred to the Irish enclave of South Boston. "I graduated BC and Harvard School of Journalism and became a freelance journalist in the late seventies. In the eighties I was hired to write an article about famous Boston criminals of the sixties and seventies. I included you in my story."

"Why?"

"I wrote about the Emperor of Chinatown, Danny Dong."

"That miserable son of a bitch," I grumbled at the memory of the drug-dealing cop killer. "Did you write how I shot him between the eyes while he was holding a knife to a prostitute's throat?" William took one step back and a second look at me.

"I did," Mick said. "You were twenty feet away. It was a great shot. Any regrets?"

"Yes. I'm sorry I didn't shoot him in the balls first." I gulped my Jameson's and slammed my glass down on the bar. Mick did the same.

"Fuck Danny Dong," I said.

"Damn right," Mick said.

"Two more," I told William.

"Damn right," Mick said again. "I'll buy."

"If you insist."

"I don't insist but it's my turn."

"I'll get the next one," I said.

"I was counting on that."

"Who else did you write about?" I asked.

"The Winter Hill Gang—"

"Whitey Bulger, Howie Winter," I interrupted, feeling a whiskey buzz. "I knew those guys."

"I know you did. I wrote about the hoods at the Tap Royal bar in Somerville, Raymond Patriarca in Providence, Joe McDonald from Southie, and that MDC cop Russell Nicholson, who turned gangster."

"I knew him too, that sneaky bastard. What about Wimpy Bennett?"

"Sure, and his brothers, Willie and Walter," Mad Mick said with a twinkle in his eye. He was enjoying the memories. "I wrote about the McLaughlin brothers, Vinnie, the Animal, Barboza, Fat Tony Ciulla, Kevin Weeks, Jerry Angiulo, Doc Hurwitz."

"Was I the only cop you wrote about?" I asked, not mentioning my recent connection to Doc.

"No, but you were the most colorful."

We gulped our drinks and I ordered two more. I don't know why. I was already buzzing like a hornets' nest. My burger arrived just in time to save me from oblivion.

"What have you been doing with your life since Boston, Mick?" I asked him, chewing on a mouthful of fries.

"Enjoying it and following my muse. I was in Central America for a few years covering the civil wars. I decided I didn't like the contras much so I did my fighting with my typewriter and had to get the hell out of there while I could. Back in the States I got a job covering the drug wars in Tijuana and lived in Redondo Beach, California, for a while."

"Sounds like an exciting life."

"It was until someone close to me got killed and I dropped out of the fast lane," Mick said sadly. "I took my forty-foot sloop, the *Fenian Bastard*, and sailed into the sunset with an adventurous friend of mine who needed a ride to Panama. We took three months to get there."

"Seems like a long time to be at sea."

"When you're mourning, you lose track of time. Plus we made plenty of stops along the way: Mexico, El Salvador, and some really small islands. When we got to the Caribbean side of the canal, my friend got off in Panama and I went on to the Antilles."

"What are the Antilles? I'm geographically challenged."

"They're a series of islands," he told me. "Some are big, like Cuba, Hispaniola, Jamaica, and Puerto Rico. Some are small, like Anguilla, Antigua, Aruba, and Grenada."

"Didn't the US invade Granada?"

"Yeah, I missed that one," he said, smiling. "I spent a full year sailing those waters, and when mourning turned to loneliness, I docked in Key West and never left. And here I am in Tallahassee on assignment. What about you? I read about the Boca Knight stuff. What brings you to this city?"

I told him about my detective agency and my pill mill case with Doc.

"Didn't Hurwitz burn down Suffolk Downs in the eighties?" I nodded.

"I remember he had a daughter," Mick said.

"She disappeared."

"Probably drugs, if I remember her correctly. Too bad."

"Too bad about all the children who get involved with this shit," I said.

"So let me get this straight. You drove up here from Boca not knowing anyone in state government or anything about state government and figured you'd work it out when you got here."

"That's it," I said, feeling pretty dumb. "I don't even know the name of the representative from Boca."

Mick closed his eyes and thought. "District Ninety," he said, opening his eyes again. "Representative Liz Frem, second term."

"Do you know all their names?" I asked, impressed and woozy.

"Most of them. It's my job."

"Could you introduce me to someone who might be able to help me?"

"Do you pay well?" he asked, downing half his drink.

"No."

"How much are you offering?"

"Nothing."

"If you're prepared to double that offer, I'll take it," Mick said.

"It's a deal."

"On one condition."

"What?"

"You guarantee me an exclusive on the pill mill story when it's done," he said.

I thought it was a reasonable request so I said, "No."

"Come on." He finished his Jameson's and ordered another. "It's a reasonable request."

"It is. But I give all my stuff to a newspaper friend of mine in Boca. I'm very loyal that way."

"I respect that, but I'm talking about a magazine article . . . not a news report? Your friend can get the news story for his paper first, and I get the sexy details for my magazines a month later. I could collaborate with your friend."

"What if I say no?"

"I'll help you anyway."

"In that case, I'll say yes. I've got stories that will make you a star."

"I'll drink to that," Liam Michael Murphy said. "When do I get these gems?"

"After I take care of my business. It'll be worth the wait. Trust me."

He held out his hand. "Deal!"

We had another drink. I needed more alcohol like I needed another hole in my head.

"Where do we start?" I slurred my words because my lips were numb.

"There are one hundred and twenty representatives and forty state senators. I know a lot of them. Some were poking around the pain-clinic industry a couple of years ago . . . mostly fact-finding. One of them is a friend of mine . . . James Field from District 120 . . . Monroe County . . . which includes Key West. I'll set up a meeting."

I tried to thank him but I hiccuped instead.

"Are you drunk?" Mick laughed.

"Dizzy," I managed.

"I'll drive you to your hotel."

"You drank more than me," I protested.

"Yes, but I'm a professional."

Outside I tried to get into my Mini, but Mick stopped me and stuffed me into his unidentifiable car. The ride to the motel was a blur. All I remember is Mick saying he would call me in the morning around eleven o'clock and not to worry about my car.

"No one will steal that piece of shit," he assured me.

Chapter 36

Mad Mick Murphy, Part 2

Never again, I promised myself the next morning.

I brushed the film of Jameson's off my teeth and the mohair from my tongue, then placed my palms over my ears to prevent my brains from sliding onto the tile. I took a cold shower, but all that did was freeze my balls together. I figured I was doomed until dusk.

At nine o'clock I went to the lobby for the free continental breakfast. Five glasses of water and three cups of coffee provided some comfort . . . but the prune Danish was a big mistake. I rushed back to my room.

Promptly at eleven, Mick called. "Good morning," he chirped.

"No, it's not," I said in a thick voice. "All I've been doing since I woke up is rehydrating and moving my bowels."

"Are you sick?"

"I think John Jameson tried to kill me last night. How are you feeling?"

"I feel great," he said with the enthusiasm of an Amway salesman. "I was at the statehouse this morning at nine and set up an appointment with James Field for six o'clock this evening. He's very excited about meeting the Boca Knight."

"He's heard of me?" I asked, rubbing my temples.

"According to him, everyone in South Florida has heard of you. I think he sees you as a vote getter."

"Whatever works."

"I'll pick you up in half an hour. We'll retrieve your oxcart, have lunch, and then you're on your own till six."

"That should give me enough time to kill myself," I told him.

"Your eyes are bloodshot," Mick said when I got into his white Jeep Wrangler with a soft Bikini top.

"I'm making progress. A few minutes ago they were bleeding."

It was a beautiful March day in Tallahassee, the kind of day that makes you glad to be alive unless you're so hungover you wish you were dead.

Mick clutched, shifted, and pulled away from the motel. "Four-wheel drive, five gears on the floor, short wheelbase, narrow frame."

I tried to pay attention but I couldn't. I tried nodding my head but even that hurt.

My Mini was across the street from the State House Steak House, and it started as sluggishly as I felt. I drove behind Mick a few blocks away to a restaurant named Zaxby's. On the way I decided the funky old Jeep Wrangler was made with Mad Mick Murphy in mind. His shaggy red hair and full beard waved in the wind, and his denim shirt fluttered under his sleeveless, light-weight Windbreaker. His bumper sticker, I'D RATHER BE SAILING, was totally believable. Like Joy Feely and Lou Dewey, they were made for each other.

At Zaxby's, Mick ordered a Zaxby's Zenzation Zalad and I

chose one of the Big Zax Snax Chicken Fingers with Texas Toast. We both ordered Coke.

"No Jameson's?" I asked, rubbing my temples.

"Later," he promised.

"So what did you learn this morning?"

"Field wants to work with you. A year ago he was on a House subcommittee that dug up a lot of information on these pain clinics. Unfortunately the committee wasn't able to garner much support from his fellow reps. It just wasn't on the top of anyone's agenda."

"What *is* on top?" I asked, unhappy.

"There are twenty-five hundred pieces of legislation in front of the Senate right now and thirteen hundred bills in the House. It's a matter of priorities."

"You want to talk numbers and priorities? Six or seven Floridians die every day from drugs purchased through pill mills, which is three times more than die from cocaine or heroin. Florida is the number one source of this shit. What legislation is the Senate considering this session that's more important than saving lives?"

"Well, today there's a vote concerning saltwater fisheries—"

"You must be kidding." I raised my voice. "Who cares about fish?"

"Fishermen. And consumers. Seafood is a natural resource that has to be regulated. The legislation today proposes carefully considered rule changes and improved record keeping. There are provisions for stricter penalties and injunctions for violations, state-grant considerations, quality-standards enforcement, tougher licensing requirements, improved conservation programs, updated equipment regulations, more stringent illegal-importation restrictions, and preventative measures against the illegal use of nets. Millions of dollars and thousands of lives will be affected by this bill. It's actually very important legislation."

"Not more important than saving lives," I said. "What else is on the agenda?"

"State energy plans, sex offender laws, the state budget, consumer initiatives, statewide insurance, labor laws, and green legislation . . . all worthy causes."

"They're not any more worthy than mine."

"Maybe not, but they're more politically correct," he said. "Legislators would rather support ecology and the economy than worry about addicts killing themselves with illicit drugs. I'm not saying every bill being considered is more important than your crusade. I told you about the breast-feeding bill. I say let women breast-feed whoever they want wherever they want. But, the breast bill has gone through the system for several years and finally made the docket. You just started, and even if you get on the docket someday . . . there's no guarantee your bill will pass."

"Do you think I'm wasting my time?"

"No. You'd be wasting your time if you did nothing," Mick said. "I just wanted you to know that you're fighting an uphill battle."

"I'm good at that."

The Zalad and Zax Snax arrived and we ate with enthusiasm.

I followed Mick to the statehouse. He got out of his Jeep and approached my car.

"I have appointments the rest of the afternoon," he said, leaning down so we were face-to-face. "You'll have to kill four hours before we meet with Field. You feel like sightseeing?"

"What's to see?"

"The easterly view of the Tallahassee statehouse is one in a million."

"What's so special?"

"You'll have to see for yourself. Drive east on Apalachee for about a quarter mile . . . make a U-turn . . . and drive back toward the statehouse. You won't believe what you see. After that I suggest a tour of both statehouses. The Observation Deck on the twenty-second floor of the new statehouse has a beautiful view of the city. I'll meet you at quarter to six at the Steak House."

I followed Mick's directions and approached the statehouse from the east on Apalachee. The building was a perfectly vertical, unadorned mini-skyscraper. On either side of the tower were low, domed office wings. As the image took shape, I started to laugh and picked up my cell phone. I punched in Mick's newly entered speed-dial number.

"What do you think?" he asked without a greeting.

"I've never seen a pornographic statehouse before."

"It's the only twenty-two-story erection in the world. And the domes at the base on both sides side make it the full package. It's referred to locally as the the *cock-and-balls building.*"

"Thanks for the colorful description," I said, noting that journalists swore like cops. "Any other phallic symbols I should check out?"

"No, that's about it. Don't forget to visit the old statehouse. It's interesting."

"Where is the old statehouse?"

"Right in front of the scrotum sack of the new one," he joked.

I would have chosen other words to give directions, but he got his point across.

"Hey, Senator," Mick said. "Wait a second. I have to talk to you. Eddie, gotta go."

"Go get him, reporter," I said.

The original statehouse was built in 1845, and changes were made over the years until the $45 million *cock-and-balls* building opened for business in 1977. The old statehouse was almost torn down, but the city decided to refurbish and open it to tourists like me. Elegant columns lined the entrance, and the Florida State seal hung over the front doors. An impressive stained-glass, dome ceiling window looked down on the foyer. Rooms filled with artifacts from Florida's past lined the corridors, and the Rotunda walls were filled with civic awards, including the Congressional Medal of Honor. A display case in one room contained a pair of beat-up hiking boots worn by former governor Lawton Chiles during a 1,003-mile march from Pensacola to Key West. He did it to draw attention to his candidacy for governor. It worked. He won.

I visited the restored Senate and House chambers, then went outside to the courtyard that separated the past from the present. A replica of the Liberty Bell, crack and all, served as a reminder of how this country started. A plaque affirmed that Florida had fought for the Confederacy, and a statue of Martin Luther King confirmed that things had changed. I entered the phallic symbol's lobby and took the elevator to the twenty-second floor, where I looked out over downtown Tallahassee. I had seen New York City from the observation deck of the Empire State Building and the Dead Sea from the flat summit of Masada. The view of Tallahassee didn't impress me . . . but it didn't disappoint me either. Everything is relative.

I returned to earth and sat on a bench in the courtyard, people watching. My first observation: people from Tallahassee were different from people from Boca. Tallahassee people are primarily from Tallahassee. People in Boca are usually from Snow Bird Nation: New York, New Jersey, Philadelphia, Chicago, Detroit, Boston, Hartford, and Toronto. In the winter Boca becomes a melting pot for frozen Jews from the North, while Tallahassee is always Tallahassee. I decided that the permanent people of the Panhandle and the seasonal citizens of Palm Beach County were not better or worse than each other . . . just different.

I'm glad I got that settled.

With the sun warming the holes in my head, I slouched my butt forward on the seat, rested my head on the back of the bench, crossed my ankles, and fell asleep.

"Are you all right, mister?" I heard a young woman's voice ask. I opened my eyes slowly and looked at her. She wore a concerned expression on her freckled face and an oversize FLORIDA STATE sweatshirt from her shoulders to her knees.

I rubbed my eyes and sat up straight. "I'm fine."

"You didn't move for so long I was afraid . . ." She hesitated.

"That I was dead."

"Well, yeah," she said, embarrassed. "At your age . . ."

"How old do you think I am?" I thought I looked pretty good for sixty-one.

"In your fifties," she said hesitantly, not wanting to insult me.

"I'm sixty-one," I told her proudly.

"Wow. That's wicked old."

"No, it's not. Sixty is the new forty-five."

"Forty-five is old."

I laughed. "How old are you?"

"Eighteen."

Wow. That's wicked young.

I was forty-three years older than her. My wife had died before this kid was born. It was like comparing the view from the

Empire State Building to the view from the top of the penis building . . . everything is relative. I glanced at my watch. It was after five. I had been asleep for the blink of an eye, relatively speaking.

"I gotta go," I said to the college girl. "There's no time to waste, remember that."

CHAPTER 37

POLITICS AS USUAL

James Field was an energetic, dark-haired man in his late forties, athletically built and handsome. He was in his second term as Monroe County's state representative and planned to run for the state Senate in the next election. I was impressed by him and he seemed to be impressed by me. I wanted to talk about pill mills, but he only wanted to talk about my anti-Nazi rally two years ago in Palm Beach and the thousands of people who joined my crusade. They were potential votes for him.

"I hope I can inspire people the way you did that day," he told me.

We talked about the low-income clinic I helped establish in Delray, the Russian Mafia I shut down, and the kidnapping case I solved just last year.

"A lot of people in South Florida respect what you have to say," he told me. "I'd love to have your support in the next election."

"Are you saying you'll help me if I help you?" I asked skeptically.

"Not at all." He held up both hands defensively. "I was involved in a pill mill investigation long before I met you. But I'd be lying if I said I didn't want to earn your support."

Fair enough. "Understood, I'll consider it."

"Excellent. Now let's talk about the pill mills."

I told him everything and he took notes.

"Fort Lauderdale is District Ninety-four," Field said. "Don Diccicio is the rep. Good man. He was on the pill mill committee with me. We gathered a lot of information but not much legislative support. Other issues took priority."

"Mick explained how that works."

"It's complicated. Maybe we're better off focusing on closing down the No Pain-U-Gain Clinic, nailing this doctor, and getting some publicity. Gaining support for legislation will be easier if we raise awareness with a high-profile arrest."

"I agree," I said.

"I'll call Diccicio right now and see what he thinks."

Field scrolled a list of numbers on his cell phone and pressed a button. Mick winked.

Connected people push a button and doors fly open.

"Don . . . it's James," Field said. "Sounds like you're at a party." He listened. "That's where I am, at a booth in the bar. I'm with Mick Murphy and a friend of his, Eddie Perlmutter, the Boca Knight." Pause. "Yeah, that's him. I'd like you to join us for a minute. Mr. Perlmutter is looking for our help." Field closed his phone. "He's here. He'll be right over."

A minute later Don Diccicio, state representative for Fort Lauderdale, was at our booth, holding out his hand. "Eddie Perlmutter, the Boca Knight," he said, smiling. "It's an honor to meet you." Even in his politician's blue suit, Diccicio looked like a tough guy and seemed genuinely excited to meet me. I never thought of myself as a celebrity, but I guess I was to some people. Celebrities get special treatment. I needed special treatment. I told him it was an honor to meet him too. He pulled up a chair, sat down, and asked what he could do for me. I repeated my clinic story for his benefit, finishing up with the No Pain-U-Gain facility.

"I know that place," Diccicio said, turning to James Field. "They were part of our original investigation."

Field shrugged. "I don't remember."

"How long have you known about this clinic?" I asked.

"Two years," Diccicio told me.

"Why haven't they been closed down?" I asked, remembering the raid I witnessed on Federal Highway with Fort Lauderdale police officers Antollini and Curley. It seemed like an eternity ago.

"Closing them down doesn't accomplish anything unless there's a lot of publicity involved," Field interjected. "Another shop will just open down the road."

"James is correct," Diccicio said. "If we can prove the doctor and the clinic are in a conspiracy to break the law, we can close the place, pull the doctor's license, and put a bunch of people in jail. Do that enough times and we can get support for statewide legislation."

"What kind of legislation do we need?" I asked.

"We need a commonsense bill," Diccicio said. "All these mills sell is drugs. If we pass a bill that says only fifty percent of a clinic's square footage can be used to sell drugs, we create a problem for illegitimate pharmacies. If we require that all doctors be registered and not have criminal convictions on their records, we'll eliminate a lot of them. If we have a bill that says doctors cannot work only at pill mills, we could eliminate Twilight Doctors."

"What are Twilight Doctors?" I asked.

"Doctors in their twilight years who want to be busy and earn some serious money," Diccicio answered. "Pill mills are their only source of income. Without Twilight Doctors, the clinics would have a labor problem. It's not a solution. It's just one step. We also need stiffer penalties for violations. We need legitimate examinations to accompany all prescriptions. No more bullshit MRIs that a phony doctor can interpret any way he wants. We need to regulate the number of pills a clinic can issue to one person a day, a week, or a month. And then we need to ban advertising so these places are not so easy to find."

"This is beginning to sound like the fishing bill Mick told me about this morning," I said. "The loopholes never end."

"Legislation is an imperfect tool to fight crime, but it provides guidelines for enforcement," Field said.

"Okay, let's get back to the Fort Lauderdale clinic," I said. "What would you need to close it, arrest the doctor, and prosecute everyone involved?"

"We'd have to catch them in the act of willfully breaking Florida law," Field said. "Right now they're working within an unregulated system and it's tough to prove anything. They're always one step ahead of us. The MRIs I mentioned are the biggest loophole. If a patient comes into a clinic with an MRI, the doctor can interpret that MRI any way he sees fit and supply drugs based entirely on his opinion. An MRI interpretation is so subjective it's impossible to challenge. Plus, the MRI clinics are part of the racket. Some of them open up in trailers behind the clinic."

"One-stop shopping," I said. "Clever. Do you know anything about Patel?"

"He's a Twilight Doctor who uses the MRI racket almost exclusively," Diccicio said. "He's also a greedy bastard. He writes prescriptions for six clinics owned by a Cuban gang out of Miami. Getting to them is almost impossible with all the protective layers they have from top to bottom. But if we can close enough of their clinics, then pass legislation, we can put them out of business."

"Let's make a deal right now," I said. "If I can catch a doctor and a clinic deliberately breaking the law, get the clinic closed, the doctor prosecuted, and generate a lot of public attention, you two guarantee to support a new legislative effort."

There were nods all around.

We had a light dinner and said our good-byes outside the restaurant. The politicians departed, leaving Mick and me alone on the sidewalk.

"What do you think?" Mick asked.

"I think I have a lot of work to do," I said. "I better head back to Boca and get started."

"I think you should take some time off and rest. You've been through a lot."

"I could use the rest. But after you've seen the penis building, what's left to see in Tallahassee?"

"Have you ever seen the Gulf of Mexico?"

"Never been there," I told him.

"It's only forty miles from here. I can get you a small rental cottage on a lake with a dock. You can relax, listen to the Gulf, watch the sun, and get ready for war."

And that's what I did.

CHAPTER 38

SITTING ON THE DOCK OF THE BAY

It took a little over an hour to drive the forty miles from Talla-hassee to Ochlockonee Bay using state roads 319 and 98 South. Through one of his local connections Mick arranged a three-day rental of an isolated, sparsely furnished one-bedroom cabin with a water view, a dock, and cell phone service courtesy of the many politicians who visited the area. I bought provisions in a general store nearby, and by midday I was settled. I walked to the end of the twenty-foot-long, low-slung boardwalk and sat on the edge. I dangled my feet in the warm water, squinted at the sun, and asked myself what I was doing in the middle of no-where, Florida. It was all so random.

I called Lou Dewey.

"Where the hell are you?" he asked, sounding annoyed. "I was worried."

I told him where I'd been, what I'd done, and where I was.

"I'm glad you took a break," he said.

"I had to. How are you and Joy?"

"Still in the hospital. She's a rehabilitating maniac . . . works out all day. My burns hurt but I'm okay. We've been spending a lot of time going through magazines looking at wedding dresses and artificial legs."

"Find anything?"

"We picked out a dress no problem," he said.

"The leg?"

"Pending."

"Are you planning a big wedding?"

"No, but she insists on a wedding dress even if there's only the four of us," he told me. "Claudette hasn't been around to visit so Joy hasn't asked her about the maid-of-honor thing."

"I told Claudette not to visit until I was comfortable with the Grover situation."

"Okay, no problem. I'll tell Joy."

"I'll be back in Boca in a couple of days," I said. "When I get there, I'm going all out on every case we have. You up to it?"

"I can't handle any physical stuff."

"You never could."

"True, so I guess we're all set," Lou said. "What about Claudette?"

"I'm going to call her right now."

Claudette sounded happy to hear from me. "Where are you now?"

I told her.

"Never heard of it," she said.

"It's a very remote place. I'm just relaxing and getting my strength back. What have you been doing?"

"Queen and I made a voodoo doll of Grover and we've been sticking pins in it."

"I appreciate that," I said. "Stick one in his ass for Lou."

"Do you think he's planning to come after you again?"

"I don't know. I sent him a pretty strong message through one of his cohorts which should have slowed him down. And I don't think he wants this to turn into a shoot-out. He had his chance to make it look like an accident and he blew it. He has to be more cautious now."

"When will I be able to see you?" she asked.

"Soon."

"Not soon enough."

I noticed a flimsy lawn chair lounger on the shore near the cottage. I retrieved it, carried it halfway down the dock, set it up, and lay down. I closed my eyes and let the sun work its magic. I fell into a deep sleep and had a troubling dream about the nine people killed at Kugel's because of me: Dave, the owner, the African-American college kid, the happy foursome sharing a dessert, the unhappy elderly couple, Herb Brown. I was dreaming about bloody faces when I jolted awake. The sun was going down.

"Bastards," I shouted. "You don't have to come after me. I'm coming after you."

Two days later I was on the road again, feeling better, driving east through the Panhandle before turning south toward Boca. I used the long ride to plan a series of showdowns. After I met with Lou, I would know where to start.

CHAPTER 39

A LEG TO STAND ON

I got to the Boca Raton Community Hospital midafternoon after a seven-hour drive. Joy and Lou had been moved from intensive care to rehabilitation. The nurse at the reception desk told me they were in the exercise room and pointed to two policemen at the door. I shook hands with the two officers and looked at Joy and Lou through the window. Joy was in a wheelchair with a light blanket on her lap. Lou sat in a straight-backed chair, pounding away at his laptop. They didn't look happy.

I opened the door. "You aren't even married yet and you're arguing already."

"Eddie," Joy said, and held out her arms to me. I bent down and slid into her arms. She squeezed me hard.

A good sign.

"I missed you," she told me.

"I missed you too," I said.

"Don't I get a hug?" Lou grumbled.

"No . . . you're giving my girl a hard time."

"Oh, hug him," Joy said with a sigh. "He's very sensitive."

Lou stood up and we hugged the way friends do. "Don't pat my back," he cautioned. "My burns." He sat down and I pulled over a chair.

"What are you arguing about?"

"Joy's wooden leg," Lou said.

"Prosthesis, for the thousandth time," she said, rolling her eyes.

"Okay, prosthesis." Lou sighed. "She wants a simple, practical one."

"What's wrong with that?" I asked.

"It's a metal pole in an ugly shoe."

"Athletes use them," I pointed out.

"Joy wouldn't be an athlete if they gave her a nuclear leg," Lou said. "She got tennis elbow watching a match on television."

"That only happened once," Joy said.

"What kind of prosthesis do you want, Lou?" I asked.

"Wait a minute," Joy protested. "It's my leg."

"It's no one's leg yet, and I'm entitled to an opinion," Lou said. "I've been doing research."

"I'd like to hear what he has to say," I told Joy.

She shrugged.

"Okay. Listen. Joy had a transtibial amputation, which means it was below the knee," he explained. "She has total use of her regular knee and only needs to replace her lower leg and foot. I want her to have an energy-storing prosthetic foot."

"And what is that, Dr. Dewey?" I asked.

"It stores and absorbs energy, adjusts to ground variances, and rotates to change direction. It does everything a normal foot does."

"I'm impressed with his knowledge," I said to Joy.

"Hey, this is my fiancée we're talking about," Lou said. "I'm trying to learn everything."

Joy touched Lou's knee affectionately. They smiled at each other.

"The best material to use is lightweight, sturdy carbongraphite," Lou continued. "But without cosmesis—cosmetics for artificial limbs—it will still look like a metal pole in an ugly shoe."

"With cosmesis?"

"An artificial limb looks like the real thing," he said. "Doctors rubberize a shaped prosthesis with silicone, then apply a pigment that makes the artificial limb look exactly like the real one right down to freckles and hair."

"Are you saying I have hairy legs?" Joy joked.

"So Joy will have this beautiful leg that matches her other beautiful leg," Lou said. "Which is then attached to her beautiful knee with a suction suspense system, and that's inserted into a beautiful replica of her former right foot, toes and all."

"Sounds unbelievable," I commented.

"It is," Lou said. "And I saved the best part for last. The artificial foot is adjustable, up and down at the heel."

"Why is that so important?" Joy asked.

"So you can wear those high heels you love," Lou said with a big smile.

Joy started to cry the way women do when they're happy. "How much is all this going to cost?" She sniffled.

"I don't care," Lou told her. "Every time you look at your beautiful leg, I want you to remember how much I love you."

That did it. She was bawling like a baby. "I'm so lucky to have you," Joy sputtered.

"I'm so lucky to have *you*," Lou replied.

"I'll be lucky if I don't have diabetes with all this sweetness,"

I said. "The truth is, you're both lucky to be alive. If your garage hadn't been filled with stacks of clothes, stuffed boxes, computer equipment, two old mattresses, and four worn tires . . . and if you hadn't been having sex at the time . . . you wouldn't be here talking about saving money on body parts."

Lou and Joy were startled.

"How do you know we were having sex?" Joy asked, spooked.

"The nature of your injuries. Lou was burned on the crown of his head and down his back. His left arm was burned. Therefore he had to be on his stomach because the blast traveled from left to right, from the garage to the bedroom. Joy had burns to her right arm and her right leg was so badly damaged she lost it. Neither of you suffered facial injuries."

"I still don't understand your logic," Joy said.

"First of all, you guys have sex all the time. So it was a logical assumption. Secondly, your wounds clearly show that Lou was on top whispering something in your right ear—"

"He was nibbling," she told me. "He's a big nibbler."

"Okay . . . so he was nibbling on your right ear. You have your right leg wrapped around his back. Your right hand was rubbing his right shoulder when, *boom* . . . the flash explosion hits whatever parts of your bodies were exposed. Of course the blast was greatly diminished going through all the junk in the garage and all the stuff between the garage and the bedroom, otherwise you'd both be toast, literally."

"You're amazing," Joy said.

"You two are amazing having sex at two in the morning," I said.

"We actually started at two-fifteen," she said.

Did you hear that, MJ?

"Enough about our sex life," Lou said. "Can we talk about Grover now?"

"What do you want to do about him?" I asked.

"I want to go after him immediately," Lou said.

I looked at Joy. She nodded. "Me too."

"Okay, but you two are in no condition to go after anyone," I said. "I'll handle it."

"You can't do it alone," Joy said.

"Yeah, you need us," Lou argued.

"No, I don't," I told them. "The three of us almost got killed and nine people were killed because I let Lou influence my judgment. I'm not doing that again. You two just focus on getting better and let me handle Grover. That's what I do best. I'll let you know when I need you."

I went to my office and reviewed Lou's files on Grover. Harry Chan's mathematical equation of trades made was still the most damning evidence. I copied the files I deemed necessary and fell asleep reading them on the office couch, my Cobra in my lap.

Chapter 40

Lunch Is on Me

I called Chief Frank Burke the next morning and told him I was ready to talk. He didn't ask any questions and agreed to have lunch with me at Mizner Park. We met at Mendy's Grille and sat at a table outside. The mid-March air was delightful. I gave him the details of the Grover case. Frank listened intently, and when I was done, he said, "This is huge. Fraud and attempted murder. I think Grover's involvement in the violence could be tough to prove. In the interest of time the fraud case should come first."

I agreed.

"It's a federal crime," he said. "We need to get the FBI involved."

"I don't want any bureaucratic delays."

"These things take time," he insisted.

"This has already taken too much time. The SEC was told about Grover's fraud years ago and did nothing. Thousands of people have been sucked into this Ponzi scheme since then, and they'll be financially ruined when it blows. There's nothing we can do for them now, but I'm not going to let it keep happening to other people."

"Assuming the FBI will do anything, what do you want?" Frank asked.

"Search warrants for B.I.G.'s trading tickets and stock certificates. According to Lou, these documents either don't exist or they're forgeries. If he's right, Grover's empire will collapse overnight. We might even find organized crime involved."

"Russians?"

"I don't know," I told Frank. "Maybe Cubans. Maybe no one."

"A search warrant requires cooperation between the FBI, the DA's office, and a federal judge. That won't be easy or fast."

"You must know someone in the FBI," I said.

"I know a special agent in their Miami Field Office. He might do me a favor."

"Can you call him?"

"I'll call him in the morning."

"Call him now," I said. "People are getting sucked in every day. Maybe some phony financial consultant is trying to sell the B.I.G. fund to your uncle Brian right now."

"I don't have an uncle Brian."

"Your hypothetical uncle Brian."

"Oh, him." Frank laughed. "Eddie, I told you I didn't want to join your crusade."

"I'm not asking you to join. I'm asking you to help jump-start the process. Come on. I'll buy lunch."

He smiled, nodded his head, and picked up his menu. "I'll call him after lunch."

"Thank you, Frank. By the way, you can't tell the FBI the name of the company I'm talking about. It has to be kept confidential until they agree to participate."

"Okay."

Our waiter came to the table. "What can I get you two gentle-men?"

"Nothing for me," I said, getting up. "I'm too busy." I put down a twenty-dollar bill on the table. "When he's spent this much, shut him off."

"You're a piece of work," Frank called after me, and I heard him laugh.

Chapter 41

Your Prescription Is Ready

I was at my office late that afternoon studying Big Game Hunter's file when the chief called.

"I spoke to Special Agent Tyler Sloan," he said. "He's willing to meet with you."

"That was fast."

"I can't take credit. Your name is magic in South Florida."

"Which name . . . Eddie Perlmutter or the Boca Knight?"

"Both," Frank told me. "When he heard you were involved, he jumped right on it and promised to contact you. Unfortunately he's going on a two-week fishing trip with his buddies."

"I can't wait two weeks. Can you find me another agent?"

"Sloan's the best."

"Can I talk to him?"

"Be my guest." Frank gave me the number.

I pressed a series of buttons until Special Agent Tyler Sloan came on the line. I introduced myself.

"Eddie Perlmutter," he said enthusiastically. "I just talked to Frank Burke, a mutual friend of ours. I told him I'd call you when I got back from vacation."

"Yes, I know, but that time frame is unacceptable."

"Excuse me?" Sloan said, surprised.

"Didn't Frank tell you this was an urgent matter?"

"He said it was a large fraud case."

"That's like saying King Kong was a monkey," I said. "I'm talking about the largest Ponzi scheme in US history."

"How long has it been going on?"

"Twenty years or more."

"That doesn't sound like an emergency."

"It should have been stopped a long time ago," I told Sloan. "I just picked it up . . . and I'm trying to make up for lost time."

"Why is this so important to you?"

"I'm sure you heard about the shootings at the deli in Boca."

"Sure, it was a big news story. Nine dead, two survivors—"

"I was the target and one of the two survivors. Nine people died because of me, and it's eating me up alive. It's all connected."

"When can you get here?"

"I'd say I can be there in a little over an hour," I guessed. "Who should I ask for?"

"Ask for me."

"What about your vacation?"

"I'm not going anywhere until I meet with you," the G-man said.

"Thank you, Agent Sloan."

I grabbed my briefcase filled with Lou Dewey's files and was out the door. I checked my cell phone for messages on the drive to Miami. I hadn't checked in for a while.

I had ten new messages. Beep.

"Hi, Eddie, it's Claudette. I just called to say I love you." Beep.

"Eddie, it's me . . . Bailey. Call me." Beep.

"Bailey again. My sister is feeling better. I had my stitches out. Hey, I saw roadkill on Federal yesterday that looked like the raccoon who attacked me. I hope it was the little bastard." Beep.

"Eddie, Doc Hurwitz. Call me." Beep.

"Eddie, Jerry Small. Remember me . . . your favorite newspaper reporter? Where's my story? Call me." Beep.

"Having a Jameson's and thinking of you pal. William says hi." Beep.

"Eddie, I think we found just the right wooden leg—"

"Louie, it's a prosthesis," I heard Joy in the background.

"Right, sorry. Anyway, it's a beauty, wait till you see it." Beep.

"Eddie, Chief Burke . . . how did it go with Agent Sloan? Thanks for lunch." Beep.

"Mr. Perlmutter, it's Teofilo Fernandez. I'm just calling to see if you're feeling okay. I'll call again." Beep.

"Mr. Perlmutter, this is Isabella from CVS. The Viagra prescription for your father is ready." I heard her giggle before the beep.

I had no more messages.

The last one was enough.

Special Agent Tyler Sloan looked like a recruiting poster for the FBI—big, rugged, and clean-cut. I estimated he was at least six foot five, 230, and somewhere in his thirties. His handshake was firm but not painful. His smile looked genuine.

"It's an honor to meet you, Mr. Perlmutter." I believed he meant it. "That rally you led a couple of years ago against the skinheads was an inspiration for me."

"I hope I can inspire you again," I said.

"You're a man who obviously won't take no for an answer."

"This is too important, Agent Sloan."

"Let's talk." He led me to his office. The sign on his door read SPECIAL AGENT IN CHARGE.

"I didn't realize you were the boss," I said, sitting down opposite his desk. "Thanks for your time."

After a knock on the open door, a slightly smaller version of Special Agent Sloan entered the room. He didn't look happy to see me.

"Mr. Perlmutter, meet Special Agent Tom Mack," Sloan introduced us. We shook hands. "Agent Mack is in charge of our Financial Crime Section. He'll look into your complaint. I usually don't sit in on these preliminary sessions, but this sounded important enough for me to listen."

Mack sat next to me in front of Sloan's desk.

"Mr. Perlmutter, I'm honored to meet you," he said sincerely. "But I have to be honest. I don't believe a financial fraud of the magnitude you described to Agent Sloan is unknown to this office. Who are you talking about?"

"This has to remain strictly confidential," I said.

"You have my word," Agent Mack said, and Sloan nodded.

"I'm talking about Benjamin Israel Grover . . . B.I.G. Investments."

Mack smiled. "We are well aware of B.I.G. Investments. That company has been investigated more than once by the SEC and cleared of any wrongdoing."

"The SEC is wrong."

Agent Mack said with a sigh, "With all due respect, Mr. Perlmutter—"

"Agent Mack, in my experience, when someone begins a sentence saying 'With all due respect,' it usually means they think I'm full of shit."

"In no way do I think that. I do think you may be misinformed."

"I think you're the one who's misinformed."

Mack's face turned red. "We work very hard in this office and pride ourselves in keeping current with every financial fraud in South Florida. B.I.G. is old news and we don't have time to waste on old news. No offense."

"None taken, but I suggest you make time to review these documents," I said politely, and handed him a full file folder. "You can save time by reading the top page very carefully."

Mack opened the folder and glanced at the top sheet. "Who compiled these numbers?"

"They're a matter of public record."

He started reading.

Sloan and I sat silently while Mack scanned the page. He looked up after several minutes. "I'm going to read this a second time."

I nodded, and Sloan leaned forward in his chair. A few minutes passed before Mack looked up again. "If the statements and numbers in this document are accurate"—he directed his remarks to his boss—"B.I.G. Investments claimed to have made more trades in 2005 than all the trades concluded on the exchange that year, by all the brokers combined."

"That's not possible," Agent Sloan said.

"It may not be possible to do," I said, "but it's not impossible to claim."

"You're positive this information is correct?"

"Absolutely, and there's a lot more where this came from," I said.

"I owe you an apology."

"You owe me nothing but your cooperation to bring this guy down."

"You've got it," Mack pledged.

Sloan picked up his phone and punched in a number. "Gus. Something urgent just came up and I can't leave with you guys. I'll try to join you later. Catch one for me."

Sloan put down the phone, rolled up his sleeves, and loosened his tie. Mack did the same. I took several thick folders out
of my bulging briefcase and handed them to the two FBI agents.

"You're not going to believe some of this stuff," I told them.

"I'm looking forward to it," Mack said, and the end of B. I.
Grover began.

For the next four hours Sloan, Mack, and I read reports and exchanged comments.

"Here's a trade on Spartan International a year after the firm
changed its name and stopped selling to new accounts," Mack
said, pointing at a line Lou Dewey had highlighted. "It doesn't
exist but Grover is claiming it as a trade. Whoever summarized
these documents did remarkable work."

"My partner, Lou Dewey, did it," I said proudly.

"Here's another one," Sloan said. "Hartford Financial, a
feeder fund, copied Grover's statements onto their own stationery
but never mentioned Grover to their clients. Everything was a
secret. I'm no mathematician, but you'd have to be blind not to
see through this farce."

"Or looking the other way," Mack said.

"This is willful ignorance," Sloan said.

"It gets worse," Mack said. "Grover is front-running some
of these trades."

"What's that?" I asked.

"Insider trading."

The list of offenses went on and on . . . "No audits, no due
diligence, total nondisclosure, intimidation, third-party hedges,
outrageous interest charges, falsified records . . ."

"How did he get away with this for so long?" Sloan wanted
to know.

"No one wanted it to stop," Mack said. "The insiders were
making millions. Did you see the Big Game Investments file?

The man gave one hundred percent of his investors' money to
Grover, did no due diligence and no analysis . . . never revealed
Grover's name and made over fifty million dollars in commis-
sions last year."

"I know the man," I said. "He's the weak link in Grover's
fraud chain. He'll fold like a wallet and make a great witness if
we pressure him. Most important, we need warrants for Grover's offices, houses, and storage facilities. When we don't find
the alleged trading tickets or the claimed stocks and bonds, you
guys can huff and puff and blow his house down."

"We're good at that," Agent Sloan said.

"The best," I said.

"We'll go to the US Attorney's Office first thing in the
morning," Sloan said. "Convince them to issue search warrant
requests for a federal judge to sign, and we're in business."

"Get a warrant for Big Game Investments while you're at it,"
I told them. "He'll panic right away."

"You got it," Mack said with enthusiasm.

"Another thing," I remembered. "When you search Grover's mansion in Palm Beach, there's an automatic front gate. It
has to be opened by remote control from inside the house, and
there's a helipad out back. If he panics, he could delay opening the
front gate and take off in the helicopter. He could claim later
that he never heard the bell."

"We'll need a no-knock warrant or a knock-and-announce,"
Sloan said.

"Thanks for the tip, Eddie," Mack said. "Anything else you
can think of?"

"I'm afraid that's it. He never invited me to his office or his
penthouse in New York."

"You're not on the A-list." Mack laughed.

"See you in the morning," I said, getting up and stretching.
I was stiff from sitting so long. "Tomorrow should be exciting."

At midnight I was still feeling the effects of an adrenaline rush when I heard a voice.

Hey, Eddie . . . Eddie . . . it's me.

I looked under the blanket. Mr. Johnson was standing at attention, like a rookie recruit.

Private Parts reporting for duty! he said.

Welcome back, soldier, I said.

There is no man-made stimulant comparable to a person's natural passion for life.

CHAPTER 42

NO-KNOCK WARRANTS

The next morning Sloan, Mack, and I blew into the US Attorney's Office like three Category 5 Florida hurricanes. We didn't have an appointment, but a kid named Chuck Rodman, one of the younger assistant attorneys, was familiar with both G-men and recognized my name. He took us to a conference room and listened intently to our presentation. Within two hours Rodman was filling out search warrant requests for B.I.G.'s corporate headquarters in New York City, Grover's homes in Westchester and Palm Beach, and the storage facility Grover claimed held all trading documentation and certificates. His offshore offices would come later. Separate warrant requests were also issued for Big Game Hunter's office and home. By midafternoon a federal judge had signed the warrants, and they were sealed and delivered to FBI headquarters in Miami.

While the FBI agents were mobilizing their search plan, I drove to my office in Boca and returned calls.

I told Frank Burke that his contact at the FBI had been helpful. I didn't tell him about tomorrow's raid. There was no need for him to know.

Doc Hurwitz sounded relieved when I called. "I hear we almost lost you in Kugel's," he said.

I told him I was fine and brought him up to date with my pill mill investigation, including my trip to Tallahassee.

"I'm glad you're making friends with our elected officials, but my case comes first, remember." I thought he sounded tired.

I assured him I remembered. "It's all part of a puzzle, Doc. I'm putting the pieces together. Trust me."

"If I can't trust the Boca Knight, who can I trust?"

"You don't sound so hot, Doc. Are you okay?"

He told me he felt good but I didn't believe him.

Three Bag Bailey was under the boardwalk when I reached her on her cell. She told me Weary Willie was the same.

"That's too bad," I said.

"He's not getting worse." Her sister was still a basket case, she said, but that was normal. "I had my stitches taken out a few days ago. It hurt like hell. What about yours?"

"They dissolved."

"See how they treat poor people in this country," Bailey complained. "Your stitches dissolved . . . mine had to be yanked with pliers."

I apologized for the medical system. "As soon as I wrap up some loose ends, I'm going to get back on Willie's case."

"He's not going anywhere," she said.

I called Mad Mick and told him I was going to make him famous.

"Jameson's on me for everyone," he shouted. "My friend is going to make me famous."

"Where are you?"

"In my apartment, indisposed." He laughed.

I gave him Jerry Small's phone number. "He's the newspaper friend I told you about. I'm giving him a lead on a sensational story that will probably break tomorrow morning. Call him tomorrow night and tell him I want you to do the follow-up article for one of the magazines you work for. The two of you should really do well with this. Maybe you'll become a team."

"Thanks, Eddie," Mick said seriously, before reverting to form. "By the way, you'll be happy to know that the legislature voted to allow women to breast-feed anywhere in Florida providing they're feeding their own babies. No substitutions allowed."

"A lot of adult male babies are going to be disappointed."

I left a message for Claudette: "It's almost over. Thank you for making it easier for me."

I was home in bed, just me and my Cobra, when I finally heard from Tyler Sloan. "We're hitting all locations simultaneously at nine a.m. tomorrow morning."

"Fantastic. Great job," I enthused. "Where's Grover?"

"Our sources say he's in Palm Beach."

"Good. Can I come with a friend?"

"I can't stop you or your friends from being in the area," he said, "but you're officially not involved in federal business. Don't get in the way."

"Don't worry."

I called Jerry Small. "Did Mick Murphy contact you?"

"Yeah," he said, not sounding happy. "What's this sharing nonsense?"

"It's not sharing. It's added exposure for both of you. It's part of the deal."

"I trust you."

"Meet me in front of the Kravis Center tomorrow morning at eight o'clock," I told him.

"Who's appearing there at that hour?"

"Just you and me. Bring a camera. This is big."

"Tell me," he urged me.

"You won't be able to sleep."

"Enough said. Good night."

I turned out the light.

It's just like old times, I heard a voice under the blanket say.

I peeked and there was Mr. Johnson standing at attention for the second night in a row.

It's nice to have you back, I told him.

I'm excited to be here.

CHAPTER 43

A RIDE INTO HISTORY

It was a beautiful March morning in Palm Beach. Unfortunately, lives would be ruined today when imaginary fortunes disappeared and dreams were shattered. My only comfort was in knowing that we would be making the financial world a safer place by destroying a monster.

"Hey, Eddie, you look beat," Jerry Small said as I stood in the Kravis Center parking lot.

"Late night," I said, getting in the car. "Let's go."

"Where are we going?"

"We're riding into history."

"Do we have time to stop at the Dunkin' Donuts first?"

I checked my watch. "Sure."

I got a large French vanilla coffee with milk and two Sweet'n Lows. Jerry had a plain cruller and a bottle of milk. We ate at the counter and within fifteen minutes resumed our historic ride. I parked across the road perpendicular to Grover's street and turned off the engine.

"Are you going to tell me now what we're doing?" Jerry asked.

"We're witnessing a house invasion of the evilest man on the planet."

"Kim Jong Il?" Jerry asked, referring to the president of North Korea.

"Worse." I checked my watch again. It was four minutes to nine. "In four minutes the FBI is going to come around the corner, turn right on that street, and raid the Grover mansion."

"Thank you, Godfather," Jerry said, reaching across the seat and patting my shoulder. "If you wore a ring, I'd kiss it."

Squealing tires got our attention. We turned in our seats and saw four black sedans negotiate a sharp right turn across the street.

"They're early," I said, starting the engine.

"They couldn't wait. Let's go."

I considered peeling a strip of rubber off my hundred-thousand-mile tires but wasn't sure I would have enough remaining tread to get me back to Boca. I cruised sedately instead, stopping behind the four government sedans parked outside the impressive gates of Grover's mansion. The agents were already out of their cars.

"Stay out of their way," I warned Jerry. "We just happened to be in the area."

"No problem."

I saw Special Agent Sloan press the button on the intercom box. Twenty agents stood behind him awaiting his orders. It must have seemed like barbarians at the gate to anyone inside looking out. Sloan fidgeted and looked nervously at his watch several times. He wasn't happy. My prediction about delays was looking like a good one. Less than ten minutes passed before Sloan turned and pointed at one of the black sedans behind him. The car's engine growled to life, and with an underhand throwing motion Sloan signaled the driver to lead the charge.

The engine roared like a rocket and the guided missile raced toward the gates. I noticed the car's front bumper had been reinforced for ramming . . . and it did its job magnificently. The impressive gates collapsed and were crushed under the reinforced wheels of the mobile battering ram. Armed agents in black jackets poured through the gap in the wall and disbursed . . . scurrying like ants. I had given Sloan a rough layout of the mansion, as I remembered it, and hoped I had covered every escape route. Jerry and I walked by the crushed gate like tourists who just happened to be in the area. We heard an engine start, quickly followed by the whirring of helicopter blades. Someone was attempting to fly away. A loud blast erupted from behind the house . . . than another.

Shotgun! I know the sound.

The rotor blades went silent.

"What was that?" I said to Jerry Small, but he wasn't there. I was standing alone where the front gate used to be. I stepped forward tentatively and peeked inside. A silver Rolls-Royce burst through one of the four-car-garage doors. I couldn't see the driver, but the car was without a doubt headed toward me. I was the only barrier between the Rolls and the road . . . unless you counted the King Cobra in my belt. I removed the handgun, held it with two hands, and aimed at the windshield. I was hoping to intimidate the driver with a "Stop or I'll shoot" threat, but he wasn't intimidated and he didn't stop. I fired. The car swerved and smashed into the wall to the right of the destroyed gates. I had aimed several feet above the car, so I must have scared the driver into swerving into the solid-stone wall. Smoke was coming from under the Phantom's crumpled hood. I opened the door and saw the driver slumped over the steering wheel. I picked up his head by the hair and looked at him. It was the son of a bitch who had washed my Mini and attached the tracking device. His forehead was bleeding into his eyes, which seemed focused.

"Are you all right?" I asked.

He nodded.

I held up three fingers. "How many fingers am I holding up?"

"Three," he said quickly, totally alert.

"Do you know who I am?"

He stared at me for a moment, focused. "Eddie Perlmutter."

"You're fine." I placed my palm on the back of his head and shoved it forward. His forehead met the steering wheel with just enough force to knock him senseless. The horn blasted until I pulled his head back. I held up four fingers. "How many now?"

He didn't answer.

"Take a break," I said, and let his head fall forward against the wheel.

CHAPTER 44

ECHOES OF TINO

Dark-skinned landscapers arrived just as Grover was being escorted from the house by men wearing windbreakers with FBI written on the back. The workers did a hurried about-face and vamoosed in the general direction of Mexico.

If Grover was in the image-management business, as Lou had suggested, he was out of business. He looked bewildered and disheveled being escorted, in handcuffs, from his palace. He had bed-head, with randomly spiked stalks here and there. He wore wrinkled shorts, a silk pajama top, and maroon bed slippers with gold emblems on top. His stylish glasses were tilted oddly on his eagle's beak nose. The helicopter pilot followed in cuffs, head down, trying to avoid the FBI photographers. I noticed Jerry Small, inside the gate, snapping pictures like a tot in a toy store. He gave me a thumbs-up and I gave him a one-finger salute, motioning him to get the hell out of there.

When he was standing next to me again, he said, "I couldn't resist. What a show. Lou should be here."

"You're right." I called Lou on my cell. "We got Grover, Lou. The FBI raided the mansion this morning with a search warrant."

"No way," Lou shouted, and repeated my words to Joy.

"Way to go, Eddie," I heard her in the background.

"The FBI is leading him away in cuffs as we speak," I continued.

"How's he look?" Lou asked.

"Terrible."

"Fabulous," Lou crowed. "I wish I was there."

"You are here, Lou. Your research nailed this bastard."

"Yeah, and almost got us killed."

A hyper, thin woman with a surgically enhanced face was being escorted from the house, screaming, "Do you know who I am?" at two agents holding her arms.

"I think they just took Mrs. Grover away," I told Lou.

"You think our names will be mentioned on television?"

"I asked that the FBI keep our names out of it. We don't need the publicity, do we?"

After a moment's hesitation Lou said, "No, we don't."

Live and learn.

I watched as the *boko* of Wall Street was loaded into the backseat of a government sedan. I was witnessing history: the end of Wall Street Wonderland; the mythical place at the bottom of the rabbit hole also known as the Bottomless Pit.

The search of Grover's mansion went on for hours with agents carrying box after box from the house. I had no idea what the cartons contained, but I knew it wasn't good news for Grover or his investors.

Special Agent Mack approached me. "I received a call from the agents in New York City. The raid on B.I.G. headquarters will take much longer than this. There are two floors of records to cart away."

"What about the warehouse with the stock certificates and trading tickets?" I asked.

"That search is still ongoing, but from what I'm hearing, it's a farce. They've opened a few hundred out of maybe a thousand boxes. All they've found so far are old records from the auto supply company that owned the warehouse before Grover rented it. The records go back to the 1980s but have nothing to do with Grover's businesses. Interestingly enough, all the boxes are stenciled B.I.G."

"Grover was hoping no one would ever open the boxes," I said. "It reminds me of the Tino De Angelis scam of the early sixties."

"I remember that. De Angelis filled empty salad-oil tanks with water and used them as proof of assets. He topped the water off with a slick of salad oil, and the authorties never checked below the surface. The guy stole millions before they caught him."

"The world will always have suckers," I said. "Any news on the raid on Hunter's office?"

"All I know is Hunter collapsed, claiming he was having a heart attack. He was rushed to the hospital."

"He's faking it. I hope the search continued?"

"We didn't miss a beat. This is going to be one hell of a story. You sure you don't want any credit?"

"You can have it," I told Mack. "I want to stay anonymous until I find the shooters and bombers."

"I'll do some checking for you through our records. See if we have anyone on file with that kind of MO."

"Thanks, but I doubt these guys will be on file. Speaking of shooters, what were those gunshots I heard?"

"Grover tried to escape in his helicopter," Mack said. "He was in his pajamas and bathrobe running across the back lawn. When the pilot started the engine, one of our guys fired a warning shot in the air. Grover dove for the ground and the pilot jumped out of the copter with his hands up."

"Why the second shot?"

"The pilot forgot to shut off the engine. The empty copter was in gear and starting to rise. The agent blasted the rotors to keep the damn thing grounded."

"If Grover was trying to escape in pajamas, why was he wearing shorts when he came out of the house?"

"His pajama bottoms got stained in all the excitement. We let him change."

We both laughed and started walking away, then Mack asked, "What's with the Rolls against the wall?"

"It looks like an accident to me."

He looked at the unconscious man in the driver's seat. "You know this man?"

"Yeah, he washed cars for Grover and planted a transmitter under my Mini."

I told Mack the story and that I still had the tracking device.

"His prints are probably still on it," Mack figured. "When can I have it?"

"Now. It's in my car."

"Let's get it," he said, looking in the Rolls's window again. "This guy looks pretty bad."

"He'll live."

We went to my car and got the transmitter. Agent Mack shook my hand. "It was a pleasure working with the Boca Knight."

"It was an honor working with the FBI."

I walked to my car and turned the key in the ignition. The

little engine sprang to life like a power lawn mower. Jerry joined me. "Let's go home, ace reporter," I said.

"Don't forget my car at Kravis," Jerry said.

"Did you have a good time?" I asked as he got into his car.

"You're the best."

CHAPTER 45

THE THRILL OF VICTORY

I went directly to the hospital to celebrate with Joy and Lou. They looked much better. Joy's face glowed like my red veil, and Lou looked like himself again, a skinny version of Elvis with braces on his teeth.

We exchanged hugs and stories. I got the biggest laugh with Grover's pajamas.

"Have you called Claudette?" Joy asked.

"Not yet," I said. "I'm evaluating the fallout."

"I think it's safe," Lou said. "The damage is done. Grover is finished. Our names weren't mentioned and the FBI is taking credit."

"I'll wait until the story comes out," I decided. "Leave the TV on for any special bulletins."

"It's only been a couple of hours," Lou said.

"In a digital world that's a lifetime," Joy pointed out, and Lou nodded.

A few minutes later a bulletin began scrolling across the bottom of the screen: SPECIAL REPORT—THE OFFICES AND HOMES OF B. I. GROVER WERE RAIDED TODAY BY THE FBI. MORE TO FOLLOW.

"Armageddon has begun," Lou said.

My cell phone rang. "It's Steve Coleman," I said, looking at my caller ID.

"To the lifeboats," Lou said. "Women, children, and morons first."

"Eddie, did you hear the news about Grover?" Steve asked when I answered.

"Yes."

"Do you know what happened?"

"Yes."

"Tell me," Steve insisted.

"I told you already."

"Is it as bad as it sounds?"

"Yes." I disconnected and looked at Lou. "I feel terrible."

"You did what you could for him," Lou said.

"He'll lose a lot of money."

"He'll survive. A lot of people won't."

At five o'clock that afternoon the shit hit the fan and splattered in the face of the international financial world.

"At nine o'clock this morning," a television newsman announced, "FBI agents in New York and Florida, armed with federal search warrants, raided the offices and homes of B. I. Grover, founder and CEO of B.I.G. Investments . . . the largest hedge fund in the world."

Pictures of B.I.G. headquarters in Manhattan and Grover's mansion in Palm Beach flashed on the screen. A video showing FBI agents swarming into a New York City office building came next.

"FBI agents swept into the Commerce Building offices of

B.I.G. and shut the company down. Employees were ordered to leave while agents confiscated printed records and computer hard drives. The process could take days."

Videos of employees leaving the building and FBI agents lugging cartons out the front door filled the screen for a few seconds, followed by an obligatory flash of palm trees and a sign that read WELCOME TO PALM BEACH. Great footage showed the front gates being run down. A voice droned over the action, "In Palm Beach, agents had to force entry into the Grover mansion when no one in the house responded to repeated requests from the FBI."

"I was there," I told Joy and Lou. "I didn't see anyone shooting a video."

"B. I. Grover was removed from the premises in cuffs after attempting to flee in a helicopter."

A brief shot of the helicopter was followed by Grover being led away in cuffs . . . wearing rumpled shorts and a pajama top.

"There's Jerry Small." Joy pointed, and there he was, snapping pictures and giving a thumbs-up.

"FBI sources told FLN News that the raid was the culmination of a ten-year investigation started by the late forensic mathematician Harry Chan. The FBI believes that Grover's financial empire is nothing more than a multibillion-dollar Ponzi scheme. More news when it happens."

"The FBI source must have been Tom Mack," I said. "Good man."

"Call Claudette right now," Joy said. "She deserves to share this moment with us."

I punched in her mobile number. No answer. "Call me," I said to the answering machine, and disconnected, disappointed.

The phone rang five minutes later, but it wasn't Claudette. It was Dr. Glenn Kessler.

"What's up, Doc?" I asked, knowing that everything was down.

"I just saw Grover on the news. What can you tell me?"

"I could tell you . . . I told you so. But I won't."

"Do you think I'll lose everything?"

"Ask your financial adviser."

"Hunter's in the hospital . . . under arrest," Kessler told me.

"Maybe you should ask someone else."

"Anything you can do to help me?"

"I tried," I reminded him. "Now it's too late."

My call waiting vibrated again. "I've got another call." I clicked off.

"Eddie, Steve Coleman again. What can you tell me?"

"I told you before but you wouldn't listen."

"I'm listening now," he said. "My group stands to lose about seven million bucks."

"You only invested five million."

"We made almost two million in only a few months."

A blast of red flashed in my head and my cheeks burned. It felt as if I were holding a hair blower two inches from my face. "What is the matter with you?" I raised my voice. "You didn't make any profit."

"Yes, we did. I have all the statements. I'm the group treasurer."

"The statements are all false. Don't you get it?"

"They are not. I accounted for all the trades," Steve defended himself. "I checked them."

"It was a fraud, Steve. All of it."

"How could he do this to us?" Steve asked, reluctantly getting the picture.

"Because you let him." I disconnected. I turned to Lou again. "How stupid can people get?"

"The sky's the limit," the former con man said.

The phone rang a half hour later. It was Claudette. "Where were you?" I said, sounding like a little kid.

"Surgery," she said breathlessly.

"Guess what?"

"I'll be home in an hour," she said without waiting for an explanation.

We met at the apartment within the hour. It was awesome.

"Wow," Claudette panted. "What a pill."

"I didn't take a pill." I told her about Mr. Johnson's two impromptu visits. "I guess he got stimulated when he realized I was going to nail the world's biggest fraud."

"Foreplay is less dangerous."

"Maybe I need the excitement."

"Were you bored with me?" she asked.

"No, I was bored with *me*. I went into a 'Is that all there is?' funk. . . . I felt irrelevant."

"You are the most relevant man I ever met."

"Thanks," I said. "But feeling irrelevant doesn't require a unanimous vote."

"You're an aging rock star like Mick Jagger."

"The Girl Scout who sells me Viagra thinks I'm a dirty old man."

"You are. Thank God."

"Maybe, but I can't depend on life-threatening events to give me erections."

"That would be too stressful," she agreed. "Do you think you're okay now?"

"I'm okay for now. I can't say how long this feeling will last."

"No one knows how long anything will last. Let's just enjoy what we have now."

Chapter 46

The Grover-thon and the Secret of St. Mary's

Grover Mania spread like a virus.

The day after the raid the *Post*'s front-page headline shrieked:

BEND-OVER-GROVER

Three days later the cover of *Money Matters* magazine proclaimed:

GROVER IS OVER

But the best headline was the first one, published the afternoon of the raid in a special edition of the *South Florida News* under Jerry Small's byline:

B.I.G.—P.I.G.

A photo of Grover staring blankly at the camera was splashed across the front page. He was in cuffs, having a bad hair day, wearing wrinkled shorts, maroon velour slippers, and a silky, flowered pajama top. Sales of the *South Florida News* tripled.

A Grover-thon followed with new revelations daily: securities fraud, wire fraud, mail fraud, money laundering, perjury, false statements, looted employee funds, obstruction of justice, and false filings with the SEC and IRS.

Rumors were rampant:

Thousands of investors lose billions of dollars.

B.I.G. feeder funds knew it was a fraud.

Many charities close.

It was an international disaster. Distraught women wailed on television, "We've lost everything."

Angry men gritted their teeth and growled, "If that rat bastard was here right now, I'd kick him in the balls."

Pitiful couples looked into the cameras moaning, "How could Benjamin do this to us? We were friends."

Sadness replaced smugness.

"I've been had" replaced "I've been blessed."

I watched the carnage with a mixture of sadness and sadism.

I'm sorry you lost your money, but what the hell did you expect?

Two weeks after the raid, Lou was released from the hospital. I picked him up midafternoon and drove him to a nearby Embassy Suites Hotel. I had rented a standard suite for him customized with new computer equipment installed by Boca Nerds, a local group of high-tech geeks. I filled the refrigerator with Lou's favorite foods, and the closet contained little Elvis-style outfits I'd selected. I helped him get acclimated and checked his bandages when I was ready to leave. I handed him a business card with the name and number of a limousine service. "They're on call for you twenty-four hours a day. They need fifteen minutes' notice."

"Thank you," he said, and we hugged carefully. "I'll get to work on the pain clinics right away."

"Take your time. Regain your strength and be there for Joy."

"I'm your man."

I went to the office and checked the phone messages. Bailey wanted to do lunch. Steve Coleman and Glenn Kessler had each called five times in two days. Their calls were always the same: what could I do for them? Neither asked how I was feeling. They had lost their money. I had only been shot in the head.

Most people only think about themselves. Friends shouldn't do that.

Frank Burke left a message asking for an update. I returned his call and told him everything. He congratulated me on bowling over Grover, and I thanked him for his help with the FBI.

"What's next?" he asked.

"Weary Willie. How are you guys doing with that?"

"Not good. You?"

"I've got a few things going," I said.

"I'll say a prayer for you tomorrow at Sunday mass."

Click! "Do you go to St. Mary's in Boca?"

"I used to go there but switched to St. Katherine's in Delray a few years ago," Frank said.

"Why?"

"I lost faith in Father Vincent Pestrito shortly after he transferred here from Brooklyn. St. Mary's got into big financial trouble after he took over."

"Do you think he's dishonest?"

"I'd prefer to think he's disorganized," Frank said. "But I do know that St. Mary's would have closed if a wealthy widow hadn't died and left the church four million dollars."

Click! Click! Click! The tumblers fell into place and the secret of St. Mary's was revealed.

Follow the money.

"Why your sudden interest in local Catholicism?" Frank asked. "You're Jewish."

"I'm flexible."

I called Three Bag Bailey and invited her to Sunday brunch. "Tomorrow's Tuesday," she insisted.

I convinced her it was Sunday by counting the days since Harold Trager last served osso buco at the soup kitchen.

"I want to go to IHOP for pancakes," she said.

"Okay, but we're going to morning mass first."

"No way. I don't do God."

"We're going to St. Mary's to check out the priest and pray for Willie," I said. "If you know what I mean."

To my surprise she understood me. "What should I wear?"

We sat in the last row of the sanctuary. Father Vincent took the pulpit in flowing white robes. He reminded me of a middle-age Pillsbury Doughboy—round, plump, and soft. He had two chins, the lower one bigger than the upper one, and both jiggled when he talked. I watched him raise his hands in prayer, clean a wineglass, give Communion, and deliver a sermon. He sounded good to me and pious as hell.

At the end of his sermon and after the last prayer, he raised his arms to the congregation. "Peace be with you."

"And also with you," the worshippers responded.

The mass concluded and we were the first ones out the door.

"Did you like the service?"

"I was asleep at amen," Bailey said. "I want blueberry pancakes."

"No problem."

I watched Father Vincent interact with his flock at the front door, and everything looked normal on the surface. But I knew there were bogus books in the basement, blood on the building, and big bucks in the bank.

Follow the money.

I took Bailey to IHOP, where she ordered a cheese omelet and toast. I didn't say a word.

Two hours later I parked across the street from the St. Mary's rectory, where Father Vincent lived, just a few hundred yards from the church. I took the Intruder out of its new leather case, aimed it at a front window, and waited for the show to begin.

Chapter 47

March 26 Madness

The Intruder worked well and I was able to hear Father Vincent's conversations about church business, outings, confirmations, Easter pageants, Sunday school, and an interview with a religious radio program.

"Hello, Mr. Travis," Father Vincent said. "How are things at South Florida Christian Radio?"

Pause, while he listened.

"Yes, I'm ready for this week's questions. Ask away."

Pause.

"The New Testament was written sometime in the second century," Father Vincent said, answering a question I couldn't hear, and going on to answer several more.

Pause.

"What does the word *mass* mean? Well, not everyone agrees, but I believe *mass* refers to the Latin word *missa* . . . which means . . ." Yada yada yada . . .

Pause.

"CCD should not be confused with Sunday school. Confraternity of Christian Doctrine, or CCD, is taught to school-age children during the week, after regular school . . ."

I tuned out, not wanting to hear about books written in the second century by unknown authors.

I tuned back in when Father Vincent said good-bye. A moment later I heard cheering in the background and band music. I looked at my watch: 4:00 p.m. Father Vincent had tuned in to the Final Four, the NCAA Men's Basketball Championship. George Mason was playing the University of Connecticut in Houston. Based on Father Vincent's comments, it sounded like a close game that he cared about.

"Make that shot . . . God damn it," I heard over the Intruder.

Father Vincent!

It got worse.

"You asshole!" he screamed. "What kind of a pass was that?"

Whoa, Father Vincent.

"You dumb son of a bitch."

Vinnie . . . My man.

And finally . . . "How could you miss a layup, you stupid fuck!"

Yo, Vinnie! What's with you?

His phone rang.

"Hi, this is Father Vincent," he said calmly.

Pause.

"Yes, Joey, I saw the game."

Pause.

"Yes, I know I owe you another twenty grand."

Holy shit!

Pause.

"You know I'm good for it," Vinnie said to his bookie, "I've owed you more. Now fuck off."

I heard the phone slam down.

A Catholic priest with a gambling problem. What next? I was about to find out.

The phone rang again.

"Hi, Maria," Father Vincent said.

Could be his sister.

"I lost. Twenty grand, plus last week's fifteen."

Pause.

"No, a blow job would not make me feel better."

I pray it's not his sister.

"No, you don't have to sell your condo," he said. "I paid cash for that. You know how all this works."

A Catholic priest with a gambling problem and *a girlfriend for an accomplice.*

"Maybe later tonight. I'm too depressed right now. You did call on the nontraceable cell I gave you, didn't you?"

Pause.

"Good girl. Call me around eight."

I went to the office, recharged the Intruder's battery, and listened to a few messages.

Steve Coleman had called me on my cell earlier in the day and left a message: "Eddie, I owe you an apology. I've been so wrapped up in my own problems that I never asked how you were feeling since the shooting. I just assumed you were the indestructible Boca Knight and worried about myself. I'm sorry. I hope Lou and Joy are okay."

If a friendship isn't destroyed by an unforgivable act and is built on a solid foundation, it can endure hard times. Steve Coleman was a good man, but his instinct for self-preservation was stronger than his instinct for friendship. I had to remember that.

I listened to a few more messages and went back to the rectory twenty minutes early. I was across the street, aiming my

Intruder at the wayward priest's front window, when his phone rang. I heard him answer, "I'll be right over," and I started my engine.

Ten minutes later the garage door opened and a black Lincoln town car backed out. I followed it onto I-95 South, staying two cars behind. The black sedan exited on Hillsboro Boulevard East and drove over the Intracoastal to Ocean Drive (A1A) South to Southeast Eighth Street, where it went left. The street ended three blocks later at a two-level condo complex on a narrow section of the Intracoastal. The road bent sharply to the left at the building and became Southeast Ninth. The black Lincoln parked in a space marked VISITORS in front of the building, and a man who didn't look like Father Vincent got out. It took me a moment to realize he was in disguise.

Good idea for a Catholic priest visiting his girlfriend.

I reached into my glove compartment for my goofy glasses and Red Sox hat, put them on, and pulled in behind the sedan.

Two can play this game.

"Excuse me," I called to the fat man who had exited the Lincoln. "Is this Southeast Tenth?"

He turned. He was wearing his own goofy glasses and a full gray beard that hid his double chin. He was casually dressed in tan pants and a brown, collared shirt. We looked at each other.

Two schmucks in disguise.

"No, this is Eighth," he said, and smiled. "Take this sharp left onto Ninth and go to the end. That should be Tenth."

I thanked him and turned left. I watched him walk up the stairs to the second level and knock on the third door of five. I made a quick U-turn and drove toward the building just in time to see a woman open the door, throw her arms around the man in disguise, and kiss him full on the lips. He returned the kiss and patted her butt. She closed the door behind them and I made a mental note of the address and unit number.

Peace be with you, Father Vincent. I'll catch you later.

So, Father Vincent was a thief and a foulmouthed, philandering gambler. He was siphoning off the church's money, gambling it away, and using it to buy his girlfriend a condominium on the Intracoastal. His cousins Gino and Tony were involved somehow, and I'd figure that out as I went along.

I could prove a case against Father Vincent right now, but I couldn't prove how Weary Willie fell down a flight of stairs, smashed his head, and was found miles away in Rutherford Park. Gino and Tony looked like professional tough guys and could have been responsible for Willie's fall, but they'd never admit it. If Willie died, they'd be admitting to murder, and even they weren't that stupid. I'd have to set an ironclad trap for these big bad bears.

When I got home to my apartment, I kissed Claudette at the door and squeezed her butt.

"I love you too," she said, smiling.

"I just wanted to know what it felt like to be a Catholic priest."

The table was set for dinner so I sat there while she brought spaghetti and meatballs from the kitchen. I told her about Father Vincent and the Intracoastal Princess.

"Nothing surprises me anymore," she said, sitting down. "At least he's diddling another consenting adult."

"He's done worse than just break his vows. He's a criminal in a priest's clothing."

"You'll catch him," she said with a smile.

"Thanks for the confidence." I looked across the steaming meatballs. She gave me her Halle Berry smile. God, she was beautiful.

"Guess who's coming to dinner."

"I didn't invite anyone," she said.

"Neither did I, but he showed up anyway."

I stood up and introduced our unexpected guest.

"Screw the meatballs," she said.

"Can't we just leave them here?"

An hour later, in the midst of a postcoital daze, I jolted upright in bed. "I've got it," I shouted.

"You certainly do," Claudette mumbled.

"Thanks. But I'm talking about the priest and his cousins. I just got an idea how to catch them in the act."

I jumped out of bed, put on a robe, and went to the dining room table to call Frank Burke. It was only ten. I ate a cold meatball while waiting.

When Frank answered, I said, "I have a plan."

"Tell me."

"I can't. It might be illegal."

"I'm not doing anything illegal. I'm the goddamn chief of police."

"Your part is not illegal," I promised.

"What is it?"

"You have to arrest a woman who has definitely broken the law."

"Who?"

"Maria."

"Maria who?"

"I don't know," I said.

"There are a million Marias in South Florida not counting Miami."

I gave him her address, including the apartment number.

"How can you know all this information and not her last name?"

"It's a gift."

"What's the charge?"

"Start with accomplice," I said.

"When is this supposed to happen?"

"I'll give you twenty-four hours' notice." I hung up before he could ask any more questions.

Claudette came out of the bedroom, stretching and yawning. "What's up?" she asked.

"The meatballs are cold."

CHAPTER 48

A SUPERHERO IN MY OWN MIND

By midafternoon the next day Lou handed me my latest requested gadget. "This is a customized Spy Master DVR and camera," he told me. "You can shoot from up to thirty feet, which is more than you'll need. It can take nonstop videos up to a half hour in length, and with a push of a button it transfers to snapshots. It's small, compact, and can hang anywhere using the built-in hooks. It's just what you asked for."

Lou showed me the operating procedure and remote-control features. I was adept in less than an hour. When I went home, I practiced until I felt confident. My cell phone rang at 10:00 p.m. It was Agent Tom Mack.

"I haven't seen you since you destroyed a mansion and shot down a helicopter," I said.

"I didn't shoot down a helicopter." Mack laughed.

"What's up?"

"We've had some developments. About an hour ago federal judge Diforio refused bail for Grover."

"Good. Where are they holding him?"

"He probably went from the US courthouse to the detention center on Gun Club Road in West Palm," Mack said. "My guess is he's already transferred to the Miami Detention Center. Wherever he is, he's in solitary so no one can kill him."

"I'm sure he's not happy with his arrangements."

"Actually he's lucky. If he was arrested in New York City, he could be in the Metropolitan Correctional Center, the worst place in the system. Prisoners are confined to their cells twenty-three hours a day. Cell lights are on twenty-four hours a day and video cameras record every minute."

"Grover deserves everything he gets," I said.

"I feel the same. We also interrogated Peter 'Jolly' Rogers, the guy who crashed the Rolls into the wall during the raid at Grover's. He accused you of police brutality."

"I'm not the police."

"I told him," Mack said. "He changed the charge to citizen brutality. He claims you banged his head into the steering wheel."

"I did. He was resisting a citizen's arrest."

"Sounds reasonable. We showed him the tracking device you found under your car with his fingerprints all over it. He said he was only following orders."

"Whose orders?"

"He didn't say and asked for a lawyer."

"That device led to nine murders," I said.

"I understand, but we won't be able to connect Rogers to them."

"How about a conspiracy to commit murder?"

"That's a reach," Mack said.

"How do we get those guys?"

"I think we'll need inside help. We have snitches, but there are hundreds of gangbangers with guns for hire in South Florida."

"Do your best," I said, and we said good-bye.

Claudette came home from a late night at the clinic. We got in bed and talked about shooters and bombers.

"Maybe you should leave it alone, Eddie. You don't need dangerous people like them in your life."

"They're already in," I said. "I want them out."

"Finding these guys is like looking for snakes in a swamp full of alligators."

"I have to try. Those bastards killed nine people just to get to me."

"I don't want you to be the tenth." She cuddled into my shoulder and kissed my cheek.

"Don't worry," I said.

"I am worried. They're professional killers."

"They're amateurs. They wore masks but short-sleeve shirts so I knew they were African-Americans. That's dumb. They had bird shot in some of their shotguns instead of buckshot . . . and not enough gas to blow Joy's house off its foundation. They weren't professional, they were available."

"I don't understand," she said.

"There wasn't enough time between our meeting with Grover and the attacks in Boca to assemble a professional crew. They sent whoever was standing there."

"That doesn't mean they're not dangerous."

"I'm dangerous too."

"You're sixty-one years old, Superman," she reminded me. "Are you still able to leap tall buildings in a single bound?"

"Short buildings, maybe."

"Leave it alone," she advised, knowing I would do the opposite.

"I'll sleep on it."

Somewhere between awake and asleep I got an idea. I reached for the pen and paper I kept on the table next to my bed for moments like these. I scribbled a note to myself and fell asleep. When I woke up, I checked my note.

I must be crazy.

CHAPTER 49

THE MRI FACTOR
LAST DAYS OF MARCH

"You must be crazy or your brain damage is worse than we thought," Lou said the next morning in the office when I told him my brainstorm. "Are you seeing red right now?"

"Maroon, actually."

"You'll be seeing bright red when you get your fuckin' head blown off. You cannot go to Mad Dog Walken for help."

"If the shooters came from Miami, he'd know them," I said.

"For all you know he was one of them."

"He wasn't. Mad Dog can't hide behind a ski mountain never mind a ski mask. He wasn't there."

"Neither was Grover but you're sure he gave the order," Lou reminded me. "Maybe Mad Dog got the order and passed it on to someone else in his gang. Even if it wasn't him, he's not going to turn the gangbanger shooters over to you. He's not your friend."

"He told me he respected what I did with the white suprem-acist from the Aryan Army two years ago."

"Yeah, and he told you not to come back to his turf again."

"He doesn't scare me."

"Nothing scares you," Lou said. "That's your problem."

"It's who I am. Besides, it's just a thought."

"Why am I wasting my breath? You'll do what you want to do no matter what I say."

He removed a pile of manila folders from his briefcase and threw them at me. "Check this out. Maybe we can solve a case for a paying customer before you commit suicide."

I opened the first folder. "What are these . . . X-rays?"

"MRIs . . . genius," Lou said, still disgusted with me.

"Whose MRIs?"

"There's one of a gorilla," he said seriously. "One drawing of a man with a perfect body, one cadaver, one man with a woman's body . . . one deformed midget . . ."

"A bunch of counterfeit MRIs . . . I get the picture. Where did you get these?" I thumbed through the pile.

"I scanned some from actual MRIs and created others with a computer program. They're remarkably realistic."

"And your idea is to present these false MRIs to Dr. Patel and see if he prescribes drugs for them?"

"Exactly," Lou said. "We destroy his credibility and get his license pulled."

"The problem is getting to Patel. I watched him a couple of times now. He only deals with people he knows."

"Greed will take care of that. We approach him with a stack of new MRIs, which means new accounts to him and more money. I used a lab he's used before so he won't be suspicious."

"How did you know who he's used?" I asked.

"There are no big secrets in this business because no one is doing anything illegal according to our state laws. But, if Patel issues Oxy and Percocet to a gorilla, I think we can get the state to do something about him."

"What about Doc's granddaughter? That's my first obligation."

"It's all linked together." Lou produced the stack of prescription slips Doc found in his granddaughter's possession the night she died. "Doc gave these to you . . . you gave them to me. Remember?"

I nodded.

"We're going to use them as our introduction to Patel," Lou said. "But we're going to need an outsider to approach him. I can't do it and you're too recognizable. We need someone no one knows around here. Preferably we'd want a shady-lookin' character, scruffy, shifty . . . long hair . . . the kind of guy who would deal in drugs."

"When do you need him?"

"Now."

I picked up my cell and called Mad Mick Murphy.

"Yo, Mick," I said when he answered, "I need your help. The job pays nothing and is very dangerous but it could be your next great story. I need you here tomorrow."

Mick arrived at our Boca office on March 30 at five in the afternoon. I introduced him to Lou, who looked Mick up and down. "Did you get this guy from central casting, Eddie? No offense, Mick, but you look exactly like a street-level prescription-drug dealer."

"And you look like Elvis Presley with a tapeworm," Mick said. His Irish eyes were smiling, making it impossible for Lou to take offense.

"Mick's the journalist from Key West I told you about," I said.

"He's perfect," Lou said.

"My mother always thought so," Mick said. "My three wives disagreed."

It was a Thursday and Lou wanted to work his sting on a Friday. He figured the mills would be busiest on a Friday because of all the weekend parties.

"Do you think you can be prepared for Patel in one day, Mick?" Lou asked.

"Tell me what I have to do and I'll tell you if I can do it."

Lou and I talked, Mick listened. When we were done, Mick said, "I can do it."

"Are you sure?" Lou asked.

"I'm an Irish writer. Trust me."

"I trust him," I said.

We decided to go after Dr. Patel the next afternoon at lunch.

Mick stayed with Lou at the Embassy Suites and I went home to Claudette. We got into bed and she pointed at me pointing at her.

"You're doing something dangerous tomorrow, aren't you?"

The next morning I drove to the Embassy Suites and had coffee in the lobby with Lou and Mick. Lou was looking better every day. Mick looked hungover.

"Are you sick?" I asked.

"I stayed up late with Mr. Jameson."

"Can you still get the job done?" I asked.

"Better. Consider my red eyes and bad breath a disguise. I look more like an addict when I have a hangover."

"He actually does," Lou said.

Mick followed me to Fort Lauderdale in his Wrangler so we wouldn't be seen together in the area. I drove by Roxie's to give Mick the lay of the land. Patel was not at his table but the RE-SERVED sign was there. I doubled back, found a parking space across the street from the diner, and waited for Patel. Mick parked two blocks away and waited for my call. Promptly at noon Patel shuffled to his table and sat down. He was a small Indian man as brown as a berry. He walked bent forward at the waist and couldn't have weighed more than 120 pounds. A waiter looked in his direction. Patel held up an open palm, signaling, *Not now*. Five minutes later a man with a briefcase arrived. I aimed the Intruder from inside my newly tinted window.

"*Hola*, Doc," the man said with a Spanish accent.

"What have you got, Jorge?" Doc asked with an Indian accent.

Folders and prescription pads came out of the briefcase and a signing began. I phoned Mick.

"I'm ready," he answered.

"The first act just started."

"I'm on my way."

Jorge was replaced by a second man with a briefcase, and they were doing business when Mick walked past their table and entered the Roxie. He sat at the counter where he could see Doc's table. He ordered coffee.

So far so good.

The man with Patel said, "See you, Doc," rising and closing his briefcase.

Patel didn't look up when he said, "Good-bye, Alex."

Four more men arrived and the transactions were quick and repetitive. It took slightly more than an hour to complete six meetings. When the sixth man departed, Patel signaled the waiter. He ordered a tuna sandwich and a cup of coffee. Mick got up from the counter, paid his bill, and walked outside. Without hesitating, he sat at Patel's table with his briefcase on his lap.

Patel was startled. "Who are you?"

"My name is Mick McGwire and I'm here to do business," Murphy said calmly.

"I don't do business with strangers."

"I'm not exactly a stranger." Mick opened his briefcase and removed the prescription slips Doc Hurwitz had taken from his granddaughter's dead body. I had written Shoshanna's name in the blank space at the top of each.

Dr. Patel looked at each slip. "Where did you get these?"

"From a young kid. Her name's on the top."

"Never heard of her," Patel said quickly.

Damn.

"Bitch," Mick said, sounding angry. "She told me she knew you." He took the slips from Patel and stood up. "I'm going to kick her ass."

Mick, what are you doing?

"It's no problem," Patel said. "You can get those prescriptions filled nearby."

"I know that," Mick responded. "I had bigger plans than just filling Shoshanna's prescriptions."

"What kind of plans?"

"Forget it. I don't do business with strangers either. This broad told me she knew you. She lied and I'm outa here."

Mick, don't push too hard.

"Actually her name rings a bell," Patel said.

"The Hunchback of Notre Dame rings bells. You either know her or you don't."

"I know her. She was a patient of mine a while ago."

"Describe her," Mick said.

"Small and skinny with dark, reddish hair. She told me her grandfather was a gangster in Boston a long time ago."

Bingo!

"When's the last time you saw her?" Mick persisted.

"Not for weeks. She stopped coming by for prescriptions."

"That's because she's in Key West."

He's good.

"Why Key West?" Patel asked.

"Her grandfather wanted to send her to rehab and she didn't want to go," Mick lied seamlessly. "I met her there and she told me about you. I wanted to meet you."

"For your bigger plans?"

"That's right."

"How did you find me here?" Patel asked. "Shoshanna didn't know about this place."

"I'm a resourceful guy. I followed you a few times. I know where you live."

"I'm impressed. Well, now that we're not strangers, do you want to talk to me about your plans?"

"Why not?" Mick removed Lou's MRIs from the briefcase. "Check these out."

My heart rate quickened. *Those phony MRIs won't fool anyone.*

Patel barely glanced at the readings. "I know this lab. They have several offices around the state. They do excellent work."

So does Lou Dewey.

CHAPTER 50

BETTER THAN WALGREENS

"I can give you prescriptions for all these MRIs," Patel said.

"I only brought five thousand with me," Mick said.

"Pay what you can and come back."

"You guys are better than Walgreens."

Mick selected three MRIs. Patel wrote on them and filled out three prescriptions for enough OxyContin to kill a gorilla.

"I don't have the cash on me," Mick said. "I'll have to get it and meet you again."

"You don't pay me anyway," Patel said quickly. "Take these MRIs and prescriptions to any of six labs in the area." He handed Mick a business card. "Here's a list of them."

"Do you recommend one in particular?"

Mick, you are an artist.

"No Pain-U-Gain is closest," Patel told him. "That's where Shoshanna always went."

Thank you.

"How does this work?" Mick asked.

"It's pretty basic. You bring me MRIs that I analyze. I write an opinion on the MRI and a prescription for an ample amount. You take the prescriptions and the MRIs to one of our six labs. They keep the MRIs on file and fill the prescriptions. When your prescriptions expire, you come back for a refill. "

"That sounds like a lot of traveling."

"Not really. My prescription amounts are quite liberal. You buy them as you need them, or, like Shoshanna, you send someone to pick them up. All we require is the prescription, a name, and cash."

Mick stood up and shook Patel's hand. "It's a pleasure doing business with you, Dr. Patel."

"Give my regards to Shoshanna. How is she by the way?"

"Her health could be better."

"Well, that's not our problem, is it, Mr. McGwire?"

CHAPTER 51

ANY LAST REQUEST

I called Doc Hurwitz immediately to make an appointment. He told me to come right over. When I got there, he was lying on his living room sofa, propped up on pillows. He was inhaling oxygen from a breathing tube attached to a tank. His skin was gray, his face skeletal, and his sunken eyes dim. The shades were drawn and the apartment was dark on a sunny day. I heard motorboats on the Intracoastal as life went on.

Doc told me he was in his third year of lung cancer, and when Shoshanna died, he stopped treatment.

"I'm fading faster than I expected."

"How long do they give you?" I asked.

"A few months maybe. I just want enough time to settle with Patel."

"I got the proof you wanted."

His eyes brightened. "I knew you would."

I placed a small recorder on the coffee table next to the sofa.

"It's all here. The Indian accent is Patel's. The other voice is a friend of mine. Are you sure you want to hear this? It's upsetting."

"Play it."

I played it and he got upset. "Scumbag," he said, grimacing. "What's next?"

"I'm getting a search warrant for Patel's office and home."

"Why bother? All you'll find are bullshit MRIs with his self-serving diagnoses. And it's all legal in Florida."

"Today Patel issued OxyContin and Percocet prescriptions to a gorilla, a cadaver, and a Cro-Magnon man. That's not legal anywhere."

"That's what your man gave him?"

I nodded.

"And he signed them?

"That's right. He never even looked at them," I said. "We can bring him down, Doc."

"How long will it take? Time is a problem for me."

"I know. It could take more time than you have."

"That's what I figured." Doc sighed.

"I'll see it through for you, Doc," I promised.

"Thanks, Eddie. I appreciate all you've done." He closed his eyes. "I'm a little tired now."

"See ya, Doc."

"See ya, Eddie," he said in a barely audible voice.

I never saw Doc alive again but I did hear from him after he died.

My cell phone buzzed at three o'clock in the morning and I answered it, expecting bad news. No one calls at that hour with good news.

It was Frank Burke. "Eddie, sorry to wake you. There's been a fire in Fort Lauderdale and I wanted to tell you. Shit, I've got another call. . . . I'll call you back."

Claudette was awake. "What's the matter?"

"That was Chief Burke. He said something about a fire."

"Why is he calling you?"

"I don't know. He got another call and hung up."

My phone buzzed again. It was Frank. "Correction. There's been two fires in Fort Lauderdale tonight."

"Frank, you're the chief of police, not a fireman," I reminded him. "Why is anyone calling you about a Fort Lauderdale fire . . . and why are you calling me?"

"The No Pain-U-Gain Clinic burned down."

Oh, shit! Doc!

"The Fort Lauderdale police knew about your investigation of the clinic," Frank said. "They're checking all leads. They want to talk to you tomorrow."

"No problem. Anyone hurt?"

"No. The strip mall had three stores. Only the clinic burned and no one was there."

"You said there were two fires," I said.

"A house in Fort Lauderdale. Dr. Venu Patel, age seventy-two. Burned to a crisp by a flash fire in his bedroom."

"I'm predicting five more fires tonight."

"What are you talking about?"

"Call me if you hear anything."

He called an hour later. "Okay, five fires, what's up?"

"Let me guess. All clinics . . . no injuries?"

"Correct. Tell me what you know."

"I know who's responsible," I said. "He's an old associate of mine."

"Give me an address and I'll have the Lauderdale police pick him up."

I gave him the information.

"Is he armed?"

"It doesn't matter," I said. "He'll be dead by the time you get there."

Chapter 52

You Have My Word

Claudette and I went to the kitchen and made coffee knowing there would be more calls. An hour later the phone rang. It was Frank.

"Right again, Eddie. Hurwitz was on the sofa . . . dead as a doornail. He had empty Oxy bottles on the floor next to him. He left one note addressed to you and one to the Fort Lauderdale police."

"What did they say?"

"I'd rather you hear it from the detective in charge," Frank said. "His name is Palley. He was first on the scene and he's got the letter. I gave him your cell."

Detective Warren Palley called a few minutes later.

"Was Doc Hurwitz a friend of yours?" he asked after a brief introduction.

"You know the old saying 'with friends like him I don't need enemies'?"

Palley chuckled. "Would you mind coming to police head-quarters and answering a few questions for me?"

"Not at all. Would you mind reading me the letters?"

"I was going to give you copies."

"I'd like to hear it now."

Palley read slowly. The first one was addressed to the Fort Lauderdale police.

Ft. Lauderdale Police
To Whom It May Concern:
I confess to setting seven fires tonight at six pill mills and one private residence in Ft. Lauderdale. I set fire to the mills to bring attention to these outlets of death. Using remote control I deliberately killed Dr. Venu Patel by igniting a small amount of napalm hidden in the pillow under his head while he slept. Patel was a drug dealer responsible for the death of my granddaughter. I acted alone. I then committed suicide with an overdose of drugs.

I have a criminal past and have given false testimony many times in my life. But this is a deathbed confession and it's all true. You have my word.
Solomon Hurwitz

I smiled when Palley stopped reading. Doc always gave his word when he was lying. If he said, "I guarantee it," you knew he was telling the truth. It was a Boston code.

"He did our job for us," the detective said.

"He certainly did," I replied, still smiling. "What does my letter say?"

Palley read to me again.

Eddie, sorry but I didn't have time to wait for the court system to work. I couldn't die in peace with Patel still alive so I

took the law into my own hands. I wanted revenge. You want
reform. Now it's your turn. You have all the proof you need.
Change the laws or change the legislators. You're the Boca
Knight. Lead the crusade.

 I'm dying, a weak old man, but I know you remember
when I commanded lightning. Those days are over now and
you don't have to worry about lightning striking the same place.
I guarantee it.
Doc

"What does that mean?" Palley asked.

"It's personal," I said, realizing that Doc was still conning
people after his death.

"Can you explain how a sick old man set seven fires in one
night by remote control? There had to be a triggering device in
each location. Who planted them?"

"Doc was getting around pretty good until recently. It's
possible he could have planted them himself when he was well
enough." *Anything is possible.*

"Was he an arson expert?"

"When he was a young man, he knew people in that business," I said.

Apparently he still did. Doc's second message to me about
how he once commanded lightning referred to Cunio Lightning.
He was telling me that his personal arsonist from Boston, Fabio
"the Fireman" Cunio, was alive and had set the Fort Lauderdale
fires for him. He also told me Fabio was out of my life forever by
writing *lightning doesn't strike twice in the same place* and guaran-
teeing it.

"I guess it doesn't matter anymore," Palley said. "We have a
deathbed confession."

I had the right to remain silent so I did.

Chapter 53

Weary Willie Moved

When the sun came up, I made a conference call to Mad Mick Murphy and Jerry Small regarding Doc's letter. Once again, Jerry's paper was first to publish the breaking news story. In an article entitled "Two Executioners," Jerry went into the lives of Doc Hurwitz and Dr. Patel and how they intersected. Mad Mick had every magazine on the East Coast clamoring for his follow-up magazine article.

I received a conference call from legislators Field and Diccicio that afternoon.

Field began, "You don't do things in a small way, do you?"

"What a breakthrough," Diccicio added. "Our names are on record for going after these clinics two years ago. Now everyone is calling us to help. We're heroes."

"Good. Now do whatever it takes to get the job done," I said.

"What can we do for you?" Field asked. "We owe you big-time for getting us involved."

"You don't owe me anything. That's not how I operate. But you could do me a personal favor."

I told them what I wanted and they told me to consider it done.

I received a return call from Jerry Small moments later.

"Weary Willie just died, Eddie."

I didn't know the man at all but I was saddened by his passing. "Does Bailey know?"

"She was with him," Jerry said. "I heard she took it pretty hard. She cried a lot and kept telling him she was sorry. When they took his body away, she disappeared. I'm going to write an article about his death. Do you want to be quoted?"

"No, and I don't want you to report his death either."

"I have to do my job, Eddie, and Willie is news."

"I need your help on this, Jerry."

"I have to print something and I don't want to lie."

"No lies," I said. "I'll e-mail you my ideas for a story."

"This I gotta see," Jerry said.

WEARY WILLIE MOVED
FROM INTENSIVE CARE
BY JERRY SMALL

Weary Willie, the unidentified sad-faced clown who was attacked and left for dead in Rutherford Park, has been moved from the intensive care ward at Boca Community Hospital. Details have not been released but I have been informed by a reliable source that there has been a dramatic change in his condition.

"You call this a news report?" Jerry said over the phone.

"I didn't lie, did I?"

"No, but—"

"No buts about it. I need some time."

"That's against the rules of good journalism," he said stubbornly.

"This will be another great story for you."

"Like I said, I love your article."

"Just keep Willie's death out of the paper for a few days and stay out of my way. Okay?"

"Okay, boss," Jerry said. "I'll be invisible."

"That would be nice."

Chapter 54

We're Not in Kansas Anymore

I went to my office and found Lou there.

"You must be feeling better," I said, sitting in front of his desk.

"I'm getting there."

"Good, get to work. I need one of your illegal reports on a Vincent Pestrito from Brooklyn, New York. He's a priest. I want to know if he has cousins named Anthony and Gino Pestrito and what their stories are."

"When do you need it?"

"Now. Drop everything."

"What about Grover?" Lou asked.

"Fuck Grover. He's being held in federal custody. Let him rot."

"Where is he?"

"Palm Beach or Miami," I said. "The Feds have a long list of people who want to kill him."

"I hope I'm on it?"

"You're second."

"Who's first?"

"Joy," I told Lou. "How's she doing?"

"The Girl Wonder is unbelievable. She does rehab three times a day."

"She wants to be ready to walk down the aisle."

He smiled. "Where should I call you when I finish this report?"

"I'm not going anywhere until you're done."

He stopped smiling.

"Weary Willie died today," I said. "Now it's murder or manslaughter. I need this information."

"I'm on it."

"It's strictly confidential."

"Understood."

Three hours later I got an e-mail from his adjoining office: *You think this is easy? I've condensed and added comments.*

Name: Vincent Pestrito

DOB: February 12, 1959

Born: Brooklyn, NY

Education: Bay Ridge High. Entered the seminary

Father: Santino, had one brother, Guido, who had two sons, Gino and Anthony

Occupation: Priest, Brooklyn, Flushing, Staten Island; 1996: Boca Raton

Marital Status: Married, 7 children—just kidding, I'm tired. Sorry.

Criminal Record: None (yet) . . .

Name: Gino Pestrito, Vincent's first cousin

DOB: April 22, 1960

Born: Brooklyn, NY

Education: 11th grade

Marital Status: Married, widower

Father: Guido; had one brother, Santino, who had one son, Vincent

Current Residence: Boca Raton, FL

Occupation: Janitor

Criminal Record: Extensive

Name: Anthony Pestrito, Gino Pestrito's younger brother

Other Facts: Same as above . . .

I drove to Rutherford Park looking for Bailey. I found her under the covers, under the boardwalk. My flashlight illuminated her face. Her eyes were closed and she was motionless. She looked dead.

"Bailey," I said in a hushed tone. "It's me, Eddie."

"Willie died today," she said, barely moving her lips.

"I know."

"Did you know he was my husband?"

"Your sister told me you were married. The way you took care of Willie made me think he might be the guy."

"His name was Brian Sweeney." Her eyes opened, glistening with tears. "I made such a mess of his life, Eddie. He had a wife he loved but she died. I fooled him into marrying me, and then I killed his unborn child because I was driving drunk. While I was in the hospital recovering, Brian ran away. I think he just snapped from all the losses he suffered and couldn't take it anymore. When I recovered from my injuries, I ran away too."

"To find him?"

"To lose *me*. I was a drop-dead alcoholic who screwed up

everything I touched. I was a burden to my parents, tormented my sister, killed my unborn child, and destroyed my husband's life. I didn't want to be Bailey Carr or Sweeney anymore. I left home with three bags of stuff and became Three Bag Bailey."

"Where did you go?"

"I was so drunk most of the time I didn't know where I was."

"How did you survive?"

"I had some money when I left home. That lasted a while, and when it ran out, I stole, worked, begged, and a few times I sold myself to men. I wasn't always old and ugly."

"Your sister said you were beautiful."

"She did?" Bailey seemed surprised. "Well, I guess I was. It didn't last long."

"You've had a hard life. You beat yourself up physically and mentally."

She nodded. "One night I woke up in a train yard in North Platte, Nebraska, with no idea how I got there. I bummed a cup of coffee in a diner and I guess I passed out. The lady who owned the place got me to a local church that had a detox and rehab facility in the basement. The priest who ran the place wouldn't let me out till I was totally clean. When I was released, I took the next train out of town and never had another drink. I can't say why."

"You were ready for a change," I said. "How did you find Brian after so much time?"

"It was totally by chance. Over a year ago I was in a Savannah Greyhound bus station trying to bum a ride anywhere. I was looking for something to eat in a trash bin and a picture in a discarded newspaper caught my eye. I took the paper out of the trash and saw it was a photo of a sad-faced clown next to an article entitled 'Weary Willie—Homeless in Boca.' It was written by your friend Jerry Small."

"Someone must have taken a bus from Boca to Savannah

and tossed the paper. Don't tell me you recognized Brian in all that makeup after more than twenty years?"

"I didn't recognize him. I just knew it was him."

"How could you?"

"Brian Sweeney idolized Emmett Kelly, the original Weary Willie. After I lost the baby, I guess Brian didn't want to be himself anymore and became Weary Willie."

Glenn Kessler, a good psychiatrist and lousy investor, told me that people will abandon one life for another if they're traumatized enough. It was possible this had happened to Brian Sweeney, but I wasn't convinced.

"Brian was a kid in the fifties when Willie's popularity was declining," I said. "In those days Brian had Ted Williams, Joe DiMaggio, and Mickey Mantle to idolize. Why pick a sad-faced, old clown?"

"Because Emmett Kelly Senior, Weary Willie the First, came from Sedan, Kansas, and so did we," Bailey said. "When Brian's life fell apart, he ran away from his hometown and chose to become his hometown's hero."

"That makes sense, I guess."

"There's an Emmett Kelly Museum in Sedan even though Senior left Kansas years ago. Emmett Junior was born in Texas and became Willie the Second. His son Paul was born in Arizona, and he became Willie the Third until he went to jail for murder. Brian Sweeney became Willie the Fourth until he died today."

"Did you go to Boca right after you saw that picture in the paper?" I asked.

"It took me a while to work up the courage."

"Did you find him right away when you got here?"

"It didn't take long, but I was afraid to approach him. What the hell was I going to say after all the years?"

"'I'm sorry' would have been a good start."

"I decided to watch after him for a while," she said. "I talked to the other homeless in the area about him. No one knew much. He was quiet and harmless. Not very social. I ate lunch sitting right next to him at the soup kitchen one day and said hello. He smiled but I could tell he had no idea who I was."

"Are you sure it was Brian? It's been a long time and you've both killed a lot of brain cells along the way."

"It was him. And as soon as I found him again, he gets killed. I'm such a jinx."

She started crying full force and put her head on my shoulder. I held her, saying nothing and letting her cry herself dry. After a half hour she pushed herself away and reached for something behind her. "Look what I got."

I shone the flashlight where her hands were fidgeting. She held a stack of clothes. It took me a moment to realize what it was. "Willie's clothes?"

"I took all his stuff," she said. "The hospital doesn't know."

"Aren't you going to bury Brian in Willie's clothes?"

"I don't know what to do. The morgue still has his body because some nitwit is delaying his burial. When they release him, I'll get him dressed proper."

I didn't bother to tell her I was the nitwit holding things up.

"I even have the fake flower he wore in his lapel."

I reached for Willie's derby and put it on my head. "How do I look?"

She sniffled. "With makeup you look like him. You're about the same size."

I took Willie's jacket and tried it on. It was baggy like a clown's suit . . . but it fit.

"Bailey, you just gave me an idea."

"I did?"

"Want to help me capture the people who hurt Willie and send them to jail?"

"Sure. What can I do?"

"I'll call you tomorrow. Get some sleep." On an impulse I kissed her forehead.

"Eddie," she called after me as I departed, "thank you for being my friend."

"My pleasure."

I drove to my apartment. Claudette asked where I'd been.

"I spent some time with my other girlfriend."

"How is Bailey?" she asked, not taking her eyes off *America's Got Talent*, on television.

"She's struggling with survivor's guilt."

"Do you really think Weary Willie was her husband?"

"It doesn't matter anymore," I said, grabbing a ladder and my Spy Master camera.

"No happy, romantic ending?"

"Sorry."

"Where are you going?"

"Making preparations to catch two thugs and a priest."

"Have fun," she said without looking up.

We all deal with apprehension in our own way.

Chapter 55

The Fighter

It was after 10:00 p.m. when I parked my car two blocks from St. Mary's and walked through the woods to the side of the church. I was carrying the little ladder, a fake pen that was really a flashlight, and my Spy Master camera. Silhouetted by moonlight, standing on top of the Dumpster, Bailey's raccoon guarded its food supply. I altered my course to avoid a confrontation with the little prick and moved quietly toward the rear staircase. I double-checked for cars in the lot. There were none.

The light over the door at the bottom of the stairs was out. It was always out and I wondered if it was broken. I went down the stairs quietly, and when I got to the bottom, I opened the short, four-foot ladder and climbed the four steps so that I was eye level with the unused light. I removed my fake-pen flashlight from my shirt pocket, turned it on, and stuck it in my mouth. I aimed it at the outdoor light fixture screwed into the stucco wall. I affixed the Spy Master camera to the top of the metal shade over the lightbulb, angling it properly so the camera could video the entire staircase. I checked the remote system and it worked. I could put the camera off and on from about twenty-five yards, which was plenty for my purposes. I folded the ladder and got the hell out of there.

The scene was set for tomorrow night.

Mr. Johnson and I woke up at the same time the next morning, surprising Claudette and me. "You must be doing something dangerous today," she said, patting Mr. J as if he were her pet schnauzer. "Regrettably I have to be at the clinic early. Sorry."

"What am I supposed to do with him all day?"

"Tell him to be patient until tonight."

"Tonight's no good. I'm working late beating up some people."

"I'm sure they deserve it, dear," she said, stroking my face.

Blind faith eliminates the need for a lot of conversation.

I went to the office. A note on my desk from Lou told me he was picking up Joy from the hospital and bringing her to the Embassy Suites. *Call me if you need me*, he wrote.

I had planned on reviewing my scripts for tonight with Lou and decided to use this opportunity to visit Doc Hurwitz's grave instead. I took a ride to the Fort Lauderdale nonsectarian cemetery where Doc had made arrangements. He gave instructions, a month in advance of his death, for a tombstone to be erected immediately after he was buried rather than waiting the customary year. It read simply:

SOLOMON "DOC" HURWITZ
MARCH 20, 1925–APRIL 3, 2006

I looked at the dash between his birth and the date of his death and thought about how he had lived his life. He was a child of the Great Depression who fought his way up in the world the only way he knew how. I had tried to put him in jail several times, but now I was at his gravesite to say good-bye.

"Hi Doc," I said to the stone, and felt like an idiot. "Your letter was a big hit and it's going to help put those clinics out of business. Thanks. By the way, I understood your message about Fabio Cunio and had a good laugh. I can't believe you're conning me even after you're dead.

"I want you to know that a new bill designed to close the pill mills will be submitted to the Florida legislature soon. Two contacts of mine are writing the legislation, and they agreed to my request that they name it the Shoshanna Bill. I hope this helps you rest in peace."

I don't believe Doc heard a word and I don't believe there's an afterlife. But when I was finished talking to the headstone, I felt better.

I returned to the office and busied myself preparing for the evening's activity. I checked my equipment, my time schedule, and my strategy. It was important to surprise, confuse, and unsettle the enemy before the battle began. As with all battle plans my success depended on many factors. But, Sun Tzu, in his book *The Art of War*, wrote, *If you know your enemy and know yourself . . . you don't have to worry about the outcome of any battle*, or something like that.

It was early afternoon when a tall, thin young man walked into the office. He looked familiar. When he smiled, I recognized him.

"Teofilo," I said, returning his smile. I got up from my desk and hugged him. "How are you?"

"Lucky to be alive."

"Me too."

We hugged like survivors.

I invited him to sit down. "Tell me about it," I said. "I didn't see much."

"It happened so fast. The gunmen walked in and started shooting. I got up from the stool and must have caught one gunman's attention. He came toward me and aimed his weapon at my face. Just before he pulled the trigger, Mr. Brown stepped in front of me and lunged at the shooter. I heard an explosion, and the next thing I know I'm on the floor with Mr. Brown on top of me. I was covered in blood. I heard a lot of gunfire after that and I guess I passed out because I woke up in the hospital. When I got home, I heard you survived and I tried calling you. I never got through."

"I've been a little busy."

"I know. I read about you in the papers."

"So what have you been doing?" I asked.

"Not much. I still have to get a job."

"Do you still want to box?" I asked, remembering our last conversation before the shooting.

"I would love to box."

"You'd need your mother's permission. Will she let you fight?"

"Since I survived the massacre, my mother believes I am destined for great things. She feels it was fate that brought us together."

"I'd like to meet her. You told me your mother had personal reasons for leaving Miami. Is there anything I should know?"

"I was her reason. We moved in with family in Miami but they were involved in many illegal things. As soon as she got a job in this area, we moved. She said it was all meant to be."

I'm not a big believer in fate. I believe life is random, like missing a boat or dodging a bullet. But anything's possible.

I called the PAL gym and got Barry Anson on the phone. Barry ran the place and coached the fighters. I asked him if he had time to look at a new prospect.

"It's a quiet day. Come over whenever you want," he said.

"How about now? I have a busy afternoon and night."

"I'll be here and Steve Doherty is working out for the next hour. Maybe Steve can take a look at him too."

Steve was a seventeen-year-old light heavyweight and our best fighter. He knew talent. "Great," I told Barry. "I'm on my way."

We were at the gym on Second Avenue in ten minutes. I introduced Teofilo to Barry and Steve. "Looks like a welterweight to me," Barry said, handing Teofilo a pair of gloves and head gear. "I'll spar with him and see what he knows."

"I'll spar with him," Steve said. "It'll be a good workout for me."

"You're too big and too experienced for him," Barry said.

"I won't punch," Steve said. "I'll just move around the ring and let him do the fighting."

When Teofilo took off his shirt to get in the ring, we were all impressed. He had a wiry fighter's build and reminded me of Sugar Ray Leonard. Steve was twenty pounds heavier, but when they faced off in the ring, he looked twice the size. "Show me what you got," Steve told Teofilo, and smiled. The kid from Cuba raised his hands and began to move effortlessly. He swayed like a cobra and mesmerized us. He struck without warning and hit the more experienced fighter repeatedly. When he threw a three-punch combination, he rocked Steve on his heels. Surprisingly, Teofilo stopped punching and with his gloves urged Steve to come after him and punch. Steve looked at Barry for guidance. Barry nodded. Steve moved forward and threw a wide-arced left hook that thudded off Teofilo's right shoulder. The force of the blow knocked the smaller man sideways, and Steve moved forward to throw a right. Instead, he was greeted with two sharp left jabs and a beautiful right cross. *Bam!* Steve went down on one knee, more stunned than hurt. He got up embarrassed, ready to go after Teofilo.

"That's enough," Barry said, and the two fighters took a step back.

"Sorry," the Cuban kid said to the bigger fighter.

"It's okay. You're good," Steve conceded. "I hope you join the club."

They touched gloves and got out of the ring. A cut was above Steve's eye.

"Where you from?" I heard Steve ask Teofilo as they walked to the watercooler.

"That kid has the makings of a champion," Barry said.

"He's got good genes," I said. "He's a natural-born fighter."

"Where did you find him?"

"At a gunfight."

"He's the kid who survived that night?" Anson asked.

I nodded.

"This was meant to be," Barry said.

Not that again.

Chapter 56

Willie Returns

The sun goes down in Boca between six and seven o'clock during the month of April. Bailey and I sat in the Mini a safe distance from the rectory and waited for dark.

"You look good," she said.

"You too."

I was wearing Willie's clothes and Bailey had done a great job painting both of us to look like him. She didn't have a clown costume, but she wore a hat and in the dark no one would notice.

"Checklist," I suggested. "Flashlight?"

"Check."

"Intruder . . . recorder . . . camera . . . walkie-talkie?"

"Check . . . check . . . check . . . check."

"Two rocks?"

"Check."

"Any questions?" I asked.

"What if you get in trouble? Can I come to your rescue?"

"You have my permission to save my life."

"Check."

"Ready?"

"Ready!"

We walked toward the house in the shadow of the trees and prepared to attack. The moon was behind thin clouds and gave off little light. Bailey moved silently to the back of the house while I remained in front. I waited until I felt certain she had reached the rear.

Now.

I hurled one of my two rocks through the front window. Glass shattered and Father Vincent was at the window in a fat man's flash, frantically looking around. I stepped out of the shadows, shone my flashlight from my chest up to my face, and stared at him. "I'll call the cops," he shouted, but I knew he wouldn't. The last thing he needed was the police near the church. Then the back window exploded.

Perfect timing, Bailey.

Father Vincent ran in the direction of the new sound and I shut off my flashlight and moved to the left-hand side of the house. By now he was staring at Bailey's version of Weary Willie's face, illuminated from her chin up by her flashlight. More holy terror, I hoped.

My second rock broke a side window. Father Vincent appeared at that window and saw me in the spotlight again. "What do you want?" he screamed, just as the window on the opposite side exploded. I saw the priest reach for a phone.

"Bailey," I said in a harsh whisper into the walkie-talkie. "He's making a call. Use the Intruder and make sure he's calling his cousins."

"Check," she said.

I dashed around the house and found Bailey. She had already removed the Intruder from its case and was aiming it at the house.

"There's some clown throwing rocks through my window," we heard Father Vincent say through the Intruder.

Pause.

"What kind of clown?" he asked, responding to a question. "A sad-faced clown, for chrissakes."

Pause.

"What do you mean you thought you got rid of him?"

Pause.

"The homeless guy sleeping in the storage room? You said you put him on a bus out of town."

Pause.

"There was a complication," Father Vinnie shouted. "Why didn't you tell me?"

Pause.

"You didn't want to worry me," he screamed. "Great. Well, I'm worried now. You're lucky he's been released and not dead." He listened again. "It was an accident until you moved his body. Get over here right away."

Bingo!

"Now the going gets tough," I said to Bailey when the Intruder went silent.

"Don't we have enough evidence taped already?"

"No. We only heard half of a two-way conversation."

She nodded.

"Stay calm and get good videos," I said.

She nodded again and was gone.

I was impressed by her calmness under fire and her clarity of thought.

I jogged from the rectory to the church, holding my derby in place. I struggled down the killer staircase, picked the new lock on the door, and entered the church. I moved quickly to the church office, nodding along the way to the statue of Jesus. I picked the second lock and entered. Nothing had changed since I last broke in. I picked the desk lock, found the ledger and removed it. I retraced my steps, not bothering to close doors or drawers or put out the lights. This was supposed to look like a break-in when Father Vincent and his cousins arrived.

"A car just pulled in front of the rectory," Bailey warned me through the walkie-talkie. "Moose one and two just went inside."

"Right on schedule."

I removed my cell phone from Willie's pants and dialed Frank Burke's cell. I had given him the twenty-four hours' notice I promised, and he was now waiting at a doughnut shop in Fort Lauderdale as agreed. He knew he was there to arrest Father Vincent's girlfriend. He had a warrant.

"Frank," I whispered. "Arrest her now."

"Okay, then what?"

"Bring her to St. Mary's Church in Boca." I disconnected before he could ask any more questions.

"They're coming," Bailey said into the walkie-talkie. "The priest just pointed at the light in the basement. The other two guys are running toward you now. This infrared stuff is cool."

I stood at the open doorway at the bottom of the stairs, the light from inside illuminating me. I pressed the remote-control button for the camera I had affixed to the light above the door. I looked up at the lens and saw the red light flash.

Lights, camera, action!

Gino and Anthony appeared at the top of the stairs and saw me dressed as Weary Willie. I was holding the ledger by my right side where they could see it. I glanced up under the brim of my derby the way they do in spaghetti westerns.

"He picked the new lock," Gino told Anthony.

"He's got the ledger," Anthony told Gino.

Father Vincent came up behind them, breathing heavily. "Good Lord," he intoned.

"Hey, bum," Anthony called down the stairs. "What are you doing with that book?"

I decided to answer. To maintain my hobo image, I thought I needed a homeless voice that sounded as if my throat were ruined by whiskey and encrusted with street grit. It had to be the voice of a man who lived outside in jungle rain, dust-bowl wind, Sahara heat, and arctic cold.

Who the hell sounded like that?

Clint Eastwood!

I tried to remember his voice in *The Outlaw Josey Wales*, *High Plains Drifter*, *Dirty Harry*, *Heartbreak Ridge*, and *Unforgiven*.

I lifted my right arm and held up the ledger. "You mean this book?" I rasped without looking up.

"Yeah, that book," Gino said. "Bring it up here."

"Come down and get it," I said like Clint.

"If I have to come down there, I'm gonna split your head wide open," Anthony threatened.

"Like the last time?" I rasped.

Father Vincent stepped between his cousins and said, "You down there, what is it you want?"

I held up the ledger again. "Money," I said, sounding as if my throat had been sandpapered. "The money you're stealing from the church."

"We're not stealing any money. The church has none," the priest lied.

Come on . . . I need a confession here.

"The widow's money," I growled. "The four million."

"He knows everything, Vinnie," Gino said.

Thank you, Gino.

"We can work something out," Father Vincent said calmly. "There's plenty for everyone. How much do you want?"

Thank you, Father. "All of it," I said to provoke them.

"No way," Anthony snapped. He rumbled down the stairs while I stood motionless and let him come. When he was standing one step above me, I made a feeble effort to defend myself, but he brushed me back like a gnat. He grabbed my shirt collar and pulled. "You little fuck. I'm going to throw you down these fuckin' stairs again, and this time you won't wake up."

Thank you, thank you, thank you.

I let him drag me up the stairs. When we were standing together, Gino tore the book from my hand. "You son of a bitch," he said, kicking me in the ass. Willie's pants were a little baggy, and my Colt slid down my pant leg, clanging on the ground. Gino grabbed it before I could turn around and aimed it at me.

"Don't shoot him," Anthony said. "We're not murderers."

"We have to get rid of him. He's got enough information to put us in jail," Gino said. "We can make it look like he tried to break in Father Vinnie's house and got shot by his own gun in a scuffle."

"That's still murder," Anthony said.

"Wait a second," the priest said. "What's a bum doing with a big, fancy gun like that? We're going too fast. This whole thing doesn't make sense."

Uh-oh!

"Think about it," Vinnie said. "Why did he break my windows?"

Good question.

"To scare you?" Gino asked.

"Why scare me?"

Another good question.

"So you would call us," Anthony said.

"Right . . . to get us all here together," the priest concluded. "Jesus Christ. This is some kind of setup."

Bailey. Are you there, Bailey?

"You got that right, dummies," Bailey screamed from the woods, and everyone turned in her direction. She stepped out of the darkness into the dim light of the moon. She was still aiming the Intruder. "Smile, morons . . . you're on candid camera."

"Good God," Father Vincent said. "Anthony, get her."

Run, Bailey.

Bailey ran.

"Get her, Anthony," Gino shouted encouragement, distracted by the activity.

Now is as good a time as any.

I dropped the ledger, grabbed Gino's right hand near the wrist and twisted it violently, counterclockwise. I heard a bone break and Gino scream. The gun hit the pavement, and Gino crumpled. His shoulder landed on the top step and he tumbled down the staircase. When he hit bottom, he groaned.

I picked up the Cobra and aimed it at Father Vincent. He stood there wide-eyed and petrified, too fat to fight.

"It's over," I said.

He nodded, went down on his knees, and started praying.

"Pray you don't get a cellmate named Bubba," I said.

Behind the priest I saw Bailey playing catch-me-if-you-can with Anthony by circling around the Dumpster. Anthony was totally unaware of what had happened to his partners, and he kept chasing Bailey futilely from one side of the garbage bin to the other. If he caught her, he'd crush her, but he would never catch her.

"I got the gun, Bailey," I said into the walkie-talkie. "You can stop now."

"Cool," she said, dashing around a corner of the Dumpster, enjoying herself.

Anthony stopped chasing her, bent over, and put his hands on his knees trying to catch his breath.

Bailey stopped but remained a safe distance away. "Hey, dummy. You want the camera?"

He looked up at her and nodded.

She tossed it into the Dumpster. "It's all yours."

Bailey! What are you doing?

She ran into the darkness.

"You better run," Anthony called before turning his attention to the garbage container.

He sighed, put his hands over the edge, pulled himself up, and went over the top . . . into the garbage. A moment later I heard him scream, "Get off of me."

He was still screaming when Frank Burke pulled up in his cruiser, followed by two more patrol cars with flashing lights. I directed the police to Father Vincent, who was still praying for his soul and a good cellmate. "There's another one at the bottom of the stairs." I pointed. "He's got a broken wrist."

"What's that screaming in the Dumpster?" Frank asked me, checking out my clown costume.

"That would be Anthony Pestrito interacting with a raccoon."

We all turned toward the bin in time to see a raccoon fly out of the blue bin and land on the pavement. We watched it get up, hiss at us, and run off into the woods.

A moment later, Anthony emerged from the garbage, bloody and torn. "I got the camera," he said before the police surrounded him with drawn guns. "When did you guys get here?"

Bailey came out of the bushes. "You got the carrying case, genius," she said, taking Vinnie's picture. "I got the camera."

Anthony crumpled to the ground and started to cry.

"Take him to the Baker center on Boca Rio Road," I told one of the cops. "They know how to treat rabies."

I gave Bailey a big hug and explained her role to Chief Burke. She didn't say a word.

"She's afraid of the police," I explained.

"I'm afraid of her." Frank walked to one of the cruisers and opened the back door. A stylish, dark-haired woman stepped out. "This is Maria Lopez," Frank said. "Father Vinnie's girl-friend. I think she's willing to cooperate."

"I remember her," I said, picturing Father Vincent's hand on her butt. "We got so much material here we may not need her, but you decide."

"May I talk to Vincent?" she asked.

"Not in private," Frank said.

"That's fine."

We approached the kneeling priest together.

The future defrocked felon looked up and saw Maria. He struggled to his feet.

"I'm sorry," he told her, opening his arms for a holy hug.

She brushed him off. "Does this mean I lose my condo?"

He nodded. "I'm sorry," he said sadly. She kicked him in the balls and he fell to his knees again.

Chapter 57

Old-Time Religion

Gino Pestrito and his cousin Vinnie were in holding cells at the Boca police station awaiting transfer to the Palm Beach Sheriff's Office. Anthony was running a high fever at the Baker clinic, where he received rabies shots and fifty-four stitches. I gave a statement to two Boca detectives, but Bailey continued her tradition of not talking to the police. When we were released, it was late, and I took Bailey directly to Rutherford Park.

"You did great, Bailey. I'm proud of you."

"Don't be proud of me," she said. "Just be my friend."

I understood. She didn't want expectations from me because she didn't want to let me down. "You got it, friend," I said.

The Pestrito boys became front-page news in Palm Beach County. Lou did some extensive research on them at his leisure. As kids, they were known in Bay Ridge as Fuckin' Vinnie and Fuckin' Anthony and Gino.

"Fuckin' Vinnie, how you doin'?"

"There's Fuckin' Anthony and Gino."

Their lifestyle was characterized in the 1977 movie *Saturday Night Fever.* They idolized gangsters such as Crazy Joe Gallo and Kid Blast. Their gang was immortalized in Jimmy Breslin's book *The Gang That Couldn't Shoot Straight.* They were familiar with Jimmy Burke and Henry Hill, who were in turn glamorized in *Goodfellas,* starring Ray Liotta and Robert De Niro. They belonged to a gang named the Dukes of Brooklyn and were arrested in a violent gang war with the Turbans. The Pestritos already had police records that included assault and battery, petty theft, and a couple of small-time felonies. An imaginative liberal judge had given the boys a choice: go to jail, the Marines, or the seminary. The Pestrito brothers chose jail, and Vinnie told the judge he'd always wanted to be a priest. So be it. He was sent off to the seminary, where he was never caught violating a rule, which was a miracle because he never stopped sinning. He was especially prolific at consorting with women, many of whom thought it would be kinky to be the one who seduced him into breaking his vows. Many succeeded.

"I'm getting laid more now than when I was a gang member," Vinnie told his cousins when they got out of jail and resumed their criminal ways. "This religion thing is a racket."

"You should have become a televangelist," Gino had told him. "Those guys make a fortune *and* get laid."

"Good things come to those who wait," Fuckin' Vinnie said.

There would be no imaginative judges this time for the Pestritos. After they were booked at Boca police headquarters, Vincent and Gino were sent to the sheriff's facility on Gun Club Road, while Anthony remained under guard at the Baker clinic. The day after their arrest the state attorney filed two separate Basis of Information forms with the South Branch of the Fifteenth Judicial Circuit Court in Delray. A motion for pretrial detention was filed at their first appearance and was granted by a Catholic judge, who was upset with Father Vincent.

I attended the legal proceedings that day, and after the hearing I talked to the state's attorney, Mike Bernstein.

"We'll have a tough time with the manslaughter charge or a wrongful-death proceeding against the Pestritos," he said. "Willie fell down the stairs, according to everyone who was there. It will be very difficult to prove he was pushed."

"I understand," I said. "What about moving the body and the embezzlement charge?"

"We'll get them for that and they'll go away for a long time. You guys did a hell of a job."

I stood outside the Delray courthouse on Atlantic Avenue and admired the beautiful April afternoon. I decided to go for a walk and enjoy the weather.

I crossed Atlantic and peered inside the Delray Tennis Center. The eight thousand seats were empty this time of year, but in season they were often filled for professional and pro-am events. I turned east toward the center of town and the freight train crossing. The train system in Delray made no sense. Freight trains roared through the busy downtown area at too many miles per hour, with no scheduled stop in the city. Conversely the Tri-Rail commuter trains that brought people to the city stopped a bus ride west of the city's most popular attractions. I remember having dinner with Claudette one night at a downtown, "hip" restaurant next to the tracks. We had just been seated when my water glass started vibrating, signaling the imminent arrival of a freight train. Our corner table near the patio wasn't thirty yards from the tracks when a seventy-car hurricane roared past, alerting me that derailment and dismemberment were only a loose rail away. The other diners seemed too hip to care so I swallowed my apprehension with a dinner roll and waited for the rolling thunder to pass. Eventually it was quiet again, and the waiter took our order while he could hear us. Apparently I was the only person worried about restaurants, hair salons, art stores, and condos being adjacent to the Cannon Ball Express. Party on!

I passed Old School Square, a block west of the railway crossing, where a Christmas tree, one hundred feet high, was displayed every holiday season. Five hundred thousand people visited the site annually to hear Christmas music and children's laughter mix with clanging bells and whistle blasts as the boxcars rumbled past the nativity scene. Season's greetings, happy New Year, and watch your caboose.

I turned left on North*east* Second Avenue, two blocks east of North*west* Second Avenue, and wondered how many tourists made the wrong turn every year. I followed a sign to Pineapple Grove not expecting to see pineapples, but the sign was inviting anyway.

When my mind stopped wandering, I was standing outside the Mystery Bookstore in Pineapple Grove. I went inside and browsed. The cozy little store was filled with thrillers and mysteries. I read a few book jackets in the Bestsellers section and thought that sometimes real life can be stranger than fiction.

CHAPTER 58

INVISIBLE BULLETS

The news was filled with Doc Hurwitz stories and pill mill details. There was talk of a march on the cock-and-balls building in Tallahassee to demand new pain-clinic legislation. Representatives Don Diccicio and James Field were spearheading the drive and winning new votes every day.

Weary Willie was put to rest in a tin urn given to Three Bag Bailey, who insisted she was his wife. No one objected. She kept his ashes under the boardwalk where she slept. Before the cremation I asked the crime lab to conduct a DNA test to determine exactly who was in that jar. Before I got the results I canceled the exam. I didn't want to know.

The Catholic church was, once again, vilified for allowing men such as Vincent Pestrito to join the priesthood. I disagreed. The church's intentions were honorable; Vinnie's weren't. The Bay Ridge boys were going to jail for their sins and St. Mary's was looking for a new priest and a janitor. The renegade priest's girlfriend, Maria Lopez, was rumored to be getting a *Hustler* centerfold and a book deal.

The Virgin Maria?

Jimmy "Big Game" Hunter came apart like a wet newspaper and told us everything he knew and claimed he was an innocent victim. Jolly Rogers confessed that Benjamin Grover had ordered him to plant the tracking device under my car. I was getting more press than I needed, but Lou Dewey couldn't get enough. He loved it. Joy Feely came home with a barely discernible limp and announced she would marry Lou in June.

Special agents Tom Mack and Tyler Sloan were awarded commendations. Jerry Small and Mad Mick collaborated on an article for *Time* on crime in South Florida. It was a big hit.

Glenn Kessler called to tell me he had lost over a million dollars with Grover and was now worried about a government "clawback" of all his profits for the last six years.

"Thank goodness for bad golf," he said, referring to his bestseller.

Steve Coleman said he would survive his financial loss with Grover but admitted he should have listened to my friend Herb when they met at Kugel's.

"If I didn't have bad luck, I'd have no luck," Steve complained.

I told him Herb had been shot to death at Kugel's.

"I'm sorry," Steve said, suddenly feeling lucky.

Perspective is a good thing to have.

Several charities closed their doors post-Grover, one feeder-fund manager committed suicide, trust funds evaporated, and wealthy widows became destitute. The initial shock of imagined losses was nothing compared to the aftershock of real losses, and it would only get worse as time went by. Lou hacked into the list of creditors being generated by investigators, and I saw some names I recognized. The large corporations didn't surprise me, but some of the small individuals listed astounded me. How could so many lose so much to so few? The fallout was spreading. Soon, individual losers would stop paying the dry cleaner, the grocer, the butcher, and the mortgage. The price of houses would collapse. Demand for labor, new homes, and new goods would evaporate. It was Armageddon, just as Lou Dewey had predicted. The sky was falling but Benjamin Grover was still trying to make deals.

He agreed to plead guilty to all charges, thus saving the government millions of dollars in court costs. As part of the deal he insisted his wife be exonerated and allowed to keep twenty million in assets he claimed were legitimate. He had no children to protect so that was his only request. The public outcry was deafening but the government made a counteroffer. They would accept his guilty plea, seek the maximum penalty against him, and allow his wife to keep two million dollars. Grover accepted the offer.

The public cried foul again. *Bullshit! Give her nothing! Put her in jail! Kill them both! I'll take two million too! This can't be! Where's the justice? Who else is involved? Where's my money?*

Legal proceedings were moving at record speed, and in early May Grover was taken to the Palm Beach Federal Courthouse to plead guilty. His police escort was huge and so was the crowd outside the courthouse when he arrived. I was there on the courthouse stairs thanks to Tyler Sloan and Tom Mack. Grover looked forlorn in his orange jumpsuit. His lion's mane was not nearly as impressive as before. The crowd pressed forward.

Fraud! Faker! Murderer! Traitor! Bastard!

The police pressed back. *Clear the way! Step back!*

Grover smiled wanly.

Bang. It sounded like a firecracker.

Bang! Bang! Bang!

Grover's smile turned to a grimace. He clutched his chest, gasped, collapsed to his knees, and rolled onto his side. He tumbled down the stairs and stopped at the bottom, headfirst. His arms were spread wide and his eyes were open.

"Where did the shots come from?" someone yelled.

People were running and screaming.

FBI Special Agent Sloan was first to Grover's side. He knelt and pressed his fingers to Grover's neck, searching for a pulse. He put his head to Grover's chest.

"There's no pulse or heartbeat," he said, looking up.

"There's no bloodstains either," I said.

Chapter 59

Keeping Pace

The *boko* of Wall Street was dead, and his bloodless death was a mystery until Dr. Barton Brass made a statement to a private group that afternoon.

"Benjamin Grover's cause of death was a heart attack," the medical examiner said.

"Was he scared to death?" Agent Tyler Sloan asked sarcastically.

"Certainly there was a moment of panic when Grover thought the firecrackers were gunshots," Dr. Brass said seriously. "A heart can misfire from fright or his pacemaker could have malfunctioned when his heart rate accelerated beyond normal limits."

"I didn't know he had a pacemaker," I said.

"I didn't know either," Sloan said.

"Apparently he didn't want people to know," Dr. Brass said.

"He didn't want people to know a lot of things," I responded.

I got a small laugh from the sparse crowd, but Dr. Brass was

stone-faced. "My job is to determine cause of death and I've concluded it was a heart attack. End of case."

Not for me.

I called my favorite internist, Dr. Alan Koblentz, and told
him I had a question about pacemakers.

"I'm not a heart specialist," he said.

"You're close enough," I told him.

"Tell that to a man with a heart condition."

"Just answer one question. Can a functioning pacemaker be
deliberately sabotaged to cause death?"

"I think it's possible."

"That's a quick answer for a guy who's not a heart specialist."

"I happened to read an article about this subject in a medical
journal recently," Koblentz explained. "The article claimed that
pacemakers can be sabotaged using sophisticated computer hacking."

"I know one of the greatest computer hackers on the planet."

"Call him," Koblentz advised.

I called Lou Dewey and gave him the doctor's information
and my theory.

"Give me an hour," he said.

Two hours later he called me.

"What took so long?" I asked.

"It's not easy to hack hackers. But I did it. I found an organization of computer nerds called MaxHax—"

"Organized nerds?"

"Scary thought," Lou said. "They even have a national convention. Some of these guys are employed by high-tech companies to find security loopholes in their systems so they can plug
them. Last year a professor from UMass, Boston, named Armand
Balfour found a huge loophole in the pacemaker industry. He
presented a paper at the MaxHax Facts convention that explained
how to hack a pacemaker. His work was financed by the pace-

maker industry. He didn't have a working model built at the time. But based on what I read, I think it's quite possible. It could be working now for all I know. Balfour's presentation was over a year ago."

"Can you explain his theory to me in a million words or less?"

"I'll try," Lou said. "As you already know from your own experience, an electrical impulse makes the heart beat. When that impulse misfires, it causes an irregular heartbeat . . . like you had."

"I remember distinctly. You saved my life that day."

"My pleasure. There are a number of ways to deal with an irregular heartbeat. A successful ablation procedure like yours can cure the condition. A pacemaker can control it."

"How does a pacemaker work?" I asked.

"Pacemakers have internal timers that determine when the next pulse should be received. Every patient has a different requirement. A computer is used to program the timing of a pacemaker, and that's where Balfour found the loophole. He discovered that no encrypted code protects the wireless connection between the control device and the pacemaker. If a hacker worms his way between the doctor's computer and the patient's pacemaker, he can assume total control of the device, turn it off, and kill the patient."

"It sounds easier said than done."

"You're right," Lou said. "And proving it would be very difficult too. The murderer could erase his codes when he's done without leaving evidence."

"Wouldn't there be an interruption between the doctor's computer and the patient's device when the hacker interferes?"

"Possibly, but that would only reinforce a malfunction theory. The connection between the two devices fails and the pacemaker malfunctions. There would be no trace of a third party."

"There can't be many people who know about this," I said.

"There's a few. When Professor Balfour made his presentation, there were several hundred hackers in attendance at the convention. The information went over the Internet to thousands of individuals and companies. Add that to the fact that plenty of people wanted to kill Grover, and your list of suspects is longer than Grover's list of victims. Why not just accept the ME report and forget about B. I. Grover?"

"I can't do that."

"I know," Lou said. "Where do you want to start looking?"

"Send me the updated list of Grover's creditors and get me a list of MaxHax members. Our killer is in there somewhere."

"I'm on it."

It didn't take Lou long to provide me with the lists. The victims' list was much longer than the MaxHax list so I started with the latter.

I had reached the MaxHax *P*'s when a name jumped out at me: Paretsky, Noah, Deerfield Beach, Florida. Noah was a former child prodigy from Chelsea, Massachusetts, who graduated MIT with honors in 1964. Noah was a genius and had attended the MaxHax convention in Washington, DC, where he would have learned about pirating pacemakers. If anyone could understand the complexities of this technology, it was Noah Paretsky. But Noah wouldn't kill anyone . . . or would he?

I set aside the MaxHax list and switched my attention to the B.I.G. creditors. Noah's name was not on that list, but his parents' names were there: Bennett and Bertha from Delray Beach.

I called Lou immediately. "Bennett and Bertha Paretsky lost almost eight hundred thousand dollars to Grover."

"I'll bet they were cleaned out," Lou said. "They weren't rich people."

"Their neighbors at 550 Delray Vista Drive weren't wealthy either."

I checked for other familiar names from the Paretskys'

building hoping that Lou's original list was wrong. Sadly, my friend Izzy Fryberg was there . . . for over a million. The Freedlanders lost six hundred and fifty thousand. Mo and Maxine Spielman were in the four hundred thousand vicinity, and Biggie Small lost over nine hundred thousand.

Wipeout.

"Lou, do a current search on Bertha and Bennett Paretsky," I said. "I got a bad feeling."

Less than an hour later Lou called me back. "Sorry, but your bad feeling was right on. Bertha Paretsky committed suicide a few days after Grover's arrest went public. She swallowed fifteen Ambien pills, got in bed, and went to sleep. Her husband found the body, had a stroke, and hasn't spoken since. He's at the Delray Medical Center. Their son, Noah, is listed as the next of kin."

I had my murderer and I couldn't have felt worse.

CHAPTER 60

THE GOOD SON

"The number you are calling is no longer in service," a recording told me when I tried contacting Noah Paretsky the next morning. I felt certain he would not leave the area with his father in critical condition.

Where would a good son go at a time like this?

I got in my Mini and drove north to Delray Beach. Twenty minutes later I parked in front of 550 Delray Vista Drive. I sat in my car looking at the unremarkable building with the remarkable tenants. Benjamin Grover had stolen their golden years from them, and though the outside of the building looked solid, the inside was ruined.

I got on the elevator and smiled. It was the haunted elevator that had brought me to 550 Delray Vista Drive in the first place, but that's another story.

The elevator went to the second floor without incident. I

remembered the Paretskys had a corner apartment to the left. I knocked on the door. No answer. I knocked again and got no response. I picked the lock and went inside. Packing boxes, some filled, others empty, were throughout the apartment. In the bedroom I saw clothing hanging in the closet long enough to belong to Noah. He had moved into his parents' apartment to await his father's passing.

I locked the front door so Noah wouldn't suspect anything when he got home. I spent some time looking around the two-bedroom unit. Most of the pictures were off the walls, already in boxes, but I saw some old photos of Noah's parents, in their happy years. They looked so young and hopeful smiling at the camera, but now all hope was gone and the smiles had faded. Life can do that.

I understand why you did it, Noah. I really do.

I sat on the sofa and waited. Within an hour I heard a key in the door and Noah entered. His tall frame looked more stooped than last year and his taste in clothes remained dreadful. His face looked older and sadder than I remembered.

He saw me and his eyes widened. "You're an amazing man."

"I'm sorry for your loss," I said, standing up. We shook hands. "Your mother was a lovely woman."

"Thank you. She didn't have the strength to start over."

"How's your father?"

"He had a second stroke. There's no hope."

"I'm sorry."

Noah nodded solemnly. "Are you here to arrest me?"

"I'm not a cop. I don't have the authority."

"Why are you here?"

"Professional curiosity and probable cause," I said.

"Anyone who knew Benjamin Grover had probable cause. But according to the medical examiner, the son of a bitch died of a heart attack."

"I don't believe that and neither do you."

He smiled and asked if anyone else shared my opinion.

"Probably not," I said. "But I don't care."

"No one cares. The man was a monster."

"That doesn't give you the right to be judge and jury."

"Or executioner," Noah said. "No one has that right, but it happens a lot."

He walked to the front door and opened it. The sun brightened the room but not the mood. "You'll have to excuse me. I have a mother to mourn and a father to bury."

"And memories to pack."

"I've got plenty of those." He opened the door fully. "I guess I should change the lock."

"Don't bother. I won't be back."

"What about the police or the FBI?"

"I can't speak for them," I said, holding out my hand to him. "I truly am sorry about your parents."

"I know you are, Eddie," he said, shaking my hand. "I'm sorry for everyone in this building and all the other Grover victims. I hope he's burning in hell right now."

"I hope so too. But I don't know if I can just walk away from my suspicions."

"You're a good man. You'll do the right thing."

I hope so.

I called Agent Sloan and arranged a meeting with him that afternoon in the Miami FBI office. Agent Mack was there when I arrived and I invited him to join us. We sat in a small conference room.

"You've had an impressive few weeks," Mack said. "You solved your hobo case, got the Florida legislature off its ass, and helped put an end to B. I. Grover."

"What if I told you I didn't think Grover died from natural causes?" I said.

"The medical examiner confirmed a heart attack and signed off on the case," Sloan said.

"Grover did die of a heart attack," I agreed. "But what if the heart attack was induced using new technology?"

"Have you got evidence or a hunch?"

"Circumstantial evidence and a strong intuition," I said.

"Do you have a suspect?"

"Yes."

"Give us the information and we'll look into it," Mack said without enthusiasm. "But don't expect speedy action. A Boca lawyer was just arrested for a smaller Ponzi scheme than Grover's, but similar. We've closed his office and put a lot of manpower on the investigation."

"On top of that," Agent Sloan interjected, "we've been ordered to open an investigation into another investment banker in Palm Beach. He's was Grover's neighbor. This could be even bigger than B.I.G."

"So I guess you're really busy," I said.

"Look around our office," Sloan said. "There's no one here. Everyone is out working on new business. Grover's old news already. But send us what you've got and we'll get to it when we can."

"I have a better idea. Call me when you're ready."

"That *is* a better idea," Mack said. "Don't call us . . . we'll call you."

CHAPTER 61

HIS FATHER'S SON

The Boca Knights Detective Agency was in bigger demand than ever thanks to Jerry Small and Mad Mick Murphy. Praise in the press is magical, and the phones at our office were constantly ringing. We were offered more cases than we could handle and even received an inquiry about a television series. Lou Dewey said he wanted to play himself. I was less than enthusiastic. My depression returned and with it a need for Viagra.

"The danger level is down and you're not up," Claudette said. "Take a pill."

I took a pill, got an erection, a headache, a blocked nose, and an unfulfilled feeling.

"It wasn't good for you, was it?" Claudette said with her head on my chest.

"This is going to take a lot of adjusting on my part."

"Practice makes perfect. And besides, I didn't fall in love

with Superman. I fell in love with a special man. Let's both be patient and go with the flow."

"Or the lack of a flow," I said, appreciating her more each day.

The day of Teofilo Fernandez's first Golden Gloves bout, Claudette and I picked up his mother, Alana Fernandez, at their apartment on Dixie Highway. A good-looking woman in her late thirties, she smiled easily but talked little. The first bout had already begun when we arrived, and over two hundred people were in the cavernous gym. Ten bouts were scheduled between twenty boxers from South Florida. In the ring were two small black kids with more enthusiasm than skill, but the crowd loved them and cheered their efforts. Barry Anson saw us standing at the door and waved us over to three ringside seats he had reserved for us. I introduced him to Alana.

"Thank you for training my son," she said. "He says you are a wonderful teacher."

Barry smiled. "He's the one who's wonderful. He already knew so much I only had to refresh his memory."

"His father was his first teacher," she said proudly.

"He did a great job." Barry turned his attention to me. "I had to move him up to a tougher division, Eddie. He was too good for the novices."

"I hope you didn't overmatch him," I said warily. "Who is he fighting?"

"Lebron Lewis. He's about ten pounds heavier than our boy and stronger."

"How many fights has Lewis had?" I asked.

"Six."

"How many has he won?"

"Six," Anson said. "I've seen him fight. Tough kid."

"It sounds like a mismatch to me," I said, concerned.

"I don't think so."

When Lewis and Teofilo entered the ring, I saw they were almost the same height but Teofilo looked like a brown feather next to a black block of marble. I was nervous. Teofilo seemed calm. He stood motionless, listening to the referee's instructions while Lewis huffed, puffed, and pounded his gloves together. His angry face glowered at Teofilo, who seemed unconcerned and relaxed. They returned to their corners, and Teofilo covered his face with his gloves and appeared to be praying. At that moment I noticed the initials on the bottom of his trunks: HB.

The bell rang and Lewis charged from his corner like a bull and started a left hook as soon as they were within reach of each other.

Bam! Teofilo beat him to the punch with a quick straight jab to the nose.

Bam! Bam! Two more blows found their mark. The crowd roared and continued cheering throughout the three rounds of boxing. Teofilo was an artist and painted Lewis's face with jabs, hooks, and uppercuts. Lewis was a tough kid and kept coming forward, but it was like a bull charging a matador. The matador was always in control. I was enthralled by the kid Herb Brown had saved. At one point I turned to his mother to see her reaction. She was crying, tears streaming down her face, her trembling hands covering her lips.

"Are you all right?" I asked when the last round ended. "Is something wrong?"

"It was like watching a ghost. Teofilo is so much his father's son. His movements, his punching, everything. I was overcome with emotion."

Teofilo was announced the winner by unanimous decision, winning every round. He was surrounded by his teammates, who pounded his back and embraced him.

"He'll be busy for a few minutes," Barry said. "I told him we would wait for him outside."

Mrs. Fernandez, Barry, Claudette, and I walked outside before the next bout began.

"That was amazing," Claudette said. "He was beautiful."

"He certainly was," I said. "He has the makings of a champion."

Teofilo joined us a few minutes later.

"Your father would have been so proud of you today," his mother said, hugging him. "Were you thinking of him?"

"Yes, of course. But I also thought of Mr. Brown before the fight and said a prayer for him. I wouldn't be here today if not for him."

Alana released her son from her embrace and turned to us. "Teofilo asked me to sew Mr. Brown's initials on his trunks. We will never forget him."

I couldn't help pondering the strange workings of fate: sixty-two years ago a helmet fell off a GI's head on a beach in the central Pacific and the world changed.

Chapter 62

Hunting Season

The shooters at Kugel's, the bombers of Joy Feely's house, and the nine victims haunted my dreams. I had to find the animals responsible and get them off the streets before I could move on with my life. The most likely place to start was Miami.

"I'm going to look for Mad Dog," I told Lou.

"You should go to the Miami police, not the Miami criminals."

"I don't want police help on this one."

"I already told you how I feel about that son of a bitch," Lou said. "There's nothing more for me to say."

The first time I met Mad Dog was by accident. I got lost in Liberty City. This time I intentionally got off I-95 at Seventy-ninth Street and trusted my sense of direction from there. I was lost after three turns.

Stopped at a red light, I heard tapping on my driver's window. I turned my head and looked into the barrel of a handgun.

A scowling, black teenage kid was pointing a .38 at my eyebrows. I watched three more scowling black kids take positions in front of the Mini, blocking my escape.

This neighborhood sucks.

I rolled down my window. "Is it hunting season already, Officer?"

"Yeah," the young man said, and smiled, showing a full grill of silver teeth. "Maybe you'd like to buy a huntin' license."

"Sure, how much?" I smiled back, wishing I had some silver to show.

"How much you got?" He touched my cheek with the tip of the gun.

"Can I check my wallet?" I asked, slowly reaching for my back pocket.

"You got a gun in that wallet?" He pressed the .38 against my skin.

"Yeah. I got a King Cobra thirty-eight loaded with Magnum forty-five shells. It will blow your head clean off."

The kid laughed, stood up, and looked at his friends. He took his gun with him. "White boy say he Dirty Harry."

"Mothuh fuckin' Dirty Harry," another boy said in a high-pitched voice, and high-fived the kid next to him. While they laughed and exchanged hand slaps, I got a grip on the Cobra's handle.

"Hey, Clint Eastwood," the kid said, still performing for his friends, "you find your mothuh fuckin' wallet?"

"Got it."

When his head appeared in the window again, the head of the Cobra fit nicely between his eyes.

"Mothuh fuckah," the kid said.

"Drop your gun on the ground." He dropped it with a clatter.

"What's wrong, Juice?" one of his men shouted from behind him.

"Dirty Harry here got a gun between my eyes, JeMarcus."

"We got three guns on him," JeMarcus announced. "We fill his white ass with holes."

"One hole in his ass enough," Juice said. "And I don't need one in my head."

I whispered in Juice's ear, "Is JeMarcus your number two man?"

"Yeah, how you know?" Juice asked in a low voice.

"I think he wants to be number one," I said, still whispering.

"Over my dead mothuh fuckin' dead body," Juice hissed.

"I think that's what he has in mind."

Juice's eyes opened wide and he nodded. "Drop your mothuh fuckin' guns," he ordered.

I heard the sound of two handguns hitting the pavement.

"JeMarcus, drop your mothuh fuckin' gun," Juice ordered.

We heard the third gun clatter.

"You better watch out for him," I advised Juice confidentially. He nodded again.

"Okay, Tarzan," Juice said loudly. "You king of the jungle now. What you want?"

"I want to see Mad Dog Walken."

Juice laughed. "Yeah, and I want to see the mothuh fuckin' Prince of Wales."

I cocked the hammer of the Colt. "I'm serious. I know the man. You know where to find him?"

"Who . . . Mad Dog or the Prince?"

I rapped Juice's forehead with the tip of the gun.

"Hey, I ain't no piñata."

"Then get serious."

"Okay, man," he said, rubbing his head. "I know Dog, but I can't just take you to him. He the T. rex of this here Jurassic Park. You don't just walk in unannounced."

"What then?"

"I can call him and ask if he wants to see your white ass."

"Call him."

"Now listen carefully, Pops," Juice said. "I'm going to take a phone out of my pocket, nice and slow, so don't go Son of Sam on me. Okay?"

I nodded.

Juice eased a phone out of his pocket and showed it to me. "See, no trigger."

I nodded again and he punched in a number. We waited. I heard someone answer. "Yo, Ice, I got a crazy old white man here with an antique gun restin' on my nose," Juice said. "Says he knows Mad Dog and wants to see him." Juice paused, then looked at me. "What's your name?" I told him. "Says his name Eddie Perlmutter." Juice listened. "Mad Dog wants to know what you want."

"Shooters and bombers."

"Say what?" Juice said to me.

"Just tell him."

"Say he want shooters and bombers," Juice said into the phone. He waited . . . said, "Okay," and disconnected.

"What he say?" JeMarcus wanted to know.

"Dog wants me to walk Mr. Perlmutter over to his block," Juice said, looking at me with new respect. "You must be a special Perlmuttah, mothuh fuckah."

"Why are we walking?" I asked.

"He's around the corner," Juice told me.

"That's cool. But I don't want to leave my Mini here."

"No one gonna touch that piece of shit," Juice guaranteed.

I followed Juice into an alley and didn't feel afraid.

This is crazy.

CHAPTER 63

WE MEET AGAIN

After a few twists and turns we exited onto a street that looked familiar. Fifty yards away was the old, four-door Buick I had seen the night I met Mad Dog. I saw gang members malingering around the car just as before, but this time Mad Dog was standing with them.

"You on your own," Juice said, and disappeared into the alley. I took a deep breath and walked toward the Overtown Outlaws while they stood motionless, watching me approach. I had seen some of their sullen black faces before. Ladanlian stood next to his mountainous uncle.

"How you doing, Ladanlian?" I asked, trying to sound more confident than I was.

The kid nodded but said nothing.

"What you want, Mr. Boca Knight?" Mad Dog asked with no expression on his face.

"I told you. I want those four shooters and the bombers."

"I know *who* you want. I asked *what* you want."

"I want justice."

"Ain't no such thing," Mad Dog said. "And why should I help you against my black brothers?"

"You tell me. You agreed to meet."

"You smart for white boy. Those shooters ain't really my brothers. They stone-cold killers."

"Some people say that about you," I said.

"I kill to survive. The boys you looking for kill for money. The night they shot up Boca, they were working for a white dude in Palm Beach who paid them big money."

"They shot a black college student that night too. Blew his head off."

"I know," Mad Dog said.

"They shot an old white man in the face when he tried to save a brown Cuban kid."

"The only color those guys see is green." Mad Dog spit. "The police were here asking questions. They figured we had something to do with it. That's bad for business."

"I want to put the shooters and bombers out of business."

"There was only one bomber and he dead. Blew hisself up makin' a bomb to kill his ammunition supplier. What's that shit about?"

"Their supplier sold them some bird shot along with their buckshot."

"How you know?"

"I got hit with the bird shot," I said. "The dead people got the buckshot."

Mad Dog nodded. "There was four brothers and one cousin that night. Cousin was the bomber. Two shooters were killed at the restaurant."

"I killed one. I shot him in the face. I shot another one in the leg but he got away."

"He didn't get nowhere. He bled to death on the way to Miami. You hit a big vein."

The femoral artery.

"Okay, I'll take the two left," I said.

"You tough enough to take them?" Roach challenged me.

"You wanna find out for yourself?" I said as the red veil darkened in front of my eyes.

"You little shit," Roach snarled, and grabbed my shoulder.

I drew the Cobra, whipped it around from my back, and pressed it against Roach's crotch. A chorus of "Mothuh fuckah" followed.

"Stop," Mad Dog growled, and we froze in place.

"Take that gun off my balls," Roach told me.

It was a reasonable request so I complied.

"Listen to me." Mad Dog pointed a long, thick finger in my face. "No matter what happens, you can't tell nobody you know me. Got it?"

I nodded. "What about your own people here?"

"I trust my people. They won't say nothin'. I ain't so sure about you."

"Don't worry about me. Now, where am I going?"

"The four Jefferson brothers lived in the back of the Jefferson Storage Warehouse, an old building their grandfather owned," Mad Dog told me. "Now only two live there. It's a big place filled with a bunch of abandoned shit. Plenty of places to hide."

"How do I find it?"

"Ladanlian will walk you back to your car and tell you how to get there."

Ladanlian took me through the alley to my car. Juice and his boys were gone. Ladanlian gave me directions to the Jefferson warehouse on the southwest corner of Sixty-seventh and Sixth. I was getting in my car when Ladanlian said, "I owe you for not killing me the last time we met."

"We're even," I told him. "But if you keep hanging out with your uncle and his gang, someone will kill you sooner or later."

"I'd be dead already without Mad Dog. This ain't like no place you ever lived. Mad Dog keeps me safe. He makes me go to school."

"He's a drug dealer and a dangerous man."

"He's more than that," Ladanlian said. "That's why he's helping you. Them Jefferson boys are pure evil. He wants them gone."

"I'll see what I can do."

"Good luck," the young man said, and walked away without looking back.

Chapter 64

The Jefferson Monument

The Jefferson Warehouse looked like a twenty-thousand-square-foot outhouse of rotting wood and metal. I picked the rusty front lock easily and entered silently. Piles of junk were everywhere, covered with dust from the last century. It was a musty hotbox in the warehouse despite the clear, mild air of a May night. In the summer it would be unbearable. I removed the Cobra from my belt and moved slowly toward a dim light on the opposite end of the floor. As I got closer to the one-room office, I could see a black man sitting at a desk wiping down an AA-12 shotgun. Another black man was watching him from across the desk.

The man with the gun put it down behind him. "Fuckin' thing a masterpiece, little brother."

"Damn near perfect, Malcolm," little brother said.

I stepped into the office holding the Cobra in both hands.

"Freeze," I shouted.

Something was wrong. The two men didn't move and smiled as if they were expecting me.

"Look who's here, Damian," Malcolm said to his little brother.

I've been set up. I can't believe Mad Dog would do that. But, then again, why not?

I felt something cold press against the back of my head and I knew it wasn't a bottle of beer.

"Welcome to the jungle, Tarzan," a familiar voice said.

It was JeMarcus, the kid who wanted to be number one. He must have been following me from the beginning.

"You was right, JeMarcus," Malcolm said. "We owe you."

"And don' you forget it like Juice did," JeMarcus said.

"You the man," Malcolm told him.

"Now drop your gun," JeMarcus said to me. "Or drop dead."

Malcolm reached back for the AA-12 and aimed it at me as he got up. I dropped my gun.

The Jefferson brothers walked in front of me and got in my face.

"Damian, you believe this little shit did so much damage?"

"Think I'll do some damage to him," Damian said, and punched me in the mouth. It was a decent shot and I felt my teeth loosen and my lips split. He looked surprised when I didn't go down and startled when I spit blood in his face.

"Tough little mothuh fuckah," Damian said. "You give it a try, Malcolm."

"I knock him on his ass," Malcolm said, and threw a left hook at my jaw. I blocked it easily with my right arm and jabbed him with a left to his face.

Malcolm grabbed his bloody nose. "Son of a bitch," he cursed. "JeMarcus, shoot that mothuh fuckah."

"I'll do it," Damian volunteered, and went for the shotgun.

"Your friend Mad Dog gonna be upset when he find you dead on his doorstep," Damian said, walking toward me.

"I don't know anyone named Mad Dog."

"You full of shit, mothuh fuckah," JeMarcus said, and rapped my head hard with his gun. "I was there when you met Juice and told him you know Mad Dog."

"I never saw you before in my life," I said.

"Maybe this'll help you remember." JeMarcus pistol-whipped the back of my head. I went down on my knees. "You remember me now?"

The Jefferson brothers laughed.

I shook my head. "Never heard of you. And I usually remember assholes."

JeMarcus kicked my ass and I fell face forward.

"Don't make no difference you know Mad Dog or not," Malcolm said. "We gonna kill that big bastard anyway, and our gang gonna take over his part of Liberty City."

"All three of you." I laughed.

"We're getting new recruits all the time," Damian said. "We'll have plenty of shooters."

"Got an opening for me?" I asked, struggling to my feet so I wouldn't pass out.

"Yeah, we gonna open a grave for you," Malcolm said, shouldering the AA-12. "I'm gonna shoot you in the face just like I did to the old man in the coffee shop."

My red veil caught on fire and I dove under the shotgun, tackling Malcolm around the waist. I heard two shots go off and waited for the pain. There was none. I knocked Malcolm on his back and pushed the barrel of the AA-12 up against his face and away from mine. I wrapped both hands around the shotgun barrel and pulled it a few inches from Malcolm's face while he pulled in the opposite direction. When I brought it down on his face, I heard a cheekbone crack and an eye socket shatter. I hit him again and his nose collapsed. Losing consciousness, Malcolm loosened his grip on the gun so I could pull it out of his hands. I lifted the AA-12 over my head and crashed the butt down on his mouth. Teeth broke as a red inferno blazed in front of my eyes. I couldn't understand why I hadn't been shot dead by JeMarcus or Damian, but I didn't let that stop me. I was focused on beating Malcolm to death for killing Herb Brown. I hit him with the butt of the gun again and again until the sight of his blood revolted me. I dropped the shotgun and stood up. Then, with adrenaline still humming through my veins, I stared at the damage I had done and was horrified.

I felt a strong hand on my shoulder. Reflexively I grabbed the fingers and twisted. The hand didn't budge. "Take it easy, little man," a deep voice said. It was Mad Dog.

"What are you doing here?" I asked, looking around the room. JeMarcus was dead on the floor, the back of his head blown away. Damian was across the room, a hole in his forehead the size of a half-dollar. I knew the exit wound was worse.

"I followed you here," Mad Dog said. "These mothuh fuckahs was so busy beatin' the shit outa you they didn't hear me come in."

I noticed he was holding a rifle with an infrared scope. "You shot them with that?" I said, pointing.

He nodded.

"You could have shot them a little earlier."

"I was busy listening to you deny knowing me," he said. "Now I trust you."

"I'm glad." I slumped down on a storage box. "I can't believe I beat that man to death."

"You'll get over it."

"I'm no murderer."

"Self-defense," Mad Dog said, trying to make me feel better.

"Bullshit. He was unconscious and I just kept hitting him. I don't think I can live with that. I'll have to turn myself in."

"Well, if you gonna mope around the rest of your life because you think you beat some evil fuck to death, we better make sure he dead."

"Of course he's dead. Look at him."

"Maybe he look worse than he is." Mad Dog squatted next to Malcolm, pressed fingers into his neck, then looked up at me. "He got a pulse."

"No way."

Mad Dog put a hand on Malcolm's chest. "He got a strong heartbeat too. You didn't kill no one, tough guy. You feel better now?"

"Are you sure?"

Mad Dog put his ear against Malcolm's chest. "Yeah, I'm sure."

Mad Dog stood up, holding his rifle by his side with one hand, muzzle down. He looked me in the eye. "Yeah, he alive for sure."

I sighed in relief.

Mad Dog casually blasted two holes in Malcolm's chest. "And now he daid."

"What's the matter with you?" I screamed. "You killed him."

"Yeah, but I can live with it."

Chapter 65

What If . . .

"Hi, sweetheart," I said to Claudette when I crawled into bed. It was four in the morning.

She was sitting up in bed waiting for me to come home or for a phone call telling her I wasn't ever coming home.

"It's over," I told her.

She looked at my battered head, then stroked it with her hand. "They must have been tough guys. I've never seen you so beat-up."

"They caught me by surprise."

"Is this craziness ever going to end for us?" she asked hopefully.

"Maybe. I can't keep up this pace forever."

"Maybe you can get involved in less dangerous crusades."

"I'll try to find one."

"Are you still seeing red?" she asked.

"I am. But it doesn't bother me too much. It's more like a warning system than an alarm."

"You'd be better off if you could see all the colors all the time. They're beautiful."

"I remember." I kissed her good-night.

I slept the entire day and woke at dinnertime. I ate with Claudette, gave her biased details of my adventure, and made love to her. It wasn't mad, passionate love, but it was chemical free and good for both of us. Before I fell asleep again, I thanked Mr. Johnson for being there.

We have some adjustments to make, I told him.

Whatever works, he said.

Are we still best friends?

Forever.

The next morning I went to the office and told Lou Dewey about the demise of the Jefferson family.

"I owe you an apology about Mad Dog," he said.

"You don't owe me anything. Mad Dog is a drug dealer and a killer, but thankfully he's selective."

"You think you'll see him again?"

"He gave me his cell number. You never know. I'm just glad to move on."

"You realize we have no cases now?"

"Yeah, but you said we have a waiting list."

"Here it is." Lou tossed me the list. I read the offers.

Community leaders from Osceola Park in Delray had asked us to investigate human smuggling from Haiti. People were dying. I knew we would take the job.

A private citizens' group in Pompano Beach had hired us to investigate gang violence in their city, which had become ground zero for the nation's gang violence.

We were hired to investigate a suspected pedophile in Delray.

A victims' group had hired us to delve into the details of a Boca lawyer's Ponzi scheme. It was a small case compared to

Benjamin Grover's, but still involved millions of dollars and hundreds of investors, dirty politics, and stupid victims. It was our kind of case.

We would turn down all marital cases except for the one involving a corpse. A local podiatrist, missing for three years, had been found submerged in his Mercedes at the bottom of a canal on Boca Rio Road. A hole was in his head. We ruled out suicide and got the feeling his merry widow shot and submerged him . . . or she knew who did. Lou's research revealed that one hundred cars had been found in one Boca canal, and many contained bodies.

"I don't think Boca Knights Detective Agency will ever run out of crimes to solve," I told Lou.

"Cool," he said.

Chapter 66

The Delray Beach Massacre

On a cloudy, windy afternoon in May, Bailey called, frantic. "Pick me up at the Rutherford. It's life-and-death."

She was at the entrance when I arrived, jumped in the Mini, threw her three bags in back, and said, "Drive!"

I drove. "Where to?"

"Delray Beach. And step on it."

I stepped on it, but the Mini's pickup was a letdown.

"Why Delray?"

"Ecological reasons. Didn't I tell you to step on it?"

"I did," I told her. "Whose life or death are we talking about?"

"Sea turtles," she said nervously. "I overheard two Rutherford bums making plans with a couple of local punks to poach nests today in Delray."

"Why steal them?"

"For money, of course. They're worth a lot."

"Why is this our business?" I asked.

"Sea turtles are endangered. And you know I love animals."

"Those cats of yours would eat every one of those turtles if they could."

"That's the circle of life. Stealing for money is a crime."

"Is it a felony?" I joked.

"Yes. Class three," she said seriously. "Those guys left for Delray a half hour ago. They'll probably raid the nests when it gets dark."

"How many eggs are we talking about?"

"A hundred to two hundred per nest."

"How many nests?"

"Hard to tell," she said. "If some nested early, there could be thousands buried there. The older ones will be ready to hatch, the new ones in sixty days. But only one in a thousand survive. Raccoons attack nests, ants, birds, dogs, cats, and people. Heat kills them during the day so they normally hatch at night, when the birds are off the beach."

"It's not safe to be a sea turtle."

"Especially after they hatch. The instant they hatch, the turtles make a mad dash for the ocean. Hundreds are lost on the way. A footprint or a ridge can stop them. Crabs eat them. It's carnage."

"So we may be saving only one sea turtle," I said.

"Maybe more. We'll be giving them all a chance."

"Where do we look for the poachers?"

"We'll find them," she said. "They'll be in a remote area carrying burlap bags."

We did find them in a quiet section of beach near several rolling sand dunes. Two of the men were digging, two were searching. They were silhouettes against a cloudy sky.

"It's dark as night," I said to Bailey. "What if the turtles get confused?"

She didn't hear me. She was running toward the poachers waving her arms. "Drop those eggs," Bailey shouted.

"Put those eggs down carefully," I said.

"Yeah, that's right," Bailey said, as she reached a young man dressed in black and tried wresting the bag of eggs from his hand.

"Get the hell outa here," he snarled, and pushed Bailey down in the sand.

My red veil pulsated as I struggled toward him through the sand.

He pointed a finger at me as if he were aiming a gun. "Get out of here before you get hurt."

I grabbed the young punk's extended right wrist with my left hand, twisted hard, and forced him to his knees. I put the bottom of my shoe on his chest and shoved him on his back. He scrambled to all fours, but before he could stand, I put my foot on his butt and shoved him facedown into the sand.

"Your poaching days are over," I told him, and shoved his face deeper into the sand with the sole of my shoe.

The other punk started toward me but stopped abruptly when I pointed at him and said, "You're about to make a bad mistake."

He believed me. "Can I help my friend up and get out of here?"

I nodded and watched them go.

The two homeless men didn't need any convincing. They put their bags down carefully and ran away.

"Good work," Bailey said, brushing sand from her dirty clothes as she approached. Suddenly we were inundated by a typical Florida tropical downpour, the kind that floods roads and halts traffic in minutes. With no shelter on the beach, Bailey and I were soaked to the skin in seconds. The sheets of rain pounded the sand like an onslaught of body punches.

"Let's get out of here," I hollered, holding my arms over my head.

"We have to bury the eggs. Rain or not."

"Absolutely not."

A minute later we were kneeling in the wet sand burying turtle eggs. Just when I thought it might rain forever, it stopped and the beach was quiet again. I heard a scratching sound and saw a shell crack . . . then another and another. These eggs had been nested early and were hatching prematurely in the cool darkness. I saw a turtle climb over the edge of the nest, paddle through the sand, and waddle toward the beach. A hundred tiny, black turtles followed. I saw one stuck in a rut in the sand.

"Poor little guy." I bent down to help him.

"Don't get involved," Bailey said. "He has to make it on his own."

I withdrew my hand.

More nests opened and countless sea turtles were scurrying to the sea. It was an amazing sight.

When the black sky turned to gray, the sun peeked through a break in the clouds.

"Damn," Bailey cursed. "If the sun comes out, the gulls will come back and the turtles won't stand a chance."

"What do we do?"

"Nothing. We can't interfere with nature."

I looked down for my favorite turtle. I was relieved to see that he had made it over the ridge and was scrambling toward the shoreline. The clouds parted like a dark gray curtain and the sun came out. It was still relatively cool, but the wind had eased and the beach was bright. I saw a gull overhead; suddenly there were dozens. They squawked and screamed as they dived for the beach like kamikaze pilots attacking battleships. It was a massacre.

"Bailey, we have to do something."

"This is the natural progression of things," she said, tears in her eyes. "They weren't meant to live."

"They weren't meant to be dug up by people and replanted

either," I called over the din of screeching birds. I was grateful that sea turtles couldn't scream.

"Stay out of it," she warned.

I watched the slaughter until I couldn't stand it any longer. I stood up and pulled out my Cobra.

"You can't shoot the gulls," Bailey shouted.

"I'm not going to shoot anything."

I could still identify my favorite turtle, struggling behind the others. I got close to him and fired a shot in the air, away from the circling birds. They scattered and the sea turtles marched on. When the dive-bombing gulls returned, I fired again. They flew off momentarily but returned in force. I felt a splat on my head, followed by two more. I touched my head and my fingers came away white and black.

Bird shit. This is war. Fire at will.

"You're slow as a turtle," I shouted at my little friend as he made painfully slow progress toward the ocean. I fired four shots in a row.

Take that.

Splat . . . splat!

Bastards.

Boom . . . boom!

A gull dive-bombed and made me duck. Emboldened, more followed, and soon I was engulfed in gulls pecking and shitting.

Sons of bitches.

I saw my turtle at the shoreline was about to become a target. I fired another shot, scattering the birds and giving my little guy time to get in the water.

Finally he made it, only to be washed ashore by a wave.

Dummy. Get out of here.

I fired another shot.

Move your slow turtle ass.

He went under the next wave and bobbed to the surface.
Get down.

A gull dove for him. I aimed at the bird but stopped.

"Enough," I said to myself. "You've done enough. You can't control everything."

The gull hit the water and my turtle went under simultaneously. When the bird resurfaced squawking loudly, I closed my eyes and lowered my head.

Bailey gently touched my arm. "Did you know that some turtles live to be eighty years old," she said softly.

"Great. Mine died at birth."

"Not necessarily. A gull can't squawk with his beak filled with food."

Really? I didn't know that. What if my favorite turtle is still alive? What if he's still alive fifty years after I'm gone and he's the one who saves his species from extinction? What if—

"I told you not to get involved," Bailey said, pointing at me.

I smiled at her. *What if I didn't get involved with you, Bailey? What if I didn't get involved with Weary Willie, Benjamin Grover, Doc Hurwitz, the Florida legislature, Mad Mick Murphy, Jerry Small, Mad Dog Walken, Father Vinnie, and the Jefferson brothers? What if I just looked the other way?*

"What are you thinking?" Bailey asked.

"I'm thinking that I'm glad I get involved and try to make things better."

"But look at you. You're covered with shit."

"Sometimes that happens to people who get involved."

I walked to the shoreline and looked at the ocean. The red veil slowly lifted and I could see all the colors again. Claudette had been right. They *were* beautiful.

Author's Note

February 2011

Drug agents raided eleven pain clinics from Miami to West Palm Beach, arresting twenty-three people and seizing 2.5 million dollars in cash and large amounts of personal property. It was the second-biggest strike against pill mills in Florida's history. Physicians were arrested and the owner of four clinics was taken into custody. The raids were made by more than four hundred federal, state, and local officers. Boxes of documents were seized.

Seven Floridians die every day from drug overdoses, and pill mills have been identified as a major contributing factor. Over two hundred clinics are still operating in Broward and Palm Beach counties.

About the Author

Steven M. Forman was born and raised in the Boston area. After graduating from the University of Massachusetts, Amherst, he founded a one-man business and built it into a worldwide enterprise. He has written two previous Eddie Perlmutter novels, *Boca Knights* and *Boca Mournings*. He and his wife divide their time between Massachusetts and Boca Raton, Florida.